Rheyzoun 45

The Beginning of the End

Book 1

Donald G. Wahl

Copyright © 2018 by Donald G. Wahl.

Library of Congress Control Number: 2018909695
ISBN: Hardcover 978-1-9845-4663-0
Softcover 978-1-9845-4664-7
eBook 978-1-9845-4665-4

All rights reserved. No part of this book may be reproduced or transmitted in any form or by any means, electronic or mechanical, including photocopying, recording, or by any information storage and retrieval system, without permission in writing from the copyright owner.

This is a work of fiction. All of the characters, names, incidents, organizations, and dialogue in this novel are either the products of the author's imagination or are used fictitiously.

Any people depicted in stock imagery provided by Getty Images are models, and such images are being used for illustrative purposes only.
Certain stock imagery © Getty Images.

Print information available on the last page.

Rev. date: 08/10/2018

To order additional copies of this book, contact:
Xlibris
1-888-795-4274
www.Xlibris.com
Orders@Xlibris.com
781882

REVIVE THE LIGHT!
(RHEYZOUN-45)

THE FALLING STAR OF THE HEART, A SPARK
DESCENDING INTO A SPIRAL OF GLOOM,
COATED IN A GLAZE OF FEAR AND DECEIT,
CUTTING THE SPARK OFF FROM ITS WOMB

JUST A THREAD OF FAITH AND HOPE IT CLINGS
AS DAYS BECOME MONTHS, BECOMING YEARS,
THEN NEMESIS OF STRUGGLES, BETRAYAL, AND DOUBTS
FOREVER MAGNIFYING THE GRAVITY OF ITS TEARS

BUT THE LOVING MOTHER HEART ANCHORS PRECIOUS LIGHT
THROUGH THE THREAD, RESUSCITATING THE SPARK
WITH THE COSMIC BLOOD OF FAITH AND HOPE FLOWING
AN UPWARD SPIRAL JOURNEYING BACK TO THE HEART

FOR MILLENNIA, FABRICS OF RESISTANCE AND DOUBT
DROWNING OUT THE LIGHT FROM WITHIN,
A DARK MISSION AND GOAL, TWO SNUFF OUT THE SOUL,
MASS CONFUSION FEEDING ITS NEGATIVE SPIN

YET OUT OF THIS GRIT GREW THE SPARK WITH A WIT,
A CONFIDENCE BEAMING FROM HEART TO HEART,
MANY VICTORIES ITS GOAL, MANY THREADS BECOMING WHOLE,
A COSMIC UNITY, CAN WE SNUFF OUT THE DARK?

INTRODUCTION

RHEYZOUN–45

IN THE NOT-TOO-DISTANT future of 2020, a cosmic council on the God Star Sirius of our Milky Way held an important, unparalleled event of grand magnitude. The time had come to make a decision on the destiny of Terra, our planet Earth.

Mankind's spiritual growth has been lagging too long, even with the assistance of spiritual beings and grants to them for certain dispensations to accelerate their paths. The rule of darkness had created a pungent fungus in the galaxy of its system, thus creating a stunting of growth and evolving of the planets surrounding it.

The great being Ramata ordered the creation of a twenty-five-mile diameter asteroid with advanced intelligent beings and twenty-five Buddhas residing in its core. The purpose of this asteroid, appropriately called Rheyzoun-45, was to act as a positive or negative catalyst, depending on mankind's choices and efforts of advancement on planet Earth.

On Rheyzoun-45's twenty-five-year journey toward earth, the Buddha and spirits would constantly send endless waves of light, love, and peace to mankind, in hopes of igniting the flame within their hearts. Each human being, a receptor of divine energy, will be accountable and responsible on how this additional cosmic energy boost would be qualified.

Hearts filled with hatred, envy, bitterness; and evil would pervert the energy to magnify the darkness prevailing on the planet. But the hearts of love, joy, hope, and peace would amplify the cosmic energy to greater heights of unity, growth, and an enlightened age, thus creating a golden age on Terra.

The Council, along with the Great Karmic Masters, sealed the project of Ramata and had an enormous ritual blessing this great mission and followed up with bursts of light immersing the path of Rheyzoun-45 to its destination: Earth.

At that moment on planet Earth, twenty-five advanced beings received inner messages unsurpassed by anything that they had ever experienced. Thousands of miles apart from one another, a twenty-five-year journey made its mark on these beings, creating a cosmic blueprint of the ultimate purpose. These consisted of ten men and fifteen women. All of them simultaneously experienced a great impulse of energy within their hearts, along with a great vision accompanying it. Unbeknownst to them, their homelands are strategically spread abroad throughout the planet.

These above-average spiritual-minded beings are as follows: The fifteen women are thirty-five-year-old Zeera of Ottawa, Canada; twenty-eight-year-old Miraki from the southern tip of South America; thirty-three-year-old Nyla of the Canary Islands; twenty-year-old Bayuni of Puako, Hawaii; twenty-four-year-old Deeka of Gjovik, Norway; thirty-seven-year-old Yoi-yu of the Hopi Mesas of Arizona; eighteen-year-old Tillow of Seward, Alaska; nineteen-year-old Amara of Perth, Australia; twenty-seven-year-old Krea of Mt. Shasta City, California; thirty-eight-year-old Fioriya of Beijing, China; thirty-three-year-old Coralee of Africa; twelve-year-old Myama of Quito, Ecuador; twenty-nine-year-old Pyrena of Kashmir, India; twenty-one-year-old Hoopti of St. Petersburg, Russia; and seventeen-year-old Yazerya of Lisbon, Portugal. The ten men are forty-five-year-old Aton of Central America; forty-two-year-old Rotussi of Prescott, Arizona; forty-five-year-old Omer of an unknown city in Norway; thirty-eight-year-old Jogil of Siberian Territory; twenty-five-year-old Vander of Stuttgart, Germany; twenty-seven-year-old Namko of Sapporo, Japan; twenty-two-year-old Tyotan of Dornbirn, Austria; thirty-five-year-old Kobin of Rugby, North Dakota; eighteen-year-old Fohran of Mosfellsbaer, Iceland; and thirty-year-old Creoki of Tecate, Baja, California.

Realizing that their world is in dire situations of evil, hatred, and calamity, these beings felt an intense sensation of urgency and a need to unite all the world on a heart level. The first step was for each being to meditate for three days, nonstop, without food or water. They all realized that their total was twenty-five, but to seek out one another was priority, so that a momentum of light could be established. This would create a strong bond of unity as a hub from which to work from.

The impending doom of Terra started many hundreds of thousands years prior, when a great light being was cast out of the heavens for her transgressions of cosmic laws. Known throughout the lands and ages as the Empress Teohta, her momentum of darkness not only polluted the minds and hearts of mankind, but also the land, sea, and air. Her aura of manipulation, fear, and control created mass confusion throughout Terra and her evolutions. Her twisted revolt in heaven, of which many fell with her, compelled her to challenge the cosmic lord Ramata. The Empress Teohta felt that within a cosmic super cycle, she could rule Terra and its galaxy, turning all beings against the light by their own free will.

Lord Ramata granted this challenge to Teohta and her Legions of Darkness. He made it well known that many light bearers would be incarnated through these times, to assure that all would be given fair chances to choose of their own free will. The time was nearing in the year AD 2020.

Numerous disciples of Ramata chose to lovingly serve their master by incarnating for many a cycle on Terra, to provide sufficient light and love to all. Humans were given every opportunity to turn to the light of their own free will.

CHAPTER 1

ON THE EVE of November 1, 2019, the twenty-five life streams of Terra received a vivid dream of a great white light radiating while they were chanting the phrase "You are a 'Chosen One'" nine times. Then the Great Spirit said, "Call upon Rheyzoun-45 to save Terra. There are twenty-five of you whose destiny is to channel your energies as one thrust of great light! Follow your intuitions and always fan and expand the spark of love within your hearts!" As the sentence concluded, the light faded away and the dreams simultaneously ended. All were mesmerized by this great message, and they were left with a great warmth in their hearts. At that same moment, an immense burst of light was transferred to all the points on Earth where these twenty-five chosen people resided. Each one of these individuals briefly saw a blurred vision of the other twenty-four, but not knowing their locations. However, a strong sense of urgency left a message that they had to seek out one another.

The twenty-five people, we shall call "The Chosen," after their vision, fell into a deep sleep, which lasted twelve hours each. On the following day at noon, they all awoke. Each was compelled to drink a quart of fresh water with a meager breakfast and a minimum one-mile walk. This was a natural intuitive act that their bodies commanded of them, knowing that this would allow a time of pondering of their recent experience. This was also a loving but firm message that this would become a daily practice that would continue to fuel their hearts with the energy and passion of their true calling, the destiny to save Terra and to help lay the foundation of a golden age to come. Again of their own free will, as each in their own way earned the right of purpose by their level of spiritual growth from many embodiments past.

Within two to four weeks in the month of December 2019, their daily meditations had begun a momentum of contacts with one another. Each knowingly received and accepted an inner oath of which a vow was made. That vow being, first, to actively maintain and increase their daily meditations; second, to expand their hearts to the rest of humanity with love, mercy, and compassion; and third, to be aware and ready to receive and attune to their intuitions while yet maintaining an alert state of discernment. Each being also aware of opposing dark forces to be reckoned with. But they were not left empty-handed for these future challenges. They were instructed to call upon the energies of each other by reciting the mantra "Ramtam Om Shivaya Om" nine times. Unbeknownst to them, the Buddhas of Rheyzoun-45 would multiply their calls tenfold, creating a great burst of light toward them, as long as the calls were rightly justified.

On the morning of December 23, contact was made while in deep meditation. Yoi-Yu, Kobin, and Krea—their locations laid a triangular force field in North America. Yoi-Yu is a medicine woman in the Hopi Mesas of Arizona. Kobin is a thirty-five-year-old park ranger in Rugby, North Dakota, and Krea is a twenty-seven-year-old teacher in Mt. Shasta City, California.

Yoi-Yu has always been a great healing tool for the "Great Spirit," as her actual birthplace is unknown. All the tribes of the Mesas revere her, and it has been said that she was born from the tear of the Great Spirit that was shed with hope and faith for all mankind.

Kobin, who resides in Rugby, North Dakota, is a devout twenty-five-year practitioner of the Tao, reveres nature, and enjoys his passion with a career as a park ranger. This six-foot-nine-inch giant gentleman supports nine-year-old twins Bessie and Trina. His wife, thirty-year-old Vanessa, homeschools the twins while enjoying their two pets, Oscar, the barn owl, and Odin, the fifteen-year-old turtle.

And lastly, there is Krea. Krea is a single, twenty-seven-year-old public middle-school teacher, residing and born in Mt. Shasta City, California. She is a recent divorcee, with no children, and her career as a teacher has become a loving substitute as she also is an only child of two loving parents. Her educating and nurturing of schoolchildren has been an answer to a prayer that's molded her life with a gratefulness and divine purpose.

These three souls would one day realize that they are kindred spirits as their ties were bound by past lifetimes in previous civilizations, but for now, their first contact and message from their intuitions were "you three are the combined action of divine love, wisdom, and power, drawn together on an urgent mission to save a planet from impending doom. By attuning to your intuitions, your works and bonding of divine purpose will yield to you a great momentum of light to saturate and bless the lands and their inhabitants with love, peace, and harmony. You must constantly hold these thoughts and emotions to feed the flame within your hearts."

Kobin's town of Rugby had been experiencing an epidemic of an unknown virus that has 25 percent of the population feeling lethargic, emotionally disturbed, and with a loss of appetite. It has been just over two months since he experienced his recent vision. The doctors and some scientists were at a loss as to what was causing this problem. They checked the local water sources and various foods grown in the area, but to no avail. Imported meats and other foods were also monitored to try and determine the cause of the sickness.

Yoi-Yu could sense this situation through their bonding spiritual union during the meditation. Her inner guides began to assist this medicine woman to help find the cause and to work on a cure as her expertise in medicines and herbs were infinitely at her disposal. Kobin could sense this and opened his huge heart as a receptacle of sacrifice for his hometown. Krea also picked up on his crisis and was open to offering her help in the matter.

Meanwhile, in the Mesas of Yoi-Yu's land, a certain number of children had been experiencing more than normal difficulties in their schooling, a deep concern for their families and elders of the tribe. Krea was touched by this situation and began to create an inner blueprint to try and determine how she could be of assistance in the matter.

In Krea's town of Mt. Shasta City, numerous high-tech companies had been recently established in the area. The townspeople were deeply disturbed as a good number of them voted against these businesses in town hall meetings. They felt that their natural habitat was being threatened. Kobin picked up on this vibration and called on his wisdom of the Tao to come up with a resolution that would help the people to find and maintain balance in their lives.

The tentacles of Teohta had dipped into the homelands of these three Chosen Ones as they were blinded by the root cause of these negative events. Divide and conquer being a major tactic of the black arts, the evil temptress Teohta subtly and ever so slowly spread her vibrations throughout the lands. A major factor in her attempt to control all, being total ignorance by the mass populations, she was rarely challenged by anybody. Most churches being caught up in various teachings and beliefs based in fear, there were scarcely any life streams aware of the divine presence within. But these Chosen Ones were equipped for battle. They had but to make calls for divine assistance with a selfless motive and for the good of all mankind, no matter what the sacrifice.

Meanwhile, as Yoi-Yu, Kobin, and Krea realized that each had an important role in each other's concerns, they could feel the light within them expand and urging them to take action immediately. A strong message of assistance came to them during their next morning meditations. "Light expand! Light expand! Light expand! Consume all darkness throughout all lands! Victory! Victory! Victory! In the light!"

They immediately made the calls, nine each. A mighty current of light energy was felt by each as the Masters of Light began to roll in motion through these beloved ones. They began to realize, more and more, that while being in a heightened state of awareness, they had become divine conduits for the light to take action on the physical plane. But for the energy to be positive and effective, thoughts of love and purity had to be maintained constantly. All three felt this powerful experience and realized that a great momentum of victory was created and they but had to maintain this great current of light. It became a huge responsibility for each and there was no turning back. They were also made aware to always focus on the light and not fear. This consistent attunement would increase the light in their lives.

CHAPTER 2

ACROSS THE GREAT Atlantic, a delightful soul, Vander of Stuttgart, Germany, was conducting a tai chi class with his twelve students in the local park. A librarian by trade, this blond-haired, blue-eyed twenty-five-year-old also developed a passion for assisting the elderly in their daily activities. Living in a small cottage, in his quiet time, he has a sensitivity for visions of future events while also believing in a higher order of spiritual beings, a brotherhood for the good of all mankind. His purity of heart attracted the hierarchy and earned him the title of a Chosen One.

During his meditations, contact was made with two souls, one of which is a twenty-one-year-old black-haired, brown-eyed young lady named Hoopti, an American Indian product born of two parents serving as ambassadors from the United States of America, serving St. Petersburg, Russia. This Russian-born girl is filled with dreams and a desire to bridge the gaps between East and West, promoting worldwide peace. This sparked her interests in the studying of cultural arts while pursuing a job hunt. Her joyous heart always fed her natural enthusiasm for life in which she had many experiences of ecstatic states of consciousness—a joyous meditation, if you will.

The other soul is that of Nyla. With a tainted past in the black arts, this thirty-three-year-old former sorceress had a near-death experience that converted her heart back to the light. This black-haired, green-eyed beloved one owns a crystal and book store based in the Canary Islands. Her companions include a male dog, Motley, and a falcon-dart. She is currently dating Brandon, who has been a tour guide for three years. Her recent conversion qualified her as a Chosen One due to the fact that a promise and commitment was made in her heart to selflessly serve the light faithfully for the rest of her life. She is a true example of divine mercy and forgiveness given by the Great Ones.

Vander and Nyla instantly felt a strong tie. Together through their meditations, Vander's eight years of tai chi made for a strong foundation in his spiritual life and his love of helping others for the good of all. These virtues and qualities were the perfect antidotes to ever expand the healing of Nyla's soul. Nyla's previous experiences from the dark side would help both Vander and Hoopti to up their guards and enhance their sensitivities of impending dangers. These three Chosen Ones began a bonding of their energies and light through their daily meditations.

Hailing from the southernmost tip of South American, young twenty-eight-year-old Miraki happily creates vases, poetry, and other various ceramics. This blue-eyed maiden with snowflake hair has a passion for and studies the ancient arts. The only daughter of parents who are owners of and work on their fishing boat, Miraki performs her own meditations in a local ancient temple. She reveres the sun and regularly communes with nature spirits. Her last meditation was a very warm and lucid experience, revealing to her a vision of like-minded beings. This was a contact and request for a commitment with a purpose. This experience deeply excited her.

On the same morning, young twelve-year-old Myama of Quito, Ecuador, had the same vision as Miraki and immediately accepted the initiation of a Chosen One. This black-haired child was a natural-born spirit guide with more invisible friends than physical ones. Her uncanny abilities were sought out by many around her as her parents had to take charge of her scheduling to help others. She also enjoys a passion for plants and herbs. She dreams of incorporating her talents and becoming a healer for all her people.

Sitting in meditation in his lovely home garden, forty-two-year-old Rotussi experienced his spiritual contact with Miraki and Myama. This gentleman, born in Buffalo, New York, currently resides in Prescott, Arizona, and owns and operates a dojo consisting of fifty tai chi students. He also sits as a board member in the local chamber of commerce. He remains unmarried and has a younger brother, Randal, and a younger sister, Sylvia. His move out west was suggested by his sensei so that he could help to spread his martial and spiritual skills with others. Do-Ling saw something special in Rotussi and knew that he needed to uproot from New York to find his true destiny. That is when Rotussi realized that his morning higher contact revealed to him as a Chosen One.

Across the Pacific Ocean, Namko of Sapporo, Japan, docks his fishing boat with a better-than-average catch. This twenty-seven-year-old fisherman is also a student of fencing and supports a deep love for poetry. His belief is that poetry is the language of the heart and is crucial in the laying of a great new spiritual divine order, a new golden age. He meditates daily before launching his boat to go fishing. However, this morning's meditation resulted in an inner contact with kindred beings. He felt a new surge of energy and purpose. He could sense a union with two souls of which he is to commune with.

One of these is Tyotan, a twenty-two-year-old auto mechanic of Dornbirn, Austria. This brown-haired, brown-eyed youngster is engaged to marry twenty-four-year-old Saraya. The two plan to own and operate a bed-and-breakfast business within five to ten years. His hobbies include hiking and backpacking with his bride-to-be. Saraya introduced Tyotan to meditation two years prior to help him to work on his patience for his auto mechanic career. Little did he realize that this allowed for a higher contact with the inner world. He sensed a contact in the morning's meditation and, with faith, accepted his role with his newfound kindred spirits.

The third contact felt the strongest impulse that morning and expressed her deepest gratitude from within. Twenty-nine-year-old Pyrena of Kashmir, India, emitted blessings to the universe for allowing her to be a part of a higher purpose. This black-haired, blue-eyed woman has developed into an amazing artist through her fourteen years of sculpting skills. She is revered and in high demand throughout her land for her amazing works of art. But she limits her projects due to her family and meditation time. Balance is important as she is the eldest of eight siblings, and strong family ties makes for a strong spiritual foundation.

These three souls feel a strong bond and made a commitment from within to prioritize their energies to the fullest extent while not knowing the time and sacrifices involved. They all received the name Ramata in their visions, along with a great wave of love and light flowing through their beings. They knew that this is the ultimate that all strive to live for.

CHAPTER 3

ABOUT HALF A world away, Coralea, of Africa, experienced a warm light and heightened sense of awareness in her early-morning devotions. This thirty-three-year-old priestess was found by hunters, Bradley and Samson, at the young age of nine. They raised the child not knowing any whereabouts regarding her parents. Coralea learned many tongues and helped many mothers in birthing their newborn. Her natural talents became famous throughout the lands, and she was/is considered a big sister to all. She considers all the jungles her homeland and birthplace.

Not far across the waters, young seventeen-year-old Yazerya of Lisbon, Portugal, was in her morning prayers and visualizations. This red-haired, green-eyed youngster is a hairstylist with a yearning to become a makeup artist for a major motion-picture company. She intensely studies the credits at the end of movies to research names to see how they received their opportunities in the industry. She also sports a passion for the special effects aspects.

Further north resides native-born Fohran of Mosfellsbaer, Iceland. He was an abandoned child at the age of seven. He woke up one morning to discover that his parents were gone. He was adopted by a couple, Albert and Hazel, whose love nurtured him greatly and motivated him to want to devote his life's purpose as a big brother. This now-eighteen-year-old especially wants to assist all abandoned children in realizing that they are still loved and cared for and can have a happy normal life with newly loved ones. The strong virtues of love, forgiveness, and acceptance have greatly enhanced his meditations, which qualified him to become a Chosen One.

These three souls made a connection with one another as the name Ramata addressed them for a higher purpose. They were instructed to commit to a more intense meditation time, thus creating a strong bond between the three. Their combined qualities and energies would be a strong factor in the near future and make for a formidable protective force field for themselves and all around them.

This continuous building of soul teams have been in the making for thousands of years as their resumes of lifetimes served as immense initiations for a far greater purpose in serving mankind and the saving of a planet. The Great Ones of spiritual hierarchy have been closely mentoring and monitoring these lifestreams on the inner planes of being. An accumulation of life spans have matured these souls on different levels that would eventually compliment and strengthen one another for an enormous task to follow.

As Tecumseh of old once quoted, "One twig by itself is weak, but a bundle strung together becomes strong." This must apply first in the spirit world to establish the creation in the physical world. The end of a cosmic super cycle was coming to a close, and the light bearers of the planet is in dire need of a group of strong souls to lead the fight for cosmic victory.

In the far north of Seward, Alaska, is native-born Tillow. This eighteen-year-old silver-haired prodigy of the classical masters of music is heading many symphonies throughout all of Alaska. Her magical talents in both violin and piano have inspired her dreams of writing her own music and performing to a worldwide audience. She feels that through her heart, she could help to create a more balanced world of peace and harmony. Little did she realize that her role as a Chosen One would definitely place her in a worldwide cause.

Across the great ocean on the island of Puako, Hawaii, twenty-year-old Bayuni has an ongoing residency in law. Her pastimes of swimming and snorkeling keeps her physically fit and has done her well in numerous Island Princess competitions. She has a fondness for turtles and dragonflies. She would also like to work on a cruise ship part-time.

Completing a triangle across the waters in Tecate, Baja, California, thirty-year-old Creoki aspires to be the ultimate tour guide in all the land. This black-haired, black-eyed gentleman sports a great passion to serve and educate the people in their culture. His interests in philosophy and cooking complements his goals in life.

This triangular connection of souls sprouted from many centuries past, where this vast ocean was long ago a great continent and thriving civilization until darkness slowly crept into the hearts of its people, resulting in a cataclysm causing its sinking. These three souls in their similarities of active traveling became the perfect magnetism to draw upward and rekindle the light of a long-lost life to be born again. All three felt a voice within summoning them as Chosen Ones for a far greater task if they were willing to accept. They all realized that their dreams were coming true but offered them a greater opportunity to grow together and to perform a greater service for mankind and the planet.

CHAPTER 4

HAILING IN THE extreme northern rural Canada, Zeera works in a mental health facility for youth. This thirty-five-year-old red-haired, green-eyed soul is unmarried and sports a passion for hiking and camping. She was born the third of five children to parents who both work in the textile industry. She has shown great success in the healing of others' emotions, thus providing them with a mental clarity and the sense of life with a purpose. The masters see Zeera as a great stabilizer of souls.

Across the great waters, Amara of Perth, Australia, population 2 million, actively pursues a degree in marine biology while continuing her training as a deep-sea diver. This brown-haired, green-eyed, nineteen-year-old has an affinity for dolphins and whales, which she feels were transported from another planet to Earth with a mission to assist mankind's spiritual growth and evolution. Her consistent inner fire of compassion sent a spiritual SOS signal to the Great Ones that her youthful passion is the perfect weapon in the fight against the hordes of darkness.

Completing this triad of Chosen Ones is forty-five-year-old Aton, a prosperous plantation owner in the Central America region. Loved by his loyal and trusted workers, the six-foot-one-inch, 195-pound black-haired, brown-eyed soul also teaches reading and writing. His father, Russi, a diplomat, and his mother Mayah, a migrant worker, met at a city market and fell in love. Two years later, an only son, Aton, was born. He was raised in an environment of love, unity, and service and matured into a natural leader.

These three kindred spirits sport a strong sense of selfless service to their fellow man. They all experienced a great vision of a light being anointing them with a bright, fluidic pearl within their hearts. As above, so below, an immediate bond was born for the three to draw on in times of need and crisis.

The last of the twenty-five Chosen Ones are a group of four souls: Omer, Deeka, Jogil, and Fioriya. These four are the base foundation of the master's choosing that unites all the Chosen Ones into one great web of light. The increasing of this web is crucial in that its increasing light is necessary to draw upon the light of the Buddhas on Rheyzoun-45. This great task and journey will determine the fate of mankind and its planet.

A product born of runaway parents, forty-five-year-old Omer is a former weightlifter who currently janitors at a local private school in Norway. This bald, bearded, mustached man was premature at birth and is an only child. His hobbies include hiking and biking. He enjoys isolated areas where he loves invoking Hindu mantras. He experienced an inner vision of a being, Ramata, calling to him as an old friend of ages past.

Not too distant from Gjovik, Norway, population 27,500, is young twenty-four-year-old Deeka. This dirty blonde, hazel-eyed woman is a seamstress with a creative talent for fashion. This single young lady adopted young Byron, age eight, and his sister, Ishi, age six. She is seeing her best friend, Abe, age twenty-six, who works as a veterinarian. Deeka's experience of many lucid dreams have prompted her creative talents in clothing styles. She strongly feels that she has been in many lands prior to her birth in this life. She experienced a confirmation of this when contacted through a strong inner surge with the softly spoken words, "Chosen One." She gladly accepted the title with great enthusiasm.

In a far-off land of the Siberian Territory is Jogil, a burly thirty-eight-year-old, six-foot-five-inch trapper by trade and friend to all towns around. As an adopted son with no siblings, this good-natured man serves as a rescuer when necessary. His parents' demise in an avalanche prompted his desire to help all in any time of crisis. Sporting a mustache complementing his black eyes, Jogil has a constant companion with his pet wolf, Zac. Jogil also has an affinity with spiritual practices and meditates often. His recent vision was an experience with two beings kindly inviting him to join a global project that would be a lifelong commitment of which he happily agreed. He was made aware that he would be working with three fellow souls of light and that their bond would be crucial for a planetary victory of the masters.

The final Chosen One, born in Beijing, China, is thirty-eight-year-old Fioriya. She has served as an interpreter for many years throughout the world. Her love and passion for her career has never allowed for any room for a family-styled life. Her strong devotion to her work has only allowed for one hobby: the reading and studying of the esoteric religions. This has only deepened her heart for what she can accomplish to help make a better world in which to live. She always concludes her evenings with a prayer and gratitude in her heart. One evening she felt a contact within that was an invitation to a higher calling. Down on hands and knees, she accepted the offer with honor.

Thus, Omer, Deeka, Jogil, and Fioriya sealed the cosmic pact at inner levels and a great rejoicing took place on the bright star Sirius. As Ramata blessed the bonds of the twenty-five Chosen Ones, millions of angels broke out in a great cosmic choir of love, light, joy, peace, and harmony. This great event created a monstrous beam of light that shut through space to Rheyzoun-45. The twenty-five Buddhas on the great cosmic asteroid in turn directed intense beams of light to the twenty-five Chosen Ones on Terra, the planet Earth. A great cosmic momentum was launched and all twenty-five souls felt a great burst of joy from within at the same moment. The great journey had begun in a battle for the victory and survival of a planet.

CHAPTER 5

AS THE CELEBRATION was concluding, Ramata distributed twenty-five micro golden discs to the twenty-five Chosen Ones. These were implanted within their heart chambers on the inner planes of being. These were great cosmic droplets of the great cosmic sun of the galaxy. These acted as super conductors of the fiery, spiritual energy [light] in which light would be magnified when sincere, intense calls were made for the great work to be done. When each team of Chosen Ones made calls simultaneously, the energy would be magnified nine times, thus making for a great offense of light while at the same time cancelling out any darkness aimed directly their way.

In the Hopi Mesa, while sitting in deep meditation, Yoi-Yu was receiving communications from Kobin on her mini crisis. The problem seemed to be that the children were being distracted and losing focus of their schooling. Kobin suggested that the students be given a special focus from Yoi-Yu on positive thoughts of nature and how they could contribute ideas for a better, healthier environment for their communities. This would help to refocus the importance of their efforts of education by applying the principles of school directly in their lives and the lives of others. Thus, the homeschooling of Kobin's family with a Tao-based environment actually complemented the public school system. Yoi-Yu was very open and eager for this idea as a healing technique for the schooling system.

Now, for Krea, in Mt. Shasta City, concern grew from the townspeople about the new companies invading their quiet little community. Kobin sent a similar idea to Krea to assist in both parties communing together on how to enhance everyone's lives without making any major changes to the beauty and natural habitat of the land. Cooperation and clear communication is necessary as a first step to progress and prosperity.

This triune communication of the three magnified the light in their hearts as a sign of a mini victory in each of their respective communities.

Yet also realizing that any future challenges and concerns would always be assistance from one another as the unity of mind and heart would be the new community building blocks, both physically and spiritually in order for overall victory in a world of universal love, joy, peace, and harmony.

Residing in the southern continent of South America, young Myama of Quito, Ecuador, was joyfully out collecting special herbs to concoct a specific remedy for healing. During her early-morning meditations, a few of her invisible friends alerted her that a faraway friend was in need of some assistance for a local virus in the community. As she gathered the herbs, she rushed home to immediately commune with the invisible friends to put together and complete the recipe. As the project was completed, she bowed in thanks for her friends' help and sent out waves of gratitude from her heart. Then she immediately sent out messages to the friend in need.

This message was received at that moment by Miraki of the southernmost tip of South America. The townspeople were suffering a virus causing weakness, nausea, and dizziness. The herbs were gathered right away, and the recipe was done in two hours. Miraki immediately sent for runners to gather doses and distribute to the community with simple directions and to rest a full twenty-four hours for the remedy to take effect. Then she graciously sent out a heartfelt thanks to Myama of Quito. A great arc of light connection was made with North and South with intense love and affection.

On the same time frame, Rotussi had received inner messages during his morning meditation and immediately sent out vibrations of love, peace, and harmony to his two soul partners. His open heart and blessings poured out and helped to bring balance and relaxation to the community during this healing process. The two received the assistance with humility and gratitude. In turn, this combined energy of love, peace, and harmony increased the light of the three and also created a vision that all shared from Rheyzoun-45.

The smile of a Buddha with the comment "Well done!" warmed their hearts while at the same time increased the momentum of great light for all twenty-five Chosen Ones on the planet. And they were admonished by the great Buddha to celebrate their victories without squandering the light, as the momentum of increase is crucial for future challenges and tasks to save the planet. He emphasized that the evil Teohta would be enraged and counter with an evil lash out to any light bearers intent to destroy her evil kingdom and plans. This the twenty-five took to heart and gave thanks for the wisdom of the Buddha.

Across the great waters, in the land of Norway, Omer maintains his low-profile career of janitor in a private school. One day while enjoying his pastime of hiking and chanting Hindu mantras, he received an inner distress call from one of his Chosen One soul partners. Young Deeka of Gjovik, Norway, came home to find that her home was broken into and robbed. Fortunately her children, Byron and Ishi, were out with her best friend, Abe. She found that certain patterns of her fashions were missing. She was keenly aware of different fashion companies that were envious of her success that might ignite an act such as this to steal her ideas and attempt to band together and put her out of business. This incident immediately sent out a distress call to her fellow Chosen Ones Omer, Jogil, and Fioriya.

The three received the inner stress call and right away joined their hearts of light directed her way. Each received a message to focus on a beam of blue light and to call to the great Buddha of protection for this incident, then to focus on a beam of fiery ruby light to seek out the perpetrators of this theft. These inner commands are crucial and need to be acted on immediately for the forces of light to exact and execute justice on the physical planes of being.

The three began an intense meditation and focus aimed at Deeka. This act heightened Deeka's sense of awareness that enabled her not to panic and to take notice of any forms of evidence that would lead to details for an investigation to be activated. When this was done, the great Buddha of the Ruby Beam instructed, "Let this focus continue for thirty minutes and then release it to the cosmos. By releasing the energy, feel the strength of faith and victory in your hearts and know that cosmic justice will prevail."

At that command, all did what was instructed of them. This was a true test of faith for all and when properly executed, would be a definite victory.

The three went about their activities after sending a deep sense of love and gratitude to the cosmic Buddhas of Rheyzoun-45. Realizing at the current moment that all could not be physically together to work on problems, they as students of the light began to realize and experience the inner forces of light as an act of divine love and harmony/unity. They began to realize that the physical has its limitations since the "fall from grace," when mankind chose to rely on his own instincts, thus cutting off the communion of the Great Spirit/cosmos by his own free will. This current incident gave them a strong sense of togetherness, unity, and loyalty toward one another.

Three days had passed since Deeka notified the authorities of the break-in and theft. On the fourth day, Deeka received a call from the authorities that they had apprehended two people with the evidence provided. A car was racing through an intersection and ran a red light. They were stopped and cited for speeding and running a red light. While they were being written up, an officer noticed that some clothes with patterns were scattered about in the back seat. From Deeka's report about the robbery, the evidence went out to all enforcement officers to be on the lookout for any unusual articles stolen within the previous week. An APB was sent out with pictures of the stolen items. This they recognized, and an arrest was made of the two suspects. It was a male-and-female couple in their midtwenties. Deeka was instructed to come and identify the couple at the precinct.

This she did immediately the same day. While she didn't know the suspects, she did recognize the clothes that they were wearing and informed the authorities that the brand of clothes being worn were of a fierce competitor that recently criticized her for trying to control the local fashion area with her ideas and influence. The authorities were keenly interested and agreed to pursue an investigation on the matter.

This pleased Deeka and also proved to her that active trust of the cosmic forces within had truly worked in this situation. She felt a deep gratitude within and also thanked her inner partner from her heart. And she also felt the urge to say a prayer for the couple responsible for the break-in and theft of her home. In her heart she forgave them knowing that they were pawns of an evil plot by one of her competitors. She felt a sincere deep sense of forgiveness and mercy. When this inner feeling was expressed, her three Chosen companions accepted this message from her and reciprocated with the same emotions.

At that precise moment, a great light being, Ramata, rejoiced with a great warmth within and a victorious message saying, "Blessed ones of my heart, this is why you are the Chosen Ones. Not only did you put your trust and faith in the light, but you laced it with mercy and forgiveness. This is a major part of the future blueprint of victory on Terra. I congratulate you all with an increase of the golden disc in your hearts. Keep on keeping on with your momentums and service in the light!" At that, all twenty-five fell in a great silence of love and gratitude.

CHAPTER 6

TURNING TO THE vast jungles of Africa, the priestess Coralea began a busy day as three pregnant mothers in adjoining communities were expecting their births that very day. She was given their names by runners of the tribe. Coralea fell into a meditative state, and by this she could determine whose baby would be born first, second, and third, so she could assist each when the time was ready. Then she instructed the runners for her preparedness and the times of her arrival.

The first young mother, Azuzu, had lost a baby from a previous pregnancy and was very nervous with this one. Coralea always sent prayers to the mothers and their babies as part of her birthing services. She would visualize newborns in a pink bubble of love outlined with a blue ring for protection. And then, as the birth would begin, she would serenade both mother and baby with a song she called "Great Spirit of Love." This would help to calm the mother and protect the baby's entrance into its new world. This time Azuzu's delivery was flawless, giving birth to a baby girl. The custom of this community was for the mother to name the baby within the first twenty-five minutes. If not, the chief of the community could either name the baby or request the father to name it. But Azuzu's first thought came within five minutes. She named the baby girl Perlu, and at that, Coralea blessed both Azuzu and Perlu.

Then she continued her day's travels to the other two places to continue her work. Her life to serve others in this manner pleased both Bradley and Samson, hunters who found and raised this wondrous child. They searched for years for her parents, but to no avail. Since there was no history of any parent, all the tribes felt that Coralea was a priestess sent from the Great Creator to bless and multiply life in the jungles of Africa. She never regretted not having her true parents and very wholeheartedly accepted Bradley and Samson as her guardians. Her heart is always filled with much love and a deep passion to serve all the tribes.

Further north, in Mosfellsbaer, Iceland, a similar kindred spirit, Fohran, was abandoned at age seven. He was adopted by two loving parents, Jacob and Misty. While an only child, he had an affinity for being a big brother to other abandoned kids. He senses a protective, positive unseen force as his guardian of life, and sports a dire passion of writing poetry.

A similar pattern of some of the Chosen Ones has been revealed. Whether abandoned, or by loss of parents, this strategy of the masters is intentional. This helps to take away any advantages that the evil Teohta could use to battle the forces of light. Any threat to one's family could always be used as a deterrence for one's mission of light. However, the adverse effect is the magnified anger that constantly provokes the wrath of Teohta.

The third of this chosen group is Yazerya, aged seventeen. She is currently struggling with her hairstyling business in Lisbon, Portugal. This has created a cramp in her use of time as she passionately pursues her goal as a makeup artist for motion-picture companies. One of her two partners left the hairstyling company, and the clientele is now dependent on two stylists only. She has three interviews for motion-picture companies this week, which conflicts with the increased hours at the hair place. This sense of urgency automatically sent out an inner distress call to both Coralea and Fohran. They both received a vision of Yazerya's situation and instantly gave prayer for a solution to her cause. Meanwhile Yazerya advertised her need of an experienced hairstylist. She also prayed to the inner guides for assistance in this matter. That immediately activated the bond of the three to seek out and inwardly contact the perfect person to fill the job. Within three days, she received three possible applicants.

Yazerya was excited yet calm as she set up interview times for the possible hires. She set aside one whole day for the interviews and gave an early-morning prayer for that day. The same was true for both Fohran and Coralea until a sense of victory was received within their hearts.

The interview process began precisely at 9:00 that morning. The first interview was a vibrant young lady that provided her credentials and did not hesitate to state that she was pursuing for a part-time position only as she was preparing for college. This candidate was respectfully declined as a full-time position was needed.

The second candidate had three jobs in the last five years and did not show a sense of stability. Her credentials were also average at best.

The third candidate was a middle-aged gentleman with a mild demeanor about him. His credentials were very impressive, yet he was not boastful about it. He wore a constant and sincere smile that pleased Yazerya. He showed an eagerness for his work and stated that he would work any and all shifts that was necessary. She felt of him as a sincere father figure and informed him of her decision the following day. This definitely felt right and all she had to do was to talk with her partner about this candidate. They both agreed to a short telephone interview and then make the decision right away.

The next day the interview began at 9:00 a.m. Yazerya and her partner, Sasha, both liked this pleasant gentleman and asked him what wage he desired for this position. His response startled them as his answer was considerably lower than they expected. They offered a bit more and he happily agreed. The decision was made to hire Bartholomew and all were happy and joyous. He was to start immediately the following Monday.

As this sense of joy filled Yazerya's heart, both Fohran and Coralea felt a surge of loving warmth within themselves. All three knew that the mission at hand was a victory for Yazerya. All three bowed their heads in gratitude, thanked one another, and praised the great light within. They also chanted the cosmic name Ramata, nine times, as a respect and thanks for their opportunities as Chosen Ones for the great cause of humanity and its planet.

Ramata responded through the Rheyzoun Buddhas, with warmth and love. "I am well pleased. Your actions of unity, trust, and faith have served you well and has magnified the light within you all. Your initiations will begin to increase and intensify as the light intensifies. Darkness responds like a moth to the light, so be constantly aware and prepared. The survival of a planet rests in your strength and the sustaining of the light."

CHAPTER 7

SHIFTING TO THE Canary Islands of the Atlantic Ocean resides Nyla, a former sorceress of the black arts, born again into the light. This thirty-three-year-old has found a new balance in her life with partner and boyfriend, Brandon, and her pet companions, a dog named Motley, and a falcon-dart. Brandon is a tour guide, and they have been dating for three years now. Nyla recently finished a complete makeover in her crystal and book store. She rid herself of all her black arts books, articles, etc., and now promotes love, healing, and positivity with all her current products. This was a most difficult but necessary transition for her as her base clientele had been those of witches, spells, incantations, and sorcery—the black arts. Most saw her as a crazed convert now and spread negative rumors about her, stating that she was judging their beliefs and tried to put her out of business. Her Chosen partners, Hoopti and Vander, sensed an uneasiness within and realized her current state of being.

They instantly responded with a warm heart of love and protection her way, and Nyla received the light beam with great love and respect. Their daily meditations consistently sent these rays of love, light, joy, and peace her way for as long as it took. Plus her companionship with Brandon was a great boost in her self-confidence and equilibrium as a new positive and bright energy began to shine in her shop.

Slowly but steadily new customers began to arrive and admire the transformation that was at one time a very dark and negative vibration that was unattractive and unappealing.

People experienced and felt a bright aura emanating from Nyla's heart and being. They were hungry and in dire need for ways to improve their lives with the proper tools of love, light, and peace. Soon the new customers started a network of sharing their new experiences with others, and within a few months, Nyla's shop was prospering beyond her dreams. A wave of gratitude and love shot from her heart to the cosmos and her inner partners. Her body shook with one mighty jolt as she felt a tremendous final release of a longtime grip that Teohta held on her.

What an awesome sense of freedom she felt. She immediately fell to her knees and bowed to the light within. "Ommm, Ramata, Ommm" was her heart's mantra as the three repeated this mantra nine times. And as she stood to admire the sunset over the ocean, a choir of blessings filled the air. With this a great message was received through Ramata and the Rheyzoun Buddhas.

"We congratulate and salute you in this hard-fought victory. A great shadow of two thousand years has been punctured but not quite totally lifted over these islands. The power of the three, when properly maintained, will continuously multiply times three when the human ego is set aside for the divine ego to intensify through the power of cosmic love and unity. You begin to see the power of twenty-five Chosen Ones when joined in a harmony of faith and unity, can lead to a great momentum of joy and hope in people's hearts. Then and only then, through their free will and following the light of the heart within, the hearts of millions can transform a planet. I thank you!"

Hoopti and Vander experienced Nyla's victory with her vision of the island sunset followed by Ramata's victory salute. Humility and gratitude filled their hearts as the inner ties of unity were celebrated.

Further west in the Central America region, forty-five-year-old, six-foot-one-inch Aton maintains 250 acres of land. As a prosperous land owner loved by his loyal and trusted workers, Aton gives blessings and gratitude to the Creator in his daily morning meditations. He is an only child born of Russi, a diplomat, and Mayah, a migrant worker. They met in a town market and felt an immediate attraction. They married and bore a son two years later.

The land they own was now being run by Aton but had been in the Russi family of three generations. Russi turned over the responsibilities to Aton at age thirty so that he could fulfill his services full-time as an ambassador. His big heart, matched with a keen wisdom, gained him respect from all surrounding lands as well as overseas. His demands were never more than what he would give of himself. Thus, he was the perfect mentor and example for Aton to admire and follow.

One morning, Aton was informed that his mother, Mayah, had collapsed and fell into an unconscious state. She had always been a robust woman of great health so all around her were completely shocked and in panic.

She was instantly administered too and rushed to the nearest hospital. Aton turned over his duties to his foreman, Byron. The local hospital was only twenty minutes away and Aton was there in ten minutes. He rushed to the emergency room desk to inquire of his mother, Mayah. This feeling of panic and fear was a first for Aton as he always has been a man of extreme self-control and calm. This feeling of hopelessness threw him out of balance, and he sent out an immediate SOS to his inner partners, Zeera and Amara. The signal was so intense that both felt an instant sharp pain in their chest.

This jolt they experienced nearly knocked them off their feet. But quickly they regained their composure and began to send signals of love, peace, and healing to Aton and his mother. This action instantly cleared Aton's head, and he felt an immediate warmth within his heart. When he regained his composure, Aton calmly asked the emergency room nurse the current status of his mother. She assured him that she would inquire as soon as the doctors finished their examination. She also asked if the husband, Russi, had been contacted.

"Oh my goodness! I forgot to call Dad!" cried Aton. The nurse said she would contact him, and Aton settled down somewhat. She did not want Aton's panicked voice to stir up Russi. She had been a friend of the family for years and was experienced in these situations as a nurse.

Soon Russi called Aton and told him he would be back in town the next day and to stay there until he arrives. Aton had finally begun to settle down and gather his composure. Amara and Zeera could really feel his trauma and stepped up their compassionate hearts and visions of the green healing ray to both Aton and his mother. Aton could feel this and asked an orderly if he could find him a quiet room to rest.

Yes, Teohta really dug in with an attack on this trio of Chosen Ones. Her dark talons of terror without mercy had punctured Aton's soul viciously as her anger had seriously amplified due to her losses to the previous recent Chosen Ones. Her rage was fed by the fear and out-of-balance soul of Aton. She was also feeling some seepage from Russi as well. This appeased her dark appetite tremendously.

Finally, finding a quiet room in the hospital, Aton began to meditate on the situation at hand. He felt ashamed within himself for allowing imbalance of his emotions to take control with fear and panic. Zeera and Amara sensed this and sent waves of mercy and forgiveness to Aton. This created a warmth that once again gave Aton a sense of peace and balance within.

Meanwhile, the doctors were at a loss as Mayah fell into a deep coma. This always healthy and robust woman had no history of illness at all through her life. The doctors could keep her breathing on life support while continuing to try and figure out the cause of this situation.

While in their meditations, the three felt their impulses increasing in intensity. It felt as though another was offering their assistance but not familiar with their vibrational pattern. To make things more confusing, the three shared a vision of a group of islands in the Atlantic. Their SOS had reached for more help as Nyla had responded to their communications. Being a former sorcerer, she had seen this experience before and it took the life of a young man.

Nyla offered her assistance along with her fellow Chosen Ones. She relayed that the deceased gentlemen was bitten by a rare and dangerous spider, but the bite was found too late to be able to counter the effect with any form of an antidote. It was a very minute puncture with no swelling around it. She told Aton to quickly alert the doctors to search her body for a non-swollen, minute insect bite. At that, he broke his meditation and rushed to inform the emergency room what the cause could possibly be and what to look for.

By this time it was morning and Russi was at the front desk area. Aton relayed his message to the doctors, and they would immediately start body scans for any signs of an insect bite that could cause this.

Now Aton could not tell Russi see how he discovered this idea, as the Chosen Ones have a pact of silence for their planetary mission. But he did not lie as he stated that the idea came to mind. This was true.

Aton felt hopeful as now the cause had been discovered and he has the light and energy of six Chosen Ones working in his favor. He excused himself and went back to his quiet room. He resumed his meditations with a new hope and fervor. Surely, this would bring a great victory for him and the planet. It did, but not in the way he expected.

At 6:00 p.m. the same day, his mother took her last breath and passed. Russi was the first to hear and went to the quiet room to inform Aton of her passing. Russi braced himself as he knew that Aton was close to his mother and that this would crush him.

While in his meditation, Aton felt a dimming in his light energy connections, which never before occurred. He felt an immediate and uneasiness that broke his concentration. At that, he rushed to the emergency room desk, only to see Russi with a long blank expression on his face. Aton stopped in his tracks and began weeping. "This can't be real! Why did this happen? Why was it allowed?" Gloom and remorse had begun to take over. His mother was gone!

Even through his shock, Aton and felt an overwhelming wave of love and empathy from his inner friends. This opened the door for a Rheyzoun Buddha to respond.

"We mourn for your loss as your mother was a strong soul of light. However, on the inner planes of being, which her conscious mind wasn't aware of, she agreed to sacrifice the remainder of this life for the greater cause. That of which your group, through the circumstances had been contacted by another group of Chosen Ones, thus a price was paid for a great light expansion was formed. She pointed out to us that she paid a great debt to you for assisting her in a like manner in a previous embodiment when you were brother and sister. Thus, this has been a great victory and gain in the light though Teohta feels she won that specific battle.

"In three days you will receive an inner message from Mayah relaying that all is well and her love for you and Russi is an everlasting love with no end. Rejoice, Aton, in your victory and new bond with Nyla and her band of three. The Buddhas salute you and the Great Ramata thanks you for your great sacrifice!" At that, Aton bowed his head in gratitude of the message and began to fully realize what is really at stake for this troubled planet.

CHAPTER 8

NOW, ACROSS THE great Pacific, hailing from Sapporo, Japan, twenty-seven-year-old Namko docks his fishing boat and makes way for his fencing class. He loves the discipline of the art and the physical aspect of keeping physically fit. And to balance his mental health, he is an avid writer of poetry. He often visualizes a divine order of living through high spiritual ethics and practices. All of these characteristics are what definitely qualified him as a Chosen One.

Now, Pyrena, a twenty-nine-year-old born in Kashmir, India, chips away on her latest block of stone for a vendor of a local shopping mall. Her skills of fourteen years has kept her in high demand. But as the eldest of eight siblings, she always creates equal time for the family. Being a sculptor does not necessarily allow for much of a social life. But Pyrena also has a passion for her spiritual meditation, which she feels also gives her creative ideas and inspiration for her artwork. Her youngest little sister, Aimee, loves for her to tell stories of her dreams and goals

Meanwhile, Tyotan and his fiancé, Saraya, 24, are absorbed in a nature's hike in the outskirts of their city, Dornbirn, Austria. The second day of a three-day hike has had its challenges as a few run-ins with some wildlife had stopped them in their tracks. But their experience with these situations pulled them through nature's testing of respect and reverence for the cycles of wildlife. Tyotan's patience and discipline as an auto mechanic serves him well in his activities of hiking, backpacking, and home restoration. His lady, Saraya, is a manager for a four-star hotel in Dornbirn. They met when she brought her car to his business for repairs. When he offered her a ride home due to the time limit of repairs on her car, it gave them a chance to get acquainted with one another. They realized that they shared similar interests and enjoyed each other's company. Saraya has a thirst for spiritual meditation, and

Tyotan loved to share his insights with her. Within two weeks, they started dating.

While on their last day of the hike, Tyotan felt an inner urge to stay closer to Saraya as there might be a possible unexpected danger awaiting them. This strong sensation was also felt by Namko and Pyrena.

The three could sense each other's inner presence and proceeded to make some calls for protection for the two. Within twenty minutes, a severe rockslide had occurred just minutes ahead on their hiking trail. Saraya had a habit of a quite extensive lead on Tyotan during their hikes together. However this time Tyotan advised her to stay closer to him and slow the pace. Had they maintained their normal pace, that would have put them directly in the middle of the rock slide with no escape whatsoever

As they slowed their pace, they heard a loud rumble from a hill just ahead of them on the trail. The huge rocks and dirt had come tumbling down the steep hill and smothered everything in its path. The dust filled the air to the point where they threw a tarp over themselves to avoid choking and smothering.

Saraya was amazed that Tyotan could sense a dangerous act in the making. He responded by explaining that his meditations had seemed to gain him a heightened sense of awareness, a sensitivity of vibrations about his being 24/7. Saraya expressed her joy and gratitude for his companionship. It was then that Tyotan had proposed to Saraya, and she happily and joyfully agreed.

Within himself, Tyotan thanked Pyrena and Namko for their energy and light, and they, in turn, shared their opportunity to share in service to one another. They also expressed their joy for him and his proposal to Saraya. Another victory chalked up for a Chosen One trio!

In that moment, an inner glow expanded in their hearts as a Rheyzoun Buddha rejoiced in their thwarting of an attack from the dark forces of Teohta. "Well done, dear hearts of light! You have become attuned greatly toward one another and have learned to take immediate action when warranted. When the light signals the heart of imminent danger, reaction with right mind is crucial as just seconds could determine the victory or defeat against the dark forces of Teohta.

May your momentum of light forever glow and shine on for this beloved planet Terra! I and the hierarchy applaud you!"

Off in the far Pacific of Puako, Hawaii, twenty-year-old, Bayuni has a new client in her law firm. She is to defend/represent a young eighteen-year-old male for possession of stolen property. She is in her first year of residency in law. When not at work, she spends her time swimming and snorkeling. Her natural beauty also permits her to actively participate in local beauty contests. Her brunette hair, complemented with brown eyes, make for an appealing contrast with her acquired tan. But her greatest passion is a desire to work on a cruise ship for a career. She also sports a fascination and love for turtles and dragonflies. She loves the adventurous life while also managing time for morning meditations.

Hailing from across the Pacific, young eighteen-year-old Tillow of Seward, Alaska, is playing a violin version of Beethoven's Fifth Symphony in a rehearsal for an upcoming concert in five days. He also plays piano and is playing a Hayden favorite on that. This young silver-haired prodigy began playing violin and piano at the age of five and was a natural for classical music. He is already in the process of writing his own compositions and recently has drawn the attention of world-renowned classical artist Yo-Yo Ma. He is reportedly going to attend her next concert, which thrills the young talented artist. Taylor is very self-disciplined and starts every day at 4:30 a.m. with a ninety-minute meditation. Because he was born of spiritual parents, this had been a daily practice of the family his whole life. Excitement was his reaction when he had received an inner signal from the hierarchy to be a Chosen One for a higher cause. He agreed and was informed not to share this with his parents. His exceptional devotion, dedication, and discipline is one of the highest ranks of all the Chosen Ones, and he is only eighteen years of age. The Buddhas said that his role in the planetary healing would mainly be provided by his music and the strong passion he has for worldwide peace and unity.

Rounding out this trio of Chosen Ones is thirty-year-old Creoki of Tecate, Baja, California. This black-haired, black-eyed man serves as a tour guide for his homeland and whose love and passion is to serve and educate the people of the local surrounding lands. His hobbies are the study of philosophy and cooking. His absorption of the philosophy prompted him to practice meditation at an early age and had helped to develop patience, understanding, and a passion to serve others. These qualities prompted his calling from the Buddhas as a Chosen One. At this contact he felt so humbled and immediately accepted his role in the effort to save this planet.

However, he received an immediate initiation upon his acceptance. One day as he awoke, a severe headache coupled with the loss of speech and a numbness in his right leg had ruled him incompetent. This sudden incident created a concern as a major tour was scheduled this day and his expertise was in great need for this special group. It was scheduled for 1:00 p.m., and it was already 5:30 a.m. He would have to call in for a replacement guide by 7:30 a.m. if he could not make it to work.

In that moment, Bayuni and Tillow felt an inner stress call from Creoki in his current dilemma. A strong focus began and Creoki felt a strong urge to play some classical music to help calm him and settle his mind. While listening to Chopin, he experienced a vision of a beautiful dragonfly fluttering its wings of very soothing colors while circling his body like a coil from feet to head. This occurred seven times, and then the dragonfly disappeared into a beautiful violet cloud. The edges of the cloud was tinted with blue and green. This vision of the cloud lasted for thirty minutes and he felt the need to immerse himself to become one with the cloud. It was now 6:30 a.m.

Bayuni and Tillow both maintained their focus and also added a strong ray of pink that was the love of their heart connecting to Creoki's heart. He fell into a soft sleep for about fifteen minutes. When he awoke, the time was 7:15 a.m. He noticed a tingling sensation in his right leg, indicating that feeling was returning. As the numbness was dissipating, his headache had reduced to a minor one. He tried a few mantras to see if he had a voice. It was very soft and weak but was beginning to return. As 7:25 a.m. arrived, he had to make a decision. Would he attempt to work that day or would he take the time off to see a doctor and have more time to recuperate?

Creoki called in to work and his boss immediately began to inform him that the tour had been cancelled and rescheduled for four days later. Apparently two people became ill and two more were delayed for that day's trip. Creoki was relieved and so happy that he did not even have to tell him about his own illness. However, he would still make an appointment to see a doctor about his recent incident.

At the end of his call, Creoki knelt down and sent a very heartfelt thank you to Bayuni and Tillow. His sense of gratitude filled their hearts as all three celebrated their joy and peace with one another. At this juncture a great silence fell on all twenty-five Chosen Ones as Ramata began a silent communion with these kindred souls of light.

"Blessed hearts, rejoice in your bonding and victories with one another for I am well pleased! You have demonstrated your commitment and devotions to one another. This was most crucial to see and determine if all were qualified to act as a great unit, a web of light if you will, and function as a mighty electrode of light from which the Rheyzoun Buddhas could set the blueprint and strategy of light to battle the dark forces of Teohta and her legions of Doom. Always remember that you are the physical conduit for the cosmic forces of light to act through. This is cosmic law and can only be activated by the right use of the human free will! Your greatest strengths are based upon your pure sense and bond of unity and purpose. There is no room in this cosmic chain for a weak link! Thus, the saying, a chain is only as strong as its weakest link!

"The passing of Mayah was, in truth, a victory for the world cause, as six of you now have formed a strong bond. From now on, the initiation of the twenty-five Chosen Ones will increase in intensity and start to become more global. I encourage all to intensify your meditations and always, always remember to call upon us for assistance in your trials. We need this on a regular basis for your light alone will not be victorious. To have complete victory for a planet is to reconnect with the cosmos and reestablish the divine cord of light with the almighty Creator! I, Ramata, and the Rheyzoun Buddhas seal you with a mighty orb of light with which to draw upon in time of great need. May your blueprint of divine love, light, devotion, dedication, and commitment shine on and expand greatly in this most crucial battle to save a planet and lay a foundation for a great golden age to come! I am your Ramata and my love for you is eternal!"

CHAPTER 9

MONTHS PASSED BY and on one early-morning spring day on April 4, 2020, Kobin was en route on one of his routine checkpoints when he received an unexpected call from Vanessa regarding the twins, Bessie and Trina. Both girls had acquired persistent coughs and were also experiencing lightheadedness, causing blurred vision as well. As a rule, the girls were very healthy nine-year-olds and had always been very energetic. Kobin inquired about Vanessa and how she was feeling. She seemed to be okay but was very troubled and concerned for the girls. He suggested to take Bessie and Trina to an urgent care facility and have them checked out.

Immediately Kobin calmly sent an inner alert call for assistance from Yoi-Yu and Krea. Their responding energy was felt instantly. Yoi-Yu's energy was exceptionally strong, as a Hopi medicine woman, while she proceeded to run an inner diagnosis on the twins' souls. This intense energy put her abilities to the extreme test as she had to make many attempts to maintain her focus on the girls to the point of near exhaustion. She made a call for assistance, and this action sent out an SOS, which made contact with Myama, the twelve-year-old herbalist of Quito, Ecuador. In turn Myama's inner partners, Miraki and Rotussi, were contacted. Miraki's strong beam of light coupled with Rotussi's tai chi presence made for an exceptional wave of light in assistance to Kobin's cause. This extra energy helped to balance Kobin's demeanor in knowing that additional help was in action. He called Vanessa to see how the twins were faring.

Vanessa's response was troubling as she reported that there were three other mothers with their children experiencing the same problematic symptoms that were slowly getting worse. What was going on? he wondered.

Teohta's tentacles were reaching out to the children of the Chosen Ones. She figured that attacking the siblings would create a fear and helplessness in their energy grids. And these tactics had been effective throughout her reign as the Queen of Darkness. Oh how she revels at the expense of others' miseries and suffering! She was sensing a great victory over Ramata and his Chosen Ones!

By the end of the day, three more families had brought their kids in with the same worsening symptoms. The doctors had decided for the families to admit their children in their nearest hospital. That hospital was called and set up a quarantine area while the problem was being researched. The children were in the best hands in case of worsening conditions that might occur.

The following morning four children had lapsed into a coma, and the other eleven had no change in their symptoms. Bessie was one of the four in a coma. Vanessa was petrified for her girls and refused to leave the hospital. Kobin had been okay with this as he figured the mother's love and light would be a positive force in the matter. This also allowed him to do some intense meditations at home without disturbance as he had put in for a temporary leave of absence for this emergency family situation.

While working on a number of plants and herbs for the symptoms, young twelve-year-old Myama remembered the instructions of the masters on how to draw the energies of all twenty-five Chosen Ones by reciting the mantra "Ramtam Om Shivaya Om!" nine times. She alerted the other five to chant this mantra quickly. They all began in an instant, and one could feel the energy soar with full intensity as now all twenty-five Chosen Ones responded to the SOS call of the mantra.

And while this abundant energy reached its peak, Kobin directed it to the hospital with a vision of the quarantine area with the children. All had received an inner message that this intense focus would have to be maintained for three days. As long as three Chosen Ones would maintain the focus in their meditations, it would equal the combined efforts of all twenty-five. So they inwardly made unbroken schedules that would keep a strong, nonstop focus of light and love for three days straight. This would require their full dedication, determination, and an unbroken discipline. This task was a successful accomplishment. Now their test of love, faith, and patience was in play.

While this inner work was being done, two more children had lapsed into a coma. The others were unchanged; no better, no worse. Vanessa had gathered the other mothers together and formed a prayer vigil for the children in the hospital chapel. Kobin was delighted when he discovered this.

Meanwhile, there was still a continuous flow of loving energy being maintained by the twenty-five. A great battle had been waged between light and darkness. Teohta was immensely hungry for a victory over Ramata. Things seem to be waning her way, and she was reveling in it.

At this juncture the Rheyzoun Buddhas received a signal from this strong impulse generated by the twenty-five from Terra. The 72-hour marathon of decrees and devotions had unleashed the clearance for Ramata and his legions to an assist in this mighty battle. He responded with an order of three legions to battle and capture a certain percentage of the worst disciples of Teohta's armies. This action would take 24 hours for the legions to capture and remove these shadow bands from the planet.

Days had passed by without any changes, but Kobin sensed this as a positive since things did not seem to appear any worse. The twenty-five Chosen Ones were still linked on their inner meditation connection when on the morning of April 20 they all simultaneously experienced a vision of a bright, powerful rainbow arcing the planet. No words were spoken as a follow-up vision of a great being was bowing to Terra and her inhabitants. Then the vision vanished as quickly as it had appeared. It definitely had a very positive, powerful effect on all the Chosen Ones.

Minutes later Vanessa called Kobin with some mixed news regarding all the children. Bessie had regained consciousness, but Trina's condition had not changed. One child passed on from his coma, and the other four coma victims remained the same. Five of the remaining nine children began to show gradual improvement. Meanwhile the doctors were still at a loss as to what had caused this strange, unknown outbreak. They had alerted other doctors from out-of-state areas as to what was happening in the town of Rugby, North Dakota.

At this point, Kobin felt a sudden urge to find a secluded spot where he could enter a meditative state. Fifteen minutes into his silence, a great being began an explanation as to what and why this battle had taken place as well as the cost of the battle.

"You have fought hard and long in this crucial battle in your city. For thousands of years your area in North America now known as Rugby, North Dakota, has been a strong focus of good and light as its location is exactly the center of your North America. Great battles have been waged in the surrounding areas due to the precious light and vibrations established here. This has been primarily done to assist and maintain a physical balance, an equilibrium to hold the Earth in its axis. Ages of this maintaining has helped to prevent any cataclysmic events or changes in the earth's landscapes. That is why it is always been a focal point of attack from the sinister forces of those such as Teohta. Teohta became the Queen of Darkness 500 of your earth years ago when she led a battle for a similar spot on the planet and was victorious. At that time there were fewer light bearers around and also they were not united as one against the forces of darkness.

"This battle was much different and better prepared. Our Lord Ramata had scoped out the earth for twenty-five Chosen Ones to band together and given the proper tools for battle. However, even this is never a guarantee as any cosmic being by universal law has to allow all human beings to act by their own free will. A victory cannot be won alone or by non-action even when the tools are provided. That is why the earth was scoured to find a minimum of twenty-five souls that qualified for the title of stalwart soldiers whose heart, passion, and right attitude in action could help to fight and maintain a certain percentage of light to hold the balance for the planet. There are millions of light souls on the planet but few who measure up to the accountability and responsibility of spiritual hierarchy and leadership in the example of the heart's passion, action, and service to life with light and purpose. A planet is a living being but does not have a consciousness of self-awareness and a natural evolution in spiritual progress and growth. So who you are and what you do or don't do is the direct cause-and-effect process that allows humans through free will to be cocreators in life, whether they are aware of this or not. Even inaction is an action but never has a positive outcome. Always be aware of the dangers of a comfort zone or lethargy. These are negative habits that have no positive use in life!

"We commend you and your band for your hard-fought victory! However, it came with a high price. Your Bessie will completely heal, but Trina will heal with some lifelong disabilities, headaches, short-term memory loss, and severe allergies in the autumn season. Two of the coma victims will pass on, and two of the remaining nine will also pass. This has been decided by cosmic law of which we cannot interfere.

"At the moment Teohta claims this as her victory, but in reality, the strength of you twenty-five has raised you to a new level of inner strength and spiritual bond. All of your alertness and heightened awareness will be much easily acquired when anyone of you desires assistance from one another. And always remember that your constant and consistent meditations alone can actually serve as preventative energies that can immediately dissolve negative causes."

At this, Kobin's meditation ceased and he knew he would be needed at the hospital to assist Vanessa in the counseling of the parents who were about to lose their little ones. The doctors still have not found a cause to the outbreak as the mysterious conditions remain unsolved.

Just a note: Bessie made a complete recovery and had displayed a certain state of peace of mind followed by a constant smile that seemed to be endless. She was informed in strict confidence by the Buddha that her life would play out an important role in the master's plan to save the world. Not even Kobin was to know what her secret mission from the Buddha would be. But for now Kobin and Vanessa were grateful and happy that their children had survived this mysterious ordeal in their lives.

CHAPTER 10

ACROSS THE GLOBE in Iceland, Fohran was in the process of writing a special poem for Taylor, a young thirteen-year-old who lost his parents by way of an auto accident at the age of eleven. Because he was an only child and had no other local family, Fohran assisted him in finding a loving couple as foster parents. The timing could not be any better.

A young couple, Chad and Kim, were looking for a son to share their lives along with their young ten-year-old daughter, Lizzie. Lizzie had been begging her parents for a big brother by her next birthday. When Fohran introduced them to Taylor, the three hit it off immediately. The next step was to introduce Taylor to Lizzie. The meeting was arranged for three days later. When Taylor was shown a picture of young Lizzie, he was ecstatic. He instantly felt the desire to write a poem for his potential new little sister. He begged Fohran to help him as he had never written anything. Fohran happily agreed. That same night he began a poem and decided that the next day he would have Taylor sit with him so he could coach him on writing from his heart and assist in his vocabulary and sentence structure.

After a brief dinner, Fohran sat in his lazy chair to relax and watch a little TV. Immediately a newsflash shot across the screen. A house break-in had just occurred, and two gunmen were holding a couple hostage. When he saw the house, his heart skipped a beat as it was the home of his adopted parents, Jacob and Misty. Fohran was beside himself. This cannot be happening! There was nothing of much value in the house and the idea of gunman was unnecessary. Fohran took a few deep breaths to regain his composure.

But his initial reaction to the situation sent a strong signal to his inner kin, Coralea and Yazerya. Coralea's maternal instincts could immediately pick up on Fohran's fear and panic when his family had been threatened. The two focused their hearts' attention in a single beam of love directed his way. This helped to calm Fohran's emotions so the three could begin a focus on the crisis at hand.

The first step was to contact law enforcement and answer any questions that might assist in the capture of the gunman holding Jacob and Misty as hostages. He was asked the basic questions: names of other possible family, any known enemies, any recent occurrences with the couple, etc. Fohran did recall that Jacob had a younger brother, Brad, who had a bit of a shady past of which Jacob never elaborated about. Ten years separated, the two brothers had not been in contact for four years. Other than that, no unusual events or situations had been experienced in their lives.

Within an hour, the parents' house had been surrounded by officers and a SWAT team had taken their strategic positions, ready for anything unexpected. And communications were in place as the captain in charge attempted contact with the gunmen.

The air was tense as only one light was on in the house—a lamp on an end table in the living room. The first attempt at communication was unanswered, no response. They did not want Fohran at the scene for safety reasons.

At this juncture, contact on the inner planes was made with a gentleman from Japan, named Namko, the fishermen of Sapporo. That connection with Namko was activated through his passion for poetry. As fellow poets of the heart, their energies resonated with one another. And when Namko responded to the inner SOS signal, his inner partners, Tyotan and Pyrena, were signaled as well. Through Fohran's situation, all had a visualization of the current crisis. They all began to chant, "Ramtam Om, Shivaya Om!" to install an invisible protective shield for Fohran and his parents, Jacob and Misty. This made Fohran a little bit more at ease. He related a message that Misty was prone to asthma attacks when battling with unexpected moments of intense fear and/or anxiety. So all focused on her heart with a calm but strong beam of energy. The rest was up to faith, courage, and her destiny. What also helped Misty is the strength and poise of her Jacob. He sports a commanding but controlled presence in any given situation. As long as he was by her side, she felt a sure sense of security.

As the couple sat silently while under siege, the gunmen were having a conversation and were mumbling some names very softly. But Jacob, being very alert with a keen sense of hearing, heard the name Brad mentioned. Could his younger brother somehow be involved? Or was it just a coincidence? He had hoped for the latter, but at least for now Misty was calm and doing okay.

Again, the captain fired up the loud horn as an attempt to communicate with the gunmen. Still there was no visual of the suspects so no further details could be established. Law enforcement had performed a neighborhood search for any suspicious vehicles parked in the area. That came up empty.

While Fohran was tuned inwardly with his partners, he suddenly received a message from a young, soft voice saying, "Four blocks southwest of the house is a red and white truck with a dog on the hood." This was all he heard, but who was this unfamiliar one? Should I trust the advice? But his inner instincts quickly responded yes quickly!

So, Fohran completed his meditation and called the police to ask if they had discovered any unknown vehicles. Their response was negative. He calmly suggested to expand their search a five-block radius if they hadn't already. They agreed and immediately expanded their search.

When this search reached out to five blocks, on the southwest side a young man proceeded to flag down a police officer. He informed him of a red and white truck that seemed unfamiliar to the neighborhood and could show him where it was parked. He stated that the truck had been cruising the neighborhood for about three days. The police thanked the young man and suggested he go home until the situation was resolved.

The officers approached the truck and ran the plates through their computers. As expected, the plates were stolen since they did not match the truck. However, there were small stickers on the truck's back window that matched the dog on the hood of the truck. They unlocked the passenger door with a slim Jim and opened the glove box. They found the registration with the name Avery Bernard and ran it. Bingo! A record of run-ins with the law was fairly extensive. A couple of break-ins, gas station robberies, and two counts of stolen vehicles completed his rap sheet.

They had radioed the captain of the rundown on one of the suspects and reported that this one, Avery, had no record of actually shooting anyone. This point would be very crucial in the handling of the current situation.

Fohran began to feel more confident now that a lead had been found. The officers thanked him for the idea to expand their search a bit further. He retorted that it was a hunch he had acquired and was glad they had agreed.

Fohran receded back to his inner sanctum of communion and expressed his gratitude and thanks to the young voice that helped to crack the investigation. Within seconds, a response came and said, "I'm Bessie and I am glad to be of service."

Apparently when Kobin's daughter, Bessie, came out of her coma, a great debt of previous embodiment was paid, which entitled her to become a young initiate of the Rheyzoun Buddhas. And she gladly accepted her role of which Kobin is unaware. She accepted a promise and a vow of silence to tell no one. She became a prime example of a seemingly defeat to Teohta, but was, in actuality, a victory for the light! Fohran had found a new friend in Bessie, of which both were thrilled.

Meanwhile, the captain attempted communications again using the name Avery and strongly encouraged him and his partner to give up. While this was in process, a record was found on Avery where an accomplice named Mitchell Dobbs also had a rap sheet of break-in. It all made sense now. The only main question now is, Why this house?

On the next attempt at communication, the captain addressed both names and requested that they put their guns down and give up peacefully. Ten minutes passed until the police heard a shout-out from one of the gunman saying, "We give up!" The front door opened, the guns were placed on the porch, and the gunmen got down on their knees with their hands behind their heads. The crisis at hand was over.

One of the officers called Fohran to inform him that the suspects had surrendered. All was well with Jacob and Misty. Fohran was beside himself. His heart was filled with love and gratitude to his cosmic partners.

After further investigation of the suspects, it turns out that they had raided the wrong house of their intentions. Three houses down from Jacob and Misty's was a couple that was extensive coin collectors. They were fairly known throughout the community, which was the gunman's target. It was a total botched plan by Avery and Mitchell. However, at any time, things could have taken a change for the worse.

On this reflection, Fohran began to receive a message from the Rheyzoun Buddhas. "The sinister forces many times over will manipulate actions that has the capability to worsen things and put more innocent lives in danger. This is because they are aware of many who have been their sworn enemies in previous embodiments. Your Jacob and Misty were responsible for the capture of certain nefarious ones of which they vowed revenge in the future. So, even though its appearance as a mistaken break-in, this was a direct attack of the evil ones! But this act was thwarted by a young neophyte of the light, Bessie. Her paid debt activated her purpose and initiation in this life. Though very young, her pure, unadulterated energy was a valuable asset to the twenty-five Chosen Ones. She is what you would term as our ace in the hole. The dark forces' worst weakness is to not realize that sacrifice is a true power and asset for the Legions of Light. We truly commend you all for your sacrifices and efforts!"

CHAPTER 11

MEANWHILE, IN THE Scandinavian Land of Norway, Deeka was enjoying a beautiful day off with her adopted children, Byron, age eight and Ishi, age six. The kids loved to hike with a light backpack load and find the perfect spot to have a picnic. Deeka would limit the hikes to a maximum of three miles so they would never be too far off the beaten path, yet close enough to the general population. The children were okay with that.

They found a patch of trees that sported a nice little grassy lawn area and decided to pitch their picnic blanket there. There were few clouds in the sky on a serene 73° day. A perfect day to play Frisbee! Deeka always expected the kids to help set up the picnic lunch before going to play. However this day, she told them to go ahead and play while she set up lunch and to not wander out of her sight. The children were much disciplined and loved their adopted mother very much.

They were enjoying their Frisbee playing when Byron over shot Ishi on a throw. It landed about 50 feet past where she was standing. She went to retrieve the Frisbee and noticed a moundlike shape where it landed. When she reached the Frisbee, she had discovered that the mound was a human body and it was not moving. She froze on the spot, screamed out to Deeka in terror, and fell to the ground.

Deeka and Byron quickly dashed over in response. Ishi had passed out, and the body found was definitely not breathing. She picked up Ishi and ran her over to the blanket and tried to revive her. Meanwhile Byron was frozen on the spot, unable to stop his glare at the body. From where he was standing, he could see no blood or open wounds on the body. But he too was frightened.

Deeka fought off a panic attack herself; however, her elevated emotions set off an inner stress signal to her partners Omer, Jogil, and Fioriya. In an instant they responded with a warm beam of energy that also acted as a protective shield for the three. When this occurred, Byron broke his frozen stare of the body and walked briskly back to the picnic blanket. In a few minutes Ishi had awoken from her unconscious state.

As soon as she was calm and fully awake, Deeka called law enforcement and reported the finding. She gave the location and was informed to stay put and that they would arrive in 15 minutes. As this was happening, Byron was holding Ishi in his arms and consoling her. Things seem to be coming back to normal.

Shortly, the authorities arrived and Deeka pointed out where the kids found the body. A few of the officers went to tend to the body while one remained back to ask Deeka some routine questions. She could now feel the others energies strengthening her body and sense of awareness. The officer did suggest Deeka to take the children to the hospital just to make sure that the incident was not too traumatizing since Ishi did pass out. She fully cooperated.

While at the hospital, Byron checked out okay, but Ishi still was a little frightened and requested that Byron remain in the room with her while being checked out. It was allowed. As Ishi was being examined, she began twitching a bit and then fell into a trancelike state. Not screaming or frightened but an intense focus with eyes wide open. This confused the doctors. Her vitals were fine, but her full conscious attention was elsewhere. She grabbed Byron's hand and began speaking to him. "The found body had suffered from an overdose of drugs that reacted badly with man's heart. He suffered some convulsions and then was gone" This explanation of Ishi's, in a monotone voice, fully surprised Byron and the two attending doctors. Byron said, "My sister has never did anything like that before! Could it be something caused by the whole incident?" he asked, very puzzled. The doctors looked at one another with blank expressions. They requested that Deeka come so they could confer with her about the situation.

When Deeka arrived, they had a consultation with her and Byron. Deeka agreed with Byron that Ishi had never experienced anything like this before. The doctors recommended that Ishi be checked out by a child psychologist, and Deeka gave her consent.

Ishi was immediately escorted to a Dr. Ramsey Clark for a psychological evaluation. Deeka and Byron both remained in the waiting room. While waiting, Deeka continued her inner attunement with Omer, Fioriya, and Jogil. Being sensitive to energies, she noticed more beings in tune with her group. She saw in her mind the name Vander. Apparently Vander had a vision of a child in a park standing by a dead body. His energy was immediately attracted and connected to Ishi's, and now his group of Chosen Ones were attuned to Deeka's circuit. Nyla projected a protective shield for the children as she knew that Teohta would look for any small opening of vulnerability to unleash her Legions of Darkness.

After 30 minutes, Dr. Clark came out with Ishi and remarked how for a child she is very strong both mentally and had an above-average inner strength. He however had no clue as to what had caused her trancelike state, explaining the cause of death of the victim. He was curious and wanted to follow up with the coroner's office on the official cause of death. So he called and left a message to inform him since he was now involved with the case by evaluating Ishi.

Ishi was released from the hospital, and Deeka decided to take the children for some pizza on the way home. This excited to the kids, and they did not realize how hungry they had become.

While driving, Deeka and the children were singing with the radio when a dog ran in front of the car. Deeka slammed the brakes and barely clipped the dog in its right rear flank. The dog gave out a yelp and ran off across the street into a field and disappeared. Ishi's reflexes caused her to grabbed Byron's arm and then she immediately entered another trance. She said, "The dog suffered a mild bruise and will be fine at his home. My brother Byron will suffer a severe viral infection and will be ill for a long time. For this I am concerned!" As she concluded her trance, her grip eased and she awoke, not knowing what had just happened. Her last memory was the joyous singing in the car but no recollection of a dog running in front of the car. Ten minutes later, Deeka pulled up in the driveway. The three scurried into the house to enjoy their pizza for an early dinner.

Deeka prepared their plates and excused herself to her room for a few moments. At this point, in a meditative state, she sensed a dialogue was about to begin preceded by a great silence by the inner attunement of her partners and those of Vander's inner group.

"The shock of which Ishi experienced had unlocked a special gift that she had acquired from a previous existence. The ability to have a keen sense of heightened awareness allows her to see events both past and present, beyond the comprehension of the conscious mind. When this is triggered, her response merely expresses the happenings that occur closest to her time frame in the moment. Whether there be a positive or negative response, she just verbally expresses a mirrorlike description of detailed events closest to her place in the current place in this three-dimensional existence. This is quite similar to what you would term as an oracle. This normally occurs at a more mature age, but due to her spiritual level and extra sensitivities, the current event she experienced activated that inner skill into this life. We don't see or perceive any danger for her; however, know that when these moments are triggered, her accuracy rate is very high indeed."

At that, the silent communion ended and all were prepared for the coming illness of Byron and on guard for one another. They also learned that when two or more chosen groups had made a connection for inner strength, the opposite was also the case. When one or two suffer setbacks, it drains the light from the total group of beings. Everything in the universe is bound by cosmic law, cause and effect. No exceptions! Thus, more accountability and responsibility would be incurred throughout these missions of light to save a planet. All would have to learn to be superhuman on many levels without boosting the human ego or making any premature actions that could hurt or destroy another's life.

Absorbing this current informational insight given, Deeka had a moment of slight doubt as to what she allowed herself to get into. Would she be strong enough to handle this great task as a Chosen One and was it fair to Byron and Ishi for their lives to be affected by her decision? As quick as the thought entered her mind, a warm and loving response was received from Hoopti and Omer. "Remember, you are never alone in this battle for the survival of this planet and we all work as one pulling together our energies along with spiritual hierarchy and battling the forces of darkness. Be most careful not to give energy to negative thoughts as wherever our intention is focused we in turn attract that energy, be it good or evil. We must all strive to keep focused on the power and victory of universal love and compassion in order for the Buddhas to be able to work through us in this battle for humanity and planet Earth."

Deeka bowed her head in deep gratitude and thanks for the positive, loving response given by Hoopti and Omer. She had realized that her oath and commitment to the group of Chosen Ones had become a permanent bond with a highly spiritual family, an order selected by higher beings, and that alone was the ultimate honor and privilege out of billions of people upon this planet. This was what was needed in this moment to be able to prepare for any and all challenges and to automatically react in a positive and aggressive manner. Deeka stepped up her prayers and meditations with a positive protective energy toward Byron in preparation for his future encounter with illness.

The following day during her morning meditations, a beautiful being began to address Deeka with some more spiritual thoughts and advice on this future bout awaiting her son Byron. Her heart was open to receive this important lesson to be given.

"Dear Deeka, feel and be blessed in the fact that your past decision to adopt these beautiful children was the main sealing act that compelled spiritual hierarchy to select you as a Chosen One for the destiny of this planet Earth. Had you not adopted the children, they would have had to still experience their lives of both good and bad karma separately with probably different parents and be less prepared for the oncoming events in their lives. Your love and passion allowed you to choose these blessed little children and allowed them the companionship of brother and sister of which they had both wished for. They have shared past lives together and have yet a greater destiny to fulfill together as they formed a previous commitment to be companions again. If you had not adopted them, there was a good chance that they would have not met each other in this lifetime. Your love, directed by right intent and a desire to adopt children in need, was the right decision for all involved. You have children that you have always wanted, and they have been reunited once again by the power and right use of the universal love inherent within you. Thus, the term right-use-ness, righteousness, has evolved in mankind to raise the vibrations of consciousness and thus allowing for the accelerated pace of spiritual involvement of mankind. So you see, your part in this is great web of life is important and crucial for the victory of a planet and its people."

At the close of this sermon, Deeka fully realized her role as a Chosen One. Now Deeka felt a new level of inner strength and confidence for the next challenge to come. And she did not have long to wait. Three days later, Byron began to feel episodes of dizziness and chronic fatigue. This led to a loss of appetite as well.

His little sister, Ishi, was by his side constantly as their love for one another was a strong bond. Deeka admired this and considered it an added strength for Byron's health and well-being. The two are so well bonded that being inseparable has sometimes been a challenge for Deeka. However, her intuition told her that Ishi would be a very crucial role in the healing process.

Byron became bedridden within a week, and Deeka decided to request a doctor to visit her home to have him examined. The doctor agreed, indicating that in case it was a virus, it would be restricted to the home. An appointment was made for the following morning at 9:00 a.m. She was instructed to make sure and keep Byron well hydrated.

The following morning, Deeka and entered Byron's room and found that Ishi was fast asleep in a chair by the bed. She lovingly picked her up and carried her to her own bedroom. It was 7:30 a.m., and she wanted to prepare for the doctor's visit. Byron was still asleep so she figured that she would wake him up at 8:30 a.m. This gave her some additional meditation time.

As Deeka quieted her mind and opened her heart, she received a "good morning" greeting from her inner compadres. The warmth of their energy of love began to fill her heart like a pitcher of cool, refreshing water. In this process she had received a special dialogue and beam of energy from Nyla. "Deeka, in order to assist in Byron's health, you must visualize a serene green ovoid shape outlined with a deep blue. The green represents healing of the body elemental and the blue ring surrounding the periphery is for protection. If all of us focus on this, young Byron should be protected while we continue on our mission of battle with the dark forces. I advise you to allow Ishi to be by her brother's side whenever she chooses. Their love for one another is part of their test/initiation to be together and evolve spiritually together. Remember, that we are all 'one' in the universal spirit of cosmic love and never divert from this thought and passion. This is what allowed me to break away from the bonds of darkness that Teohta held over me."

At the end of the dialogue with Nyla, all began a chant of "Om," which resonated and lasted for a period of seven minutes, followed by a great ever-present silence. In the conclusion of the meditation, she glanced at the clock, which read 8:15 a.m.

When she entered the hallway leading to Byron's room, she was joined by Ishi, and they held hands together with a warm smile adorning their faces. As they entered the room, Byron was just waking up and smiled back at them. Deeka asked Ishi to fetch a cool glass of water for her brother, which she gladly accepted.

With her inner eye, Deeka could see the green ovoid with the surrounding blue ring enveloped around Byron's bed. And a good thing too, for she could also see a dark cloudy substance filling the rest of the bedroom. Clearly, the dark energies were present, awaiting any opportunity to invade Byron's soul to take for themselves. Seeing and experiencing this, Deeka was very grateful for Nyla's advice and assistance, fully realizing the necessity for a group focus on these protective energies.

As she glanced at the clock, the doorbell rang. The doctor was very punctual, and she was ready for any questions the doctor had for her. After ten minutes, the doctor, a Miss Sophie, requested to be taken to Byron's room. She asked to be left alone while doing her checkup and diagnosis of his condition. Both Deeka and Ishi agreed and quietly left the room.

While Ishi began doing her homework for that day, Deeka decided to call her best friend, Abe. He was very glad to hear from her and wondered why it had been a while since he had heard from her. She felt ashamed since she had not seen him at all since the incident at the picnic in the park. But Abe also felt ashamed, stating that he had not followed the news recently and therefore wasn't there for her when needed. Both Ishi and Byron liked Abe very much and considered him to be like an uncle. But their recent events kept the three focused on one another. He gladly offered his services for them at any time necessary. They both agreed to stay in touch more often and to get together soon.

As she hung up the phone, Dr. Sophie entered the living room to converse with Deeka. She expressed concern with the fact that Byron's speech had begun to be slurred and his attention span was shorter.

Dr. Sophie recommended that Deeka admit Byron to the hospital to have some tests run to hopefully eliminate or rule out certain symptoms while stating that if it was anything viral, it was not anything of a contagious nature. Deeka inquired, "How long?" Dr. Sophie responded, "About three to five days at the least." She advised that if things worsened, he would be in the best care possible. This was reassuring on a physical level, and she knew what was needed at the inner levels of action. She agreed and made arrangements to take Byron to the hospital the following day. Ishi requested of her mother that she be able to visit her brother at least three times a week, to which Deeka agreed. She realized the important bond between the two and would never interfere with their destiny together.

With this current event of Byron, Deeka felt the need to step up her meditations. She planned on commencing with a late-night vigil of inner work from 11:00 p.m. to at least midnight and to check in with him before going to sleep. When she entertained this thought, she had received an inner message from her cohorts that they would pledge to do the same. All had realized the need and urgency of the matter set before them. The healing cloud with the blue-green outer ring had to be maintained constantly twenty-four hours a day. A great battle was being fought, and their commitment to one another was very crucial for Byron's soul and physical being. Knowing this, they all called upon the golden disc placed in their hearts of the Rheyzoun Buddhas.

When they realized that this was necessary, an immense surge of light energy was felt throughout their beings and uniting the contact of all the Chosen Ones like a cosmic SOS call. Their energies were drawn together to magnify the force field around Byron's being. This act infuriated Teohta as she was hell bent on winning this battle for the hordes of darkness.

Teohta summoned her demons of hell and responded with an action of gale force winds and black clouds of lightning in the town in which they resided. Her fury was so great that it caused a power outage that lasted for days.

While Byron was still in the hospital, its power source was running on backup generators only. Fortunately, at this point in time, any type of life support system was not necessary for his needs. Dr. Sophie was about to contact Deeka to inform her that she would be able to take Byron home with instructions of his care to be followed up by three nurse visits per week. However, phone communications were unavailable at this time.

Deeka felt the need to go to the hospital and took Ishi with her. But this was not an easy task as the lightning and winds were still intense and the street lights were out all over. What normally took 15 minutes of travel now took 45 minutes to the hospital. On their way to the hospital, there were many downed trees, some partially and some fully blocking streets for any auto travel. But they finally arrived at the hospital.

Dr. Sophie happened to be at the front desk when Deeka came in. When she gave instructions for Byron, Deeka was delighted to be able to take Byron home. She turned to tell Ishi, but Ishi had already gone to Byron's room to see him.

Deeka went to the room and saw Ishi on her knees with Byron's hands softly held by hers. As Deeka entered the room, Ishi began speaking in one of her focused trances. "Byron will be in and out of consciousness for months but in the end will be at peace within. Besides the doctor's care, his home will be his greatest place for strength and healing. This must be done soon. The doctors are yet unable to diagnose the cause but will continue to monitor his condition at the house." At this, the trance ended, and Byron woke from his sleep.

His smile met Ishi's smile as they embraced each other with a warm hug. Byron began to tell Ishi of some dreams he had been experiencing and also some visions that he did not understand. Deeka was standing by the slightly open bedroom door but did not want to intrude on their moments together. However, she could overhear what was being said.

Deeka could sense through her inner being that his dreams were interspersed with previous that embodiments and the assistance being given by the Chosen Ones while the visions experienced were quite unpleasant but he felt safe as though an observer of the dark forces around him.

Ishi responded to Byron by stating that she could sense an ever smooth and serene green cloud surrounding his body and for him to focus on this cloud as a friend. She also noticed a blue band that protected the green cloud. Deeka was surprised and delighted with the fact that Ishi had a sensitivity to feel and to understand the different energies and to sense which ones were good and bad. She stated that an invisible friend named Vander was helping to communicate things for her.

Deeka was amazed even more as she was able to name a Chosen One that she labeled as a friend. As Deeka entertained this thought, Vander began an inner dialogue with her.

Vander: "I sensed a strong tie with your daughter, Ishi, as in a previous lifetime she was a daughter of mine and our bond was inseparable. When she was twenty years of age, we were out on a hike in the woods of Montana. We came upon a river with a strong current and were preparing to make camp on the banks of the river. Twenty minutes into making camp, we heard a cry coming from upriver. A young man was aboard a half-sunken boat with a life jacket on. He was alone and in panic. Without a moment's thought, my daughter Chelsea tied a rope around her waist, gave me the other end, and jumped into the river to swim for the boy. She would always put others before herself and react on instinct. There were many that were grateful for her immediate assistance in troubled instances. I rushed to secure the rope to a tree so I could return to the shore for assistance in her rescue. She successfully reached the boy and ferociously swam for shore. The current was strong and swift, but her intensity and endurance brought the boy within my reach. Things happened so fast! I grabbed the boy and took him to safety. When I turned around to fetch Chelsea, the last

I ever saw of her was a hand in the air before she was pulled under from a strong undercurrent of the river. My Chelsea was gone!

"The spiritual hierarchy informed me that Chelsea is indeed Ishi and that the boy she saved is her current brother Byron. I am karmically tied to Ishi and was granted communication with her in this life. By assisting her currently, I am able to pay a cosmic debt and we as a chosen group will have her added to the team in the years to come." The communication concluded, and Deeka felt so blessed that the forces from on high were always monitoring and assisting mankind for the higher common good of the planet and its people.

A brief message was communicated to Deeka from a Buddha: "Please remember that your secrecy of mission is not to be revealed to your children. Even though Ishi has ever-increasing sensitivity to her inner potentials, this must solely be for the destiny between her and Byron." At that, the dialogue ended.

The following day, a brief break in the inclement weather allowed for Deeka to take Byron home from the hospital. On the same day power was restored to the town, and the trees were still being cleared from the streets. Upon the ride home, Byron noticed a rainbow glowing in the sky. This touched his heart immensely, but Deeka and Ishi did not see any rainbow at all. This rainbow was the cause in the weather break that would only last for minutes after the three returned home. It was a momentary intervention of hierarchy that was granted due to the group efforts of the Chosen Ones on this particular mission.

Minutes after entering the house, winds started to stir again and clouds with lightning once again ensued. But this time preparation was made with candles disbursed throughout the house in case of power outages in the town. A complete source of water was available to help keep Byron hydrated during his ordeal.

Meanwhile, Vander was kept very busy between his job as a librarian, his tai chi classes, and assisting the elderly part-time. He found himself putting in more hours, which was close to cutting into his meditation times, and as a Chosen One, the meditations cannot be sacrificed at any cost. He would have to make some adjustments in his other duties and responsibilities.

As soon as he entertained these thoughts, an inner warm contact was made with Nyla and Hoopti. They offered their assistance to Vander on some ideas so he could get the rest he needed without sacrificing his meditation work. This had become a common practice with all the groups as their combined energies had to be at 100 percent level at all times with one another in order to be on standby alert for anything that Teohta and her dark legions may direct their way. The use of time and timing itself was crucial.

After 20 minutes of inner dialogue and pondering, the group came up with a solution that would work to Vander's benefit. He would cut back to two tai chi classes a day instead of three, be on call to assist the elderly at two-hour intervals three days a week instead of five, and still be able to maintain his full-time job as a librarian. This pleased him greatly, and he thanked Nyla and Hoopti with a blessing and warm thoughts to them. They all three learned from his experience and also realized that at a point in time, they too will have to be open and flexible to changes in their lifestyles when it comes to their times and needs for increased meditations.

Back in Deeka's hometown of Ausland, Norway, Byron was feeling more fatigued and wanting more water. Ishi got in the habit of bringing two bottles of water when she came in his room to spend some time with him. Recently she had begun to hum some music to him and he would smile as he fell into a deep sleep. It was music Deeka had never heard before, and she had asked Ishi where it came from. "I don't know. It is a memory of some kind but I don't know its source." Deeka reasoned within herself that it must have been a favorite of theirs from a previous lifetime. But it seemed to comfort Byron and that was a positive.

Then, a few days later, Ishi had begun to feel a little ill and exhausted while doing her homework. Deeka then told her to get some rest and she could finish her schoolwork tomorrow. This was a cause for concern as Ishi, in general, has maintained a strong immune system. Then Deeka came to the realization that her visions and energies of a serene green cloud with blue lining for Byron should also include Ishi as well. Ishi is very mature for a six-year-old but still has a child's body that needs to be nurtured and protected as well. The moment she had this thought, an increase of warm energy filled her heart and being. Her inner companions heard this and immediately reacted in a compassionate manner, which transferred light energy to both her and Ishi. Then a sweet calm voice from above interjected the experience. "My dear Deeka, you have learned a valuable lesson in spirituality. In the case of Byron and Ishi, if one is the subject of an attack, the karmic partner is most likely to be affected as well. So both lifestreams require equal amounts of energy and protection directed their way, especially in the case of children. Always remember that universal energy is infinite and can be accessed at all times, whether for good or bad intentions. However, the light will always trump the darkness because there is no fear in light and the strong passion to do good will intensify the flow of light until the victory is gained. Be alert that negative or bad intentions never entertain the mind or heart for these are the tools of the sinister forces in motion. Each Chosen One represents a crown of cosmic justice made manifest in human form. With this in mind and heart, their actions and reactions will be in mind for the victory of a planet and her people." At this, the friendly advice ceased and Deeka, along with her inner partners, gained new insights to strengthen their energies and efforts.

CHAPTER 12

AT THIS JUNCTURE in time, the great cosmic council on Sirius called to the Rheyzoun-45 Buddhas for a current report on the chosen twenty-five of Terra. Lifestreams had to maintain a high level of progress in order to receive warm light energies in this ongoing mission to save a planet. Being under a year in earth time, this was still in an embryonic stage for creating a strong and firm foundation from which to work with. If they were not physically prepared, too much light could cause an excess surge within their physical shell and cause a short circuit. So caution was needed as each one was evaluated by the reading of their auric fields and chakras. The progress of their meditations combined with daily activities, decisions, and added responsibilities would determine their capacity to receive more light energy.

One of the hardest concepts for mankind to grasp is the action and acceptance of faith, prayer, and meditation in their lives. It was when man separated himself from God by becoming arrogant, independent, and self-righteous, that the flow of infinite light had begun to slowly diminish, resulting in shorter life spans due to sin, disease, and death. This was due to his own choosing, the misuse of free will.

But the mercy and compassion of the Creator has allowed these billions of souls to re-embody and hopefully realize their oneness with cosmos and the grand reality of service to one another and of all of life.

After a progress report was submitted to Ramata and the cosmic council, a verdict would be made in five earth days. Each report was scoured intensely on both an individual and at the group level. They could see that the growth in the beings as an ever-increasing bond in one another but not yet evolved enough to know when to call on the hierarchy for additional assistance in life. There is still a strong sense of separation of divinity, but nevertheless progress was heading in the right direction.

A decision was made and Ramata determined that an extra dispensation of light would be premature at this time, but due to the momentum of their growth, they should be ready to receive one close to the beginning of the winter solstice.

All were in agreement and concluded the session with song and prayer for the twenty-five souls, the Chosen Ones, and their steady progress. Their greatest accomplishment to this point was their recent use of the golden disc given to each one.

Another important factor in the mission of the Chosen Ones was the strength and bond in unity. They realized that as their energies grow together in unity, this also increased their karmic responsibilities toward one another. All things and actions have a cause-and-effect cosmic tie, and the more positive growth attained, the more intense challenges and initiations will come to follow.

Thus, Vander's group, through his ties with Ishi, daughter of Deeka, had been combined and now all have a cosmic destiny with one another. And technically since all are connected by their acquired golden disc, their future actions in this life provide the required energies to magnify and intensify their growth and eventually allow for more light to be obtained from spiritual hierarchy in the form of grants given.

A few of the Chosen Ones began to realize also that these had created karmic ties with the higher spiritual beings and that their spiritual growth progress was contingent upon those being sponsored. Thus, the true understanding of sacrifice was coming to light. When one is sponsored by another, the sponsor is giving a portion of his light energy to the disciple in the hopes that the light will be used in a positive manner and effort. If the energy is misused in any way, the sponsor also pays a karmic price for the allotted energy give into the student. This is the cosmic responsibility and accountability of both the students and teacher to pay. The student with true intent and a sincere heart realizes that his gratitude for the teacher's sacrifice of light completes the trinity of love, wisdom, and power in action.

CHAPTER 13

THE WIND WAS intensifying to the point where car alarms where being tripped by flying debris throughout the neighborhoods. A branch broke loose from a tree in Deeka's yard and broke a window in Byron's room. A big spider crack formed, but the glass did not shatter into pieces. They quickly patched the breaks with duct tape and then shut the window shutters. Byron remained sound asleep.

The following morning a nurse came to the house for a scheduled visit. All Byron's vital signs were in acceptable range, and Deeka inquired about any results of his tests given at the hospital. The nurse said that Dr. Sophie would be giving her a call in the early evening. At 5:00 p.m., Dr. Sophie called to inform Deeka of some test results. Byron's psychological evaluation was normal, and the other tests for any form of viral infections came up negative. Mild strokes were ruled out, and they did not find any insect bites on his body. It seemed a mystery as no one else in town had experienced the symptoms and conditions that Byron was currently dealing with. Dr. Sophie requested to see Byron in two weeks from that day to perform a second evaluation as long as his progress was maintained at the home. Deeka agreed.

The following morning, Ishi went in to see Byron and noticed a slight smile on his face while still asleep. She sat beside him with his hand in hers and began humming some music to him.

Fifteen minutes later, he woke with a serene smile, gazing at his little sister. He began to share with her some dreams he had been experiencing, both good and bad. He said that some dark forms would try to invade his room and also to tempt him to follow them outside the house. They could not forcefully take him out against his will. And every time that he said no, he would begin to see some beautiful light beings accompanied by some chantlike music that filled the air. The dark shadows would fade away while being replaced by the beautiful light beings. He had never experienced these kinds of dreams before and was not sure what to make of them.

Little did he realize that Omer, not far away in Froland, was doing his meditations and performing some Hindu mantras. Because he was part of Deeka's group, the energy he projected was received in an instant through the dream state of Byron. With less resistance in the dream state, a great momentum of light was building to fight the dark forces of Teohta and her bands. But being so young, the battles fought on a daily basis were very strenuous and fatigued him greatly. Thus, at times, he would lapse into states of unconsciousness but was still protected by the light of the Chosen Ones and the constant maintaining of the green healing form outlined by the blue band. Ishi by his side was the added strength of love from a soul mate.

Omer is one of the stronger souls on this mission. His many embodiments proved his commitment of passion and sacrifices made. And this life was even more exceptional. His parents, Gilmore and Ruby, were runaways from their families. At the young ages of sixteen and seventeen, they shared a deep affection for one another, which was rare, and both sets of parents did not understand the bond formed.

Gilmore and Ruby married and two years later born an only son, Omer. A healthy, premature, 13-pound baby, Omer had above-average strength and a heart to match. His love for his parents motivated him to excel in every challenge life had to offer. His parents encouraged him in school and in his new passion of weightlifting. At 5'11" and 215 pounds of solid muscle, Omer excelled in his weight division and won state champion two years in a row for his high school. However, on his third attempt as a senior, he fractured his collarbone, and this ended his competition.

Omer's second passion was his love for philosophy and the study of Eastern religions. He understood the laws of vibrations and resonated with the concept of chanting mantras. This complemented his love for hiking and biking. He thrived on the concept of oneness with nature and drew upon that for his exceptional health. He felt within himself that spiritual growth is the most important goal in life and to serve one another with humility is the ultimate path to attainment.

Omer entered the janitorial industry and embraced it fully. This field of work allowed him to apply the remainder of his time for his outdoor activities of hiking and biking. His primary goals had developed into his daily practices of chanting mantras and Eastern music.

After twenty-five years of his spiritual practices, he began to obtain insights and a heightened awareness of being with life. His intuitions were expanding more than ever and were leading to a crescendo. Then, one morning during a meditation, a great light being made contact through his heart. He was offered a mission, which he humbly accepted, and he was fully aware and ready for any challenges thrown his way as a Chosen One.

Ommmer Byron was mumbling in his sleep. He woke up to his sister's smile. To her surprise he sat up in his bed with a renewed sense of energy. The combined energy of Omer's mantras and Ishi's singing to Byron had begun to create a strong momentum of light in Byron's being, but he needed to learn to harness this energy and use it wisely when most needed.

Omer now felt a strong connection more than ever with Byron and sent him an inner message addressing him as a "little brother," and an eternal bond was formed. A cosmic passion and commitment was solidified between Omer and Byron. Deeka could also sense this and was very joyous and ecstatic.

Not far away, in Denmark, Fioriya was on assignment for her country on economic relations. During her one-week assignment, her meditations felt stronger with Deeka and Byron. She felt the urge to want to set up a time to physically meet one another but then received a strong signal indicating that it was not safe to meet at this time. She heeded the message and sent Deeka and family a message of great love for the time being. She was curious as to why the physical meeting was not encouraged at this time. Then, immediately a response was received from a Rheyzoun Buddha.

"Dear Fioriya, the sinister forces would actually like the Chosen Ones to physically meet at this time, for their strategy is to knock out two or more enemies at the same time while still young and inexperienced in their mission against the dark forces. We feel that at this time your greatest strengths are your meditations from a distance, building for a stronger bond in the combined light energies between the teams of Chosen Ones. Until a great momentum of time and buildup is formed, the prematurity of physical contact would surely result in a defeat against Teohta and her legions. But with patience and persistence, you will be able to visualize a picture born in your minds with your inner eye that will reveal the physical appearance of your specific partners. Due to the severity of this mission, we will continue to assist you in these areas as long as the questions in your minds are sincere and motivated by love and passion for the mission at hand." At this, the intercession concluded and both Deeka and Fioriya were satisfied with the explanation given. Both were in agreement with the advice given.

Back at the home front, Deeka and Ishi closely monitored Byron's condition. For the next three days, the windy weather had subsided and Byron seemed to make progress. But then, on the fourth day, things took a turn for the worse. Without warning, while in bed, Byron passed out while Ishi was at his bedside. Without panic she went to inform Deeka about his episode of unconsciousness. She checked his vitals to make sure that his respiratory status was okay then made a call to Dr. Sophie. The doctor agreed to make a special visit to check up on Byron.

When Dr. Sophie arrived, she could hear Ishi singing to her brother and was impressed by the calm and poise that Ishi was showing. Their eyes met with a smile as she began his checkup. Heartbeat and pulse were fine, breathing and color were fine, all signs appeared normal and no indications of anything such as epilepsy or narcolepsy. A strange case indeed. "So what to do? Should I recommend more tests at the hospital or leave Byron at home in the care of his family?" Dr. Sophie decided to have a little conference with Deeka and Ishi. She would allow them to make the decision as all the tests done on Byron already would just be duplicated again. Both Deeka and Ishi agreed to keep Byron home with a stipulation that any changes at all would be directly reported to Dr. Sophie at once. All agreed on the decision as Deeka saw the doctor to the door.

While unconscious, Byron began to have experiences of different levels of awareness. Some were shadowy and unpleasant while others were beautiful and full of light. His own personal battle, an Armageddon, was in process through his illness. It seemed that his stronghold was the vibrations of Ishi's singing coupled with chants from a higher source. Temptations of all sorts were being thrown at him, and as a spirit warrior, his free will was being severely tested. Through these trials and ordeals, he began to realize more and more that the heart and voice of Ishi was truly his strength and anchor in love and in the light.

The dark forces hated this terribly and intensified their attacks on his soul, causing the physical form to experience the blackouts and slurred speech. And when the pressure was almost at a breaking point, a mighty surge of light would envelop and saturate his being. Thus, a powerful surge of light immediately scattered the darkness, which was partially responsible for the gale force winds and inclement weather, which they would experience. This would occur for many weeks to pass. But the Chosen Ones' meditations were stronger than ever.

Due to the intensity of the battle being fought, others, such as Nyla, Hoopti and Vander, were also suffering mild flu symptoms in their physical beings. Thus, this shows the connections of the four levels of being making up mankind. The physical, mental, emotional, and spiritual levels were all being attacked and challenged simultaneously. The enemy would intensify its attack on the weakest link of the four levels and suck out the light of the other three like a straw. The areas of weakness could range from any traits such as envy, bitterness, jealousy, mild dislike, and gossip . . . just to name a few.

To counter these traits with love, selfless service and sacrifice is the main armor of a spirit warrior to be equipped with. The saying "All for one and one for all" is the mighty light force that one fights with and can call on in any kind of emergency.

The key to spiritual progress is the individual investment made to call upon the Legions of Light for assistance in the constant battle of Armageddon, whether it be on an individual for a group level. A price is always paid on any one of the three or all four levels of being. Selfless service with a heart of love and light is the greatest weapon of all, and when reinforced with faith and the courage to act, it cannot fail one's battles in life.

During the visions, Byron was encountering a bright gold disc outlined in blue that began to descend and stopped just in front of his eyes for him to gaze upon. It seemed endless, and then when he felt a sudden surge of heat within his heart, the vision disappeared. He knew at once that the object had entered his being. The golden disc was a well-earned award for Byron, and his battle with the forces of darkness. But the battle was not over yet.

In centuries past, the black brotherhood had won several battles and captured the golden discs of the light warriors. When this occurs, the perversion of its energies convert it to a black pearl of smoky substance that pollutes the soul's aura, decelerating the vibrational rate and instilling fear within. The fear then becomes the seeds of doubt, envy, jealousy, etc. These qualities slowly drain the life force of a lifestream, causing illness and premature death. So once acquired, strength and endurance in and of the light needs to be maintained and an increase in its momentum.

Byron finally gained consciousness twenty days later with Ishi at his side. He expressed a need for food and water and asked how long he had been asleep. Deeka told him and with a smile said she thought that he was hibernating and all three had a good laugh.

Day by day, Byron began regaining his health and vitality. Both Ishi and Deeka noticed that he began humming some songs and chanting as well. He expressed that he heard these many times in his dreams and that comforted him and soothed his soul. He also described many unpleasant confrontations and temptations, but he knew that he had to follow his heart and the light within it. One could sense a maturity complemented with the passion of a young warrior spirit. It is almost like a transformation had taken place while in the unconscious state. What used to be a child now seemed to be that of a young man.

Byron also expressed a reverence and gratitude for the spiritual support he received in his journeys. He had established a heightened awareness in which he recognized the kindred spirits assisting him in his battles. And yet he realized that his actions would determine the outcome of his personal battle with the dark forces.

Five days later Byron was able to get out of bed and walk around the house. Both his strength and appetite were increasing, and his voice was more vibrant than before. And in the early mornings, him and Ishi would meditate and hum together. Deeka was in awe of the positive changes occurring in Byron, and her heart was overjoyed with gratitude and love for her companions in the great mission of the Chosen Ones for the Earth.

Then one morning Byron began a conversation with his mother, which totally caught her off guard. His expression was projecting a serious but warm love and concern. He began, "Mother I realized through my illness that there are some evil forces at play and that a constant battle between good and evil is taking place and has been for a long time before I was born. And I also feel very strongly that Ishi and I have been together before because I feel it in my heart and soul. And Ishi feels the same as I do. And we both feel very grateful that you adopted us into your heart as family."

Deeka was both shocked and happily amazed at what her son was saying as he continued his conversation with her.

"We both feel that we have a big responsibility in this life to assist all in need who have their inner demons and conflict that creates an imbalance in their lives. And we are okay with this task in our lives, and we feel blessed that we have been offered this opportunity through our life experiences, as young as we are, to realize and work with light beings that are helping to assist and guide mankind back to the light of their own hearts, thus creating love, peace, and harmony. Like a positive virus whose goal is to spread worldwide!"

At this point, Deeka almost thought that she was being spoken to by a Buddha as Byron's speech was being presented in such a heartfelt tone and wisdom to match. She remained silent and he continued on.

"I feel that you also have your role in this but are not allowed to speak out about. Both Ishi and I respect this. Yet we have together a bond and destiny to fulfill. A mission, if we accept the call to service in the light for which we have already agreed. We both realize that more challenges and opposition will be directed to us and you, but that the three of us together can tackle these confrontations along with calls to the light beings to assist us in these battles when necessary. But yet we also have to bear the burdens brought upon mankind as a world karma has to be paid on the physical level of being. I hope you understand what I'm saying, and both Ishi and I are in this battle for the long haul as we feel that you are as well."

At this point Byron paused so that his mother could give her response to his story of the current events of his experiences.

Deeka began her response to the conversation. "My son, I'm so glad that you are feeling better and am awestruck at your firmness and ability to withstand what you, along with Ishi, have gone through. This experience has enlightened you and your sister to a great battle and the highest cause of all on this planet today. You are true that many things I cannot say or express, but I feel that what you need to know at this point will be revealed to you when the time is right on your path. And always know that as my children, we are bound in our bond together to fight as one through all challenges and opposition thrown our way. Your wisdom and understanding acquired through your illness is a blessing because you chose to not give in to your lesser self through pain and fear but to realize that we always have options that through free will can overcome obstacles with a fiery spirit and compassion that can move mountains if we maintain a sincere and positive attitude to match the heart's desire to do good on this planet. I am so proud of you and Ishi and am glad to be your mother in this life. My love for you is endless."

At that, Byron gave Deeka a big hug as Ishi entered the room from playing outside. They all smiled at one another, and Byron continued with one more point he had to share with his mother.

"I will be fully healed within a month of this current illness and also Ishi and I will be doing some morning prayers, humming, and meditations from now on." At this, they all rejoiced in song and dance to celebrate Byron's victory and growth in the light. And within their hearts they all three felt a resounding message of "Well done, my children."

Following this experience, a deep silence overcame them and a warm beam of light began with a great message of importance imparting to their minds and souls as follows: "The threads of spirituality are a divine recipe of aspects and virtues implanted within the souls of mankind that have remained dormant for numerous ages and centuries past. These sins of darkness have clouded the hearts and mankind for so long that he has lost his memory and feeling of his origins in the divine image of his creator. This fall from grace has led to the sense of separation from the divine source by thinking of a lesser self, based on fear, imperfection, doubt, and delusion. These 'clouds of delusion' are thus the creation of a sinister force. This 'sinister force' is a legion of rebels in heaven that felt the need to rule mankind for the appeasement of their arrogant egos.

"When this sinister force was thrown out of hierarchy, they descended to the earth and its cycles with an extreme wrath and vengeance toward mankind. They had the same free will as does mankind and also have to abide to the great cosmic laws of cause and effect. Their dark influences polluted the lower atmospheres of earth that created a negative imbalance of all the lands, the sea, and the air. This created a great burden upon mankind yet all have the same choices of free will to act upon and express.

"Through all millennia, all beings, be it angels or mankind, have known the difference between good and evil and have lived according to choices made and experienced through divine law and the results, good and bad karma. Now, for too long, the earth has been bearing the burdens of a dark, polluted consciousness resulting in natural disasters inflicted upon it.

"Now as the ending of a cosmic cycle is at hand, the earth has been too dark for too long and one last effort to save a planet through the victory of the light is at hand.

"All humans have experienced many life cycles in an opportunity to right the wrongs of themselves and the whole of humanity. And there have been more than enough light beings incarnated on the Earth to be a beacon of light for the planet and its people.

"Many souls of light have assisted young master Byron in his recent battles with the darkness. They projected their light energy toward you and, in turn, took on a portion of your karma in return. This caused a slight illness within each one as they exchanged the light for the burdens of karma, which by cosmic law, has to be exacted for balance and debts to be paid. So a major factor of sacrifice is an important thread of group efforts in the great battles of personal and planetary Armageddon taking place. But as you see and have experienced, the acts of sacrifice have resulted in a victory and yet a stronger bond of love, trust, and faith in the warriors of light.

"The angels of hierarchy have celebrated your victory with song and praise to Ramata and his legions of Buddhas! You are all blessed and are reminded to make the calls for assistance when needed. As long as all your efforts remain sincere and selfless, you will never ever be abandoned by the Light!" This discourse ended and a wave of peace and harmony filled the air along with a pleasant fragrance of lavender. At the same instant all the Chosen Ones involved in the battle were instantly healed as the increment of karma was balanced.

The following morning, Deeka called on Dr. Sophie for an appointment to examine Byron's condition. Dr. Sophie agreed on a time at 2:00 p.m. for the same day. At 2:00 p.m., a knock on the door was answered by Byron with a big smile. Dr. Sophie began the exam while Ishi sat in the room to observe. All his vitals were getting close to normal and all were very happy and excited.

As Deeka entered the room, Dr. Sophie requested a conference with her. She marveled at the progress Byron had made and admitted that all previous tests run on him left the doctors at a loss as to what caused his condition. She requested one last full checkup on him at the hospital to clear up his case and to declare him as fully well. All agreed and an appointment was made for the following day.

CHAPTER 14

TURNING TO THE land down under, Amara began spending more diving time on some strange behaviors occurring with the dolphins lately. Their communications seem to be more like distress calls than that of beauty and harmony being the norm. She could not see any visible changes but was fully aware of the high vibration frequencies emitted and received by these wonderful creatures. She had become friends and attuned with a group of five dolphins. She named them as follows: Apache the leader, Pearl his mate, Spike, Flint, and Cora. They all accepted her as family and happily greeted her at every morning swim. At this point she was the only human that they fully accepted, and her aura and presence always brought out the playfulness in their beings.

That very same day in the early evening on her way home, she noticed a huge fire burning uncontrolled off to her right in the nearby fields away from town. She turned on the radio and a story broke about the fire. So far the cause had not been determined, and the firefighters had only 10 percent of the fire contained. It became so huge that it created a hot wind, making it difficult for the firemen to build any form of boundaries to contain it. But at least the road she traveled on was in the opposite direction of the raging fire. The dry climate of Australia made it extremely difficult for firefighting, and the personnel always seem to be stretched thin.

Following the next morning while Amara was in her meditations, she could smell a strong odor in the air of a smoky substance. As she peered out the window, a smoggy haze had enveloped the entire city. She turned on the TV and the news was in the middle of a story about the wild fires burning out of control. Three firefighters were injured, and planes were dropping fire retardant on the massive flames. But her house had been declared in a safe zone, clear from the fire. But concern for the people threatened by the fire was a weight on her heart for their safety. This feeling had sent a signal from Amara's heart to her fellow partners of their spiritual work.

Aton could feel the intensity of her inner SOS and Zeera as well. An immediate focus of a beam of love/light was directed her way. Amara felt their energy in her heart and being but also felt a great love force from another source.

She immediately had a visualization of her five dolphin companions swimming in a formation of a heart and singing to her in unison. Her heart became filled with joy as all these wonderful beings were sharing their light/love directed her way. And then still she felt another surge of light from an unknown source but a very friendly vibration.

Young Bayuni of Puako, Hawaii, had picked up on her distress call and immediately responded with a ray of love. Amara received a visual of this lovely Hawaiian soul and expressed her heartfelt gratitude of love to her. Following the new contact with Bayuni came that of Creoki of Baja, California. He sensed the urgency of Bayuni's heart call and immediately directed his light energy Amara's way. He could envision a massive out-of-control fire as the source of emergency. Creoki has an affinity with nature and the land that his heart became one with. He began to focus on the air spirits and summoned an idea to create what he termed "back force winds." These are winds that reversed the direction of wild drafts of winds created by fires so that they reversed direction to feed back upon itself.

As he increased his intensity of focus, he could feel assistance being given by Tillow of Seward, Alaska. Her soothing but piercing energy merged with his and the others to combat the raging fire of destruction. This merging of energies was magnified by the activation of the golden discs within their hearts. The golden discs are always activated by acts of sacrifice and selfless service to others. The power of the heart and its love, when rendered to good and service, is an unbeatable force so long as sincerity of service with the utmost humility is the driving force. The human ego remains in the backdrop, not claiming credit for the ego.

Within hours the news reported that the winds of the fire had begun to decrease and actually reversed directions. This had allowed for better opportunities for the firefighters to get the upper hand for containment. Up to this point 2500 acres have already been burned and a few towns were directly in the path just twenty miles away. Not a moment could be wasted in the continuous efforts to cease the wildfire.

And the news further reported that the cause of the fire was from a cigarette butt from a few hikers who admitted to the cause. Background checks showed that one of the hikers had been previously arrested for starting a fire in an abandoned shack while camping in it. That particular individual was sentenced to jail time.

The following day the fire was 70 percent contained and burning out rapidly. There were no longer any homes or towns threatened by fire. But the air quality was still to remain unhealthy and the people were to remain in their homes for two days. Amara was grateful to her spiritual companions for their assistance in the battle and bowed her head in reverence to the light within. Gratitude filled the air with faith as its cloak and love as the armor of goodwill.

The next two days of being homebound gave Amara the chance to catch up on reports to write on her diving excursions for the marine biology projects. She was anxious to see her dolphin companions as normally she made daily dives for her work and they were used to seeing her on a daily basis. As she finished the last report, the air outside began to clear.

On the third day Amara awoke early to allow more time for morning meditations. She was greeted with a warm welcome feeling in her heart by her new inner friends Bayuni, Creoki, and Tillow. They all began to feel and realize that the adversities that would be awaiting them are the initiations of the paths of Chosen Ones necessary for the advancement of the eternal life and the victory of worlds in which constant evolving is gained and earned by the right use of free will. But also being mindful of the enemies within, the human mind and ego had to be held at bay until fully extinguished. Qualities such as envy, jealousy, greed, hate, and mild dislike and the sense of separation from the life being the grandest delusion of light and that true self.

At this time the meditation concluded with a beautiful song. Music from the heart of Tillow permeated the air with a blessing, which sent light vibrations to the hearts of all. Soon she gathered her equipment and set out to commence the next dive to commune with her friends and continue her underwater studies.

As she approached the dive spot, she noticed that a small boat was anchored about a quarter mile from her location. She shrugged and then returned attention to her dive.

After five minutes, three figures were swimming her way to greet her. Apache, Pearl, and Spike surrounded her in joy, but she did not see Cora and Flint anywhere in sight. Had anything happened to her friends, she wondered.

After five more minutes had passed, Flint and Cora came racing through the waters to greet their human friend. Amara's worries faded quickly as the five comrades circled her in joy and play. Then she continued her studies until the time to surface. However, she could sense something different, a slight change in Flint and Cora, as they would drift away for a while and then return with the rest.

When she boarded her vessel, she spotted a man on the other boat pulling up anchor to prepare to leave. She was too far away to see the name on his boat and was about to dismiss it in her mind, but then the man spotted her and gave a greeting wave. She responded as a friendly gesture. Soon both boats fired up their engines and headed for the docks.

As the sun began its descent, Amara docked her boat and then waited a few minutes to see if the other boat was close by. About five minutes later, a boat approached about five docks away from hers. She felt that it was the one anchored nearby her dive site. In an instant the man turned her direction with a wave and a smile. They mutually began toward one another for a formal meeting.

He was a pleasant young twenty-two-year-old gentleman named Nicholas, a young man on vacation looking to snorkel and explore the waters as a hobby. He also apologized to Amara, indicating that he did not intend to infringe upon her space as she informed him of her biological marine studies. She smiled in gratitude for his respect and mannerisms.

Then he shared his joy as he met two friendly dolphins during his swim. Now Amara knew why something was sensed different about

Flint and Cora. This was also sensed as a confirmation of acceptability to Nicholas and his demeanor.

For the dolphins, up to this point, would avoid human swimmers outside of Amara and her territory of studies. She consented in allowing Nicholas to anchor his boat at the same location if he pleased. They shook hands in agreement and then shared a couple of cups of coffee and friendly conversation. Then both went their separate ways to end the evening.

Morning came and Amara was immersed in her meditations. In the midst of her focus, she picked up on an unfamiliar but warm vibration resonating with a name: Nyla. It was sent as a friendly warning of possible new acquaintances in the near future, for the dark forces have cunning ways in their strategies utilizing any and all possible weak spots of an individual. At that, the communication gently faded. Her interpretation of the contact with Nyla was to be on the alert and to proceed with caution. This was followed with an assist from the higher beings "Ramtam Om Shivaya Om." At the end of the meditation, Amara felt a more acute sense of awareness, an alertness and higher sense of discerning of spirits. Yet she felt no inharmonious feelings toward her new friend, Nicholas. But they had just met.

Amara set out for her dive spot while noticing that the boat of Nicholas was not at the dock, so she figured she would see him out on the waters. However, when she had arrived at her spot, Nicholas was nowhere in sight. Maybe he searched out another spot for diving, she thought. Nothing to worry about or be concerned with. She continued with her dive, the greeting of her five companions, and marine studies.

A normal routine day ended for Amara and she docked her boat. She did notice Nicholas's boat but did not see him anywhere. Then she figured, *He'll do his own thing while I do my studies, which would have less distractions and no commitments to worry about.* But that being said, she felt it would be nice to have a collaboration with a new human friend. With her work being independent, it does not allow for a social life so far. But she does enjoy her dolphin buddies.

In the early evening, Amara decided to go out for dinner and had a craving for some pizza. Her favorite place for pizza was called Hoppin'

Toppins', and it had been a while since she indulged herself. It was only fifteen minutes from home. So she went out.

Upon arriving at Hoppin' Toppins,' the place was half full of customers. This she liked and decided to stay and eat instead of takeout. She found herself a nice little corner table and proceeded to it. Soon a waiter approached to take her order. She ordered her favorite, a medium-sized, thick-crust Pouch Popper, which consisted of sausage, olives, bell peppers, and a double dose of cheese. Her drink of choice was always root beer with her pizza. The waiter said it would be about twenty to twenty-five minutes and she nodded okay. He went to fetch her drink; a refill always came with the medium-sized pizza.

The waiter returned with her drink and asked if there would be anything else. As she answered, "No, thanks," a young gentleman entered the restaurant. Her eyes lit up.

It was Nicholas. Then her disciplined mind made her hesitate before making any sudden responses. *Should I wave him over or see if he notices me first?* She was torn as her inner child wanted to get his attention, but her mature, disciplined mind reassured maybe he just wants to be alone and not bothered. She chose to back down and let his actions of awareness rule the moment.

As soon as she decided to maintain, he waved to a friend at a table opposite the room and it was another young man waving back at him. She sighed in relief. *Thank goodness, I did not get his attention. I never entertained the thought that he might be meeting someone in the parlor. What if it would have been a young lady?* At that, Amara changed her gaze and turned her attention elsewhere.

In an instant she felt a subtle but warm warning again from her new inner contact, Nyla. She analyzed and pondered the inner message, interpreting it as maybe the person to be concerned with is Nicholas's friend, she thought without panic and just took in the moment with a deep breath. Then the inner message slowly drifted away within her heart as the waiter approached her with the pizza. He kindly refilled her glass with more root beer.

As Amara took her first slice of pizza, she could see out of the corner of her eye that Nicholas was looking her way. He recognized her and gave a slight wave with a nod of greeting. He always seemed to have a warm smile supporting his demeanor. She smiled then turned her head back.

He felt that she did not want any more than the small nod of "Hi" and proceeded to turn his attention back to his friend. Amara noticed this and was thankful that he did not get up and approach her. But yet she did not want to chance it, and after a second slice of pizza, she asked the waiter for a to-go box and a cup for her drink. Then she got up to leave without looking Nicholas's way. She was happy to see him but also glad that the evening went the way that it did. Again she felt a respect for Nicholas and began to open her heart a bit toward him. A real gentleman he seemed.

On her drive home, she hummed a happy tune and also noticed that there was not any inner messages or feelings sent her way. "So maybe Nicholas is okay and maybe his friend is the one I have to be cautious about," she pondered. At that instant, a signal in her heart confirmed the last thought. Her objective analysis was spot on. Now the challenge to handle a future situation was at hand.

The following day Amara set out for her daily routine. She turned the key in her car and nothing happened. Then she realized that she had left the lights on her car on all night and it had drained the battery. It was too early and her neighbor would not be up for another one and a half hours. He had jumper cables and a battery charger and has helped her on a couple of occasions. He was a retired navy man named Max. They are good friends, and he thinks of Amara like one of his own kids. He could be trusted and was always there when she needed. So she decided to wait for his assistance until he awoke. At least her work was not a 9-to-5 job every day and she did not have to worry about a boss harping on her for being late. So she used the time to catch up on some of her reports.

As the one and a half hours passed, she decided to see if Max was up and about. She looked outside at his driveway to see that his newspaper was gone. That meant that Max was up already as his habits were like clockwork. Amara would wait a little while longer so he could enjoy his oatmeal and coffee undisturbed. She made herself a hot cup of tea and began to wrap up her work on her reports.

When Amara went outside to see Max, he was already standing beside her car with his pleasant fatherlike smile. She walked up to him and gave him a warm hug.

"You must have car problems since you are still here so late in the day," he said. "Is it your battery again?" he added with a quirky grin like a dad to his kid.

"Yeah," she replied. "I hope I didn't ruin it this time. Three times in a year is not good for it, is it?"

Max just smiled back with a slight grin. "We will try to jump it first to see if it starts," he said. He popped her hood and connected the cables on her end. Then he pulled his truck opposite hers and finished the hooking up the cables. "Let it sit for a couple minutes then we'll try to start it," he remarked. How fortunate to have Max as a neighbor and a friend as well.

Max had no children of his own, and his wife of thirty-five years had passed away from a severe stroke five years earlier. He missed his Abigail dearly, but having Amara around was enough of a companion and a good therapy for him. They would occasionally visit, and Max would share happy stories of events that he and Abigail shared in their married lives. This made both Max and Amara very happy, and it kept Max in extremely good health.

Max gave the signal and Amara turned the key. Nothing. "Oh darn! I think I've ruined it this time."

Max nodded in agreement. "If you like, I will remove the battery and then take you to get a new one," he offered.

She returned with a pouty-looking face. "I'm afraid I can't afford a battery right now as rent is coming up and I need some groceries to last me until payday."

Max just smiled and gave Amara a hug. "I will get you a battery at my discount and you take your time in paying it back, no worries." Just like a dad would do. She felt ashamed and grateful at the same time. *What would I do without him?*

"And I won't take no for an answer," he said, with a firm but smiling and caring expression.

"Okay, okay," she replied. So they jumped in his truck and headed for the auto store. The gentleman at the counter was a friend of Max's. His name is Gus. They have been fishing buddies as Gus showed Max some pictures of his latest trip and catches. Gus applied the discount without Max even requesting it.

"It was very nice meeting you, Gus," Amara said. He also gave her a discount card of her own. Both Max and Gus smiled as though two brothers helping out their younger sister.

They drove back and Max installed the battery. Amara turned the key, and the car started up perfectly. She was so grateful that she insisted Max let her make them lunch since noon was fast approaching. He happily agreed.

Amara made lunch, and they enjoyed it on Max's front patio. It was such a beautiful day, and they both loved the great outdoors. Then they shared some iced tea and conversed for a while. Amara felt such an inner calm when around Max's company. She had realized that her day was a blessing and a lesson. The realization that it should not take a dead battery to see Max and spend some quality time with such a dear friend.

Amara had been caught up too much in her work, which caused neglect with the ones that should also require her attention. This experience really touched her heart and gave her similar sensations like those of her morning meditations. She bowed her head in a prayerful manner and gave humble gratitude for another opportunity of growth through supposed inconveniences.

The next morning arrived, and her routine was back in full force. The only difference was the promise she made to herself that she would always be more available, time wise, to those in need as these are the virtues needed most as a Chosen One advances in their spirituality.

Amara arrived at her diving spot and was greeted by her five comrades: Apache, Pearl, Spike, Flint, and Cora. It was a happy reunion as they all played for about ten minutes. Then it was back to work in their rhythmic waters. Soon, Amara would be expanding her work zone to a full mile in diameter. Her studies were progressing very well, and the results were better than expected.

On her way back to shore, she did not see Nicholas anywhere in sight. She figured that maybe he found another spot or that his vacation might be over. Sure seemed like a nice fellow, and she wouldn't mind seeing him again. But it is what it is.

Amara docked her boat and headed for her car. When the car was in sight, she noticed that the left rear tire was completely flat. Rats! What to do? She did not want to call Max and bother him, and she did have a good spare tire but no lug nut wrench. She looked around the parking lot, which was almost empty. Then she was just about to call a tow truck when a car was coming her way. The car slowed to twenty-five miles per hour, and she noticed that it was Nicholas.

"Hi stranger," he said as he halted to a stop, noticing her flat rear tire. "If you need assistance, I would be happy to help you."

"Yes," she replied. "I have a spare in the trunk but no lug wrench. Would you happen to have one?" He smiled with a "Yes" and offered to change the flat tire for her.

"There you go," he said as the last lug nut was tightened firmly and he lowered the jack. He then put the flat tire in the trunk along with the lug wrench.

"Oh, Nicholas! You put the lug wrench in the trunk and it's yours."

He smiled again and replied, "That's okay. I have another and I would like you to have it for future use."

What a gentleman and such a nice gesture! "Thank you so much! Can I at least pay you something for it?" she asked in gratitude. "Oh, how about a lunch sometime next week at your leisure?"

He replied with a shy grin, "I have four weeks left for vacation."

Amara consulted her intuition and all seemed clear to give the green signal. "Agreed! As long as I get to choose the place," she remarked.

"Deal!" he said as he wrote his number down for her and shook her hand as he gave it to her. "Until then! Have a great evening and I look forward to your call for next week." At that he dismissed himself and rode off into the sunset.

Amara's emotions were a mixture of gratitude and excitement. *He is such a nice and sincere gentleman*, she thought as she started the car and proceeded home. On the whole trip home, not one negative impulse was detected about Nicholas and that was a good sign.

When she arrived home, Amara flipped on the TV to check out the weather forecast. The next few days showed some high winds and above-average temperatures, which were unfavorable for ocean travel in her little boat. She immediately decided to not do her dives the next two days. Her reports for her work were almost caught up, and she had not taken a day off for some time. So the next two days were open for some leisure time.

As Amara pondered about what to do with her free time, an intense inner alert flared within her being. She sat calmly and focused her attention to the moment. While sitting in contemplation, she began to hear some intense classical music within her being followed with a vision and the name Tillow above it.

At the same moment, while at a violin practice session, Tillow suddenly passed out in her chair. Her two fellow violinists, Myra and Seth, rushed to her side before she could fall to the floor. Seth went to fetch some water while Myra fanned Tillow with one hand while holding her head upright with the other hand.

"What happened?" asked Tillow softly after she regained consciousness. "You just passed out," replied Myra, still fanning her slowly. "How are you feeling now?" asked Myra.

"A little pain and numbness in my forehead," Tillow answered.

"I am going to call the doctor and have you checked out," Seth interjected.

"Okay," replied Tillow.

Although her head was a bit foggy, Tillow felt a warm contact from Bayuni and Creoki. She also envisioned another young lady, Amara. The inner SOS alert call was in full contact.

At this moment, Amara committed her full time and attention to the assistance of Tillow's being, which also signaled Zeera and Aton. They envisioned a soft green cloud surrounded by a bright blue ring immersing the being of Tillow. And they all felt a natural urge to call on hierarchy for assistance in her healing and protection. As was said, that call compelled an answer.

"We have come to assist in this matter of your calls for Tillow. We have assigned 'protectors' in her defense while the energies of your visuals on the healing have been set in motion. The immediacy of your calls were crucial and spot on. This has happened due to a lack of meditation time spent for some of you. Please realize that your earthly mission as Chosen Ones are all connected as a great spiritual circuit and the energy level assessed by meditation energies was very crucial for the assignment at hand.

"We caution you and encourage you about commitment and the sacrifice of time allotted for this work is imperative. This will increasingly require your dedication and discipline of time spent on a daily basis. The more consistency spent on the spiritual work, the more sensitivity, alertness, and activity of reaction time will increase. Your inner levels of growth and awareness in spirit qualified you all as the Chosen Ones. And your growth through initiations is endless in the work of spiritual evolution. When the activity becomes inconsistent, it creates an inner short circuit and the energy/safety level is compromised. And that is when the dark energies of the sinister force leaks in the crevices creating inner conflict and off guard, which starts the seeds of the 'divide and conquer.'

"We applaud your call for assistance and also use this opportunity to remind yourself of the necessity of purpose of this mission to save a planet. The sacrifice of idle time must increase in order to prioritize more time for spiritual matters.

"Your combined progress halfway through this first year is commendable! Just remember, the more growth you acquire as a group of unity, the more we can assist you from your calls. Also keep in mind that karmic debts have to be paid in the process. Remember! Trust your instincts! Trust each other! And trust us through your calls! Strength in unity! Strength and passion!"

As the hierarchy concluded their communications, all the Chosen Ones expressed their heartfelt gratitude and a reigniting of their fiery purpose with commitment and fervor.

Meanwhile, Tillow was being tended to at an urgent care center on the physical level. She was slightly dehydrated and ran a slight fever. Exhaustion was also in play, so complete rest was ordered for the next few days' minimum. Young Myra volunteered to tend to Tillow for the next few days. Hopefully the event was nothing serious and requires a recharging of one's energies.

Due to the current event at hand, Amara decided to further intensify her commitment as a Chosen One and utilize her two days off for the focus of the mission (global) quietly in her home. As she pondered this, she felt an inner impulse from her partners, Zeera and Aton, that they agreed to do the same. Thus, their bond would increasingly grow stronger as well as the accountability and responsibility of their actions. As this thought of stepping up their activity, an inner message was received from the hierarchy with the words "Well done, dear hearts!" This message was relayed to all the Chosen Ones at the inner levels of being.

Right away Amara sensed on things to do for her preparations for the next two days so there would not be any type of disturbance veering her from her focus.

First she would see her neighbor, Max, and let him know that she would be home and not to be disturbed. Second, she would do shopping the night before so everything was properly stocked for the house. And thirdly, she would leave a voicemail message stating that she was unavailable for the following two days. A valuable lesson of preparation was stepped up, and this is an important quality that must grow as well to make substantial progress on the spiritual path. Since all twenty-five were on a path of spiritual growth in harmony and unity, what one would learn, it would automatically be shared and felt by the others. They can all sense and feel their inner and outer perspectives of life constantly growing and changing, making for better actions of cause and effect in their global efforts.

So Amara started with visiting Max to inform him of her two days at home and that her work was not to be interrupted with the exception of any emergency situation that may require her immediate assistance. Max complied with the offer that if she needed any help in any way to give him a call. They both smiled in agreement and sealed the visit with a hug. *Max is such a dear soul!* she thought to herself.

Then Amara went home and prepared herself for an intense meditation session with no time limit of any kind. As she prepared her meditation chair and lit a candle in front of her on a small homemade altar, a thought came to her on a new approach for her inner work. She grabbed her notebook from the end table on her right and began writing the three steps of her new meditation process. They are as follows: (1) Take seven deep breaths to clear the mind and focus on the lit candle, which represents the inner heart flame, giving thanks and gratitude to the spiritual hierarchy for their infinite love and assistance in daily life, becoming a living conduit of love. (2) Radiate a beam of love and light to the other Chosen Ones and to all of humanity as an offering of self through sacrifice and service. This creates a clear line of communication to all of mankind worldwide. (3) To call upon the Great Spirit for all the love, wisdom, and power needed for life's daily challenges and initiations, becoming the ultimate spiritual warrior and to be in a constant state of alertness, awareness and action. This is what she termed as the divine "Triple As of Life."

As Amara concluded her writing, she lit the candle and commenced with the meditation process. The silence experienced through the seven deep breaths created a soothing glow of soft white light within her mind. Amara could see the flame of her heart dancing as three plumes of pink, yellow, and blue. She felt that this was the igniting of the love, wisdom, and power within her being. Her "Divine Pilot Light" had been activated.

As she maintained her state of heartfelt gratitude for hierarchy, a sweet lightness of being permeated throughout her body. Such a state of relaxation complemented with a heightened state of alertness and awareness that she never experienced before.

Then the feeling of unity was truly felt as expansion of her consciousness took her beyond her physical body. Wherever her thoughts were directed, she was immediately there in the moment. Such a vividness and purity beyond expression! A total sense of freedom of spirit but with a purpose. There was no limit to where she could travel in this free state, and the feeling of total freedom was an exhilarating experience! Then a silent warning, a caution in message was directed her way.

"Dear Amara, we commend you on your progress through your expanded dedication and practice of your meditations. We also lovingly caution you that this level of awareness must be guarded as the dark forces will go to any level of action to attack and subdue those who do not protect themselves and the level of this state of purity and light. From now on, you must establish a spiritual armor as a physical warrior would sport.

"This armor would consist of a sphere of gold and fire ruby stars surrounded by a dark blue ring for your protection and sustainment of perpetual spiritual energy. Teohta and her legions cannot breach this force field at all. Only enter this level when certain actions are required for battle. Only until the darkness has been completely defeated can this level be accessed at will and still is only entered for purposes of spiritual growth. If used unwisely, access by the dark ones would surely pollute the level of spirituality and would definitely be the cause of destruction of all worlds such as the Earth." The communication ended.

Amara absorbed all this information within her spiritual blueprint of being and began to withdraw from the new level of attainment. As this was in process, she realized that what she attained would also be the attainment of the other Chosen Ones on the path. The sense of accountability and responsibility really hit home in her understanding of the cosmic laws of cause and effect. If one failed in a battle with evil forces, all would be affected in a slight or greater loss of light as well as if a victory was won, all would gain from that. The importance of dedication and commitment of purpose through actions of free will in the evolution of spiritual growth is a path that, once started, can never be turned back or stopped. To do such would result in the practice of the black arts due to the level of spiritual attainment and the perversion of the powers gained.

Before ending her meditation session, Amara focused on a soft beam of pink light in a sphere of healing green toward the heart of Tillow. As she activated this, the others did the same and a process was set in motion for the healing of their compadres. And when they all did this, they observed the energy going out from their hearts as a figure eight (8) flow of light. They pondered in their minds as to why this figure 8 (or infinity shape) was occurring. A response from the hierarchy soon followed.

"My dear ones, this figure 8 flow of energy indicates that the directed spiritual energy to assist another is being used properly. It shows that through the love and heart of the sender, the energy is being released as a sacrifice and selfless service without expecting anything back from the receiver. Thus, the nexus of the 8 severs the energy from the sender (cause) and becomes the energy and responsibility of the receiver (effect). Then the receiver projects love and gratitude back to the sender or senders, (cause/effect) thus creating the figure 8 flow of divine energy. This is a cosmic flow process used from advanced beings of other systems and worlds assisting all of life in the universe on their evolutionary paths of spiritual progress.

"Now, if one ever sends out energies directed to one and both are enclosed in the same circle, the sender is actually robbing, or sucking out, the life energies of the receiver. This is misuse of divine energy, the perversion of the dark path, and will eventually result in heavy karmic debts." At this, the explanation ended.

All were now made aware of the protection needed and the proper way of directing energies to assist one another and the penalties of the misuse of energies as well.

Meanwhile, progress was being made on Tillow's health status at inner levels. Through her bout of illness, she described visions she had experienced while unconscious to both Myra and Seth. They listened intently while she described that she was encased in some form of a protective shield, a deep blue substance, and through that she could see various dark forms and objects attempting to reach her but with no avail. She experienced dark charcoal gray orbs shooting at her but unable to penetrate her blue protective shield. In a sense it was a form of hell in her mind attempting to capture and control her soul. Wicked fires of an angry red and yellow was the birthing nest of evil shooting darts, arrows and gray orbs being directed at her. At one point, the barrage of attacks was so great she could actually feel the concussion of the objects slamming against her force field of blue, but to no avail. Then something strange but beautiful happened. Her protective shield started a counterattack consisting of a release of gold, purple, and ruby stars directed at the evil nest. Such a beautiful site and experience to behold! When the stars made contact with the evil nest, a great explosion occurred that completely decimated the nest. The resulting fallout was a beautiful pink, yellow, and violet of Aurora Borealis affect in the atmosphere.

Both Myra and Seth were in awe of Tillow's experience. The details of the action and colors mesmerized their capacity to try and visualize what Tillow had experienced. They both knew that she was endowed with an exceptional creative mind, which allowed her to be so accurate in her descriptive explanations. Tillow continued her dialogue of her experiences.

She described seeing a falcon flying high in the air majestically hovering over a dog below on the landscape. Then she envisioned a female human figure that waved at her with a big smile. Then with hands clasped together in a prayer-type mudra, the woman bowed her head to Tillow. In her mind and heart, Tillow could see and feel the name "Nyla" come to her. In response, Tillow returned the gesture filled with love and gratitude. As this took place, the blue force field around her disappeared and was followed by a beautiful flow of energy in a figure 8 shape emanating back and forth between the two. Then the sealing of the experience ended with huge raised letters of gold outlined with a deep purple spelling the words "Victory! Victory! Victory!" The battle was over, but Tillow knew that the war between light and darkness was still in full force.

But Tillow noticed and felt a slight melancholy in her heart radiating from Nyla. While assisting Tillow in her battle with evil, Nyla lost her companions Dart, the falcon, and Motley, her dog. A sacrifice was paid for the attainment of victory for Tillow. But Nyla knew in her heart that Dart and Motley were still alive and well in spirit. A great truth was reignited in the hearts and souls of the Chosen Ones: a price, good or bad, is always a debt to be paid in the cosmic laws of cause and effect. There is no escape for anyone.

The next day after a good night's sleep, Tillow woke up feeling refreshed and rejuvenated. Then, out of the blue, she felt compelled to practice her meditation at the seat of her piano. She never questioned her impulses because they always led to her seed bed of creativity. And these normally occurred with her violin. However, this time was different.

When her meditations concluded, a strange but pleasant feeling came over her, as her hands and fingers softly began to caress the ivory keys. Inspiration took over, and the creation of a new composition was born. She allowed the energy to take command and knew that this would be a great piece. An expression of her recent experience put to music.

Then an unusual thing began to occur. All the children of the Chosen Ones simultaneously heard music being played in their heads and felt within their hearts. Tillow's new composition was being experienced by the children. It was beautiful and the twenty-five were attuned to this new strange phenomenon. Their curiosity ignited contact with the hierarchy.

A Rheyzoun Buddha commenced with an explanation as follows: "Dear ones, a beautiful experience is taking place as we speak. Tillow's battle and victory has created a flowering of youthful energy and beauty. When this high-frequency energy of an etheric vibrations occur, it seeks out receptors of the same youthful purity similar to bees seeking out flowers to pollinate. But in this spirit world the divine energy will only seek out those of equal or greater high-frequency levels. The receivers are usually that of youth, purity, and innocence, which have not been smeared by lower levels of vibrations consisting of negativity, dislike, rebellion, etc. So the children of the Chosen Ones are indeed kindred spirits and already have a connection at inner levels with the divine energy inherent within as seeds of light.

"Now, when this divine chlorophyll flow contacts the seeds, it ignites with a divine spark and the seeds emerge and transforms into new buds of a spiritual flowering. Thus, the caterpillar has dissolved/transformed into the butterfly.

"We are pleasantly surprised and celebrate this occurrence as an offshoot and a foundation of a new beginning in the hopes of mankind. We eventually expected this, but even as the hierarchy, our timing of predictions are off. As a young group of Chosen Ones, what would normally take a minimum of three Earth years to develop, you have attained it in a period of nine months! Given the current mission for this planet, this new momentum of youthful divine energy has been born and the new energy will continue to seek out other seeds of light throughout the Earth. Young and innocent souls close to the vibrations of this new energy will be 'pulled up' on the inner planes by a divine gravity effect, and this foundation will begin to grow exponentially. These newborn souls will intertwine as a divine network on a grander scale worldwide. And all of this began through the victory of Tillow and the foundation of the seedlings Bessie, Trina, Taylor, Lizzie, Byron, and Ishi. As disciples of our great Guru Ramata, we salute thee!"

The response of love and gratitude from the Chosen Ones was overwhelming. This action triggered one more brief dialogue with the hierarchy.

"We wish to inform you that Myama of Ecuador (twelve years of age) is truly a stem of light that will expand throughout the country of South America. Her pure connection with the nature spirits and her natural ability as a healer will cleanse the continent from north to south, establishing a new foundation of light throughout the land. The youth is the light of the future!" The dialogue ceased.

CHAPTER 15

THE FIRST DAY of September 2020, arrived as Myama rose to breathe the morning air in preparation for her early-morning meditations. A small glass of water at her side, she lit the candle and she began her seven deep breaths in reverence to the Great Spirit within. She visualized rays of love and devotion emanating from her heart out to all on the planet. As this occurred, she could feel her companions connect with her energies and, with arms raised in receptive mudra, blessed all with infinite love and protection in their lives. She envisioned a massive pink cloud saturating the entire globe, and a response of immense gratitude from Mother Earth filled her heart in return.

This was followed by a deep silence while her relaxed but intense focus remained on the candle. From this deep silence, a faint sound of young babies crying began to emerge within her senses. As she closed her eyes to receive any visions, a great mountain standing alone appeared to her. This stalwart mound did not look familiar to any in her country as it supported a great snowcapped crown. Numerous dark green trees skirted this great mountain as the faint cries of the babies increased in volume. Then a vision of two babies appeared in front of a huge boulder centered between two towering evergreen trees.

The babies were individually wrapped in two separate blankets. One was blue and gold, the other green, pink, and lavender. Myama could sense that the babies were male and female. Then Myama began to feel the loving energy of another Chosen One, that of Krea of Mt. Shasta City, California.

As the energy was doubled between Myama and Krea, they both immediately questioned in their minds and hearts if this was a kind of trickery created by the shadow warriors of Teohta. They both learned to activate the filter of discernment to verify actions and events within their states of meditation.

Their question was answered within seconds. A blue sphere filled with a pink substance encased both babies, and they felt that this was not a vision of trickery but an actual valid vision.

This vision became more surreal to Krea as she noticed that outside of the protective sphere of the babies, a smoky substance began to appear and permeate the air around the area. She sensed that danger was prevalent in the vision and felt the urge to quickly set out on a search for the babies. The feeling of urgency altered the spirits of Kobin and Rotussi.

The male energies of Kobin and Rotussi magnified that of Krea and Myama. The protective sphere of the babies doubled in size as their energies were blended together. This allowed extra time and protection but no time to waste for Krea to begin her search.

As the meditation was nearing completion, Krea focused on the surrounding area of the vision and noticed a familiar sight. She calculated that it would take a full day's hike to reach the site and another 1 to 2 hours to reach the destination. Then Krea sent feelings of love and gratitude to her compadres as they reciprocated with the figure eight flow of energy back. The meditation concluded and she immediately began preparing for her hike to find the babies.

Krea listened to the news station on her radio to see if there were any hikers reported missing, while getting together supplies and loading up her backpack. There were no missing-persons reports announced today. It was fairly common to have people get lost or hurt as the terrain of Mt. Shasta had its challenges and wildlife to match. Krea was thankful that this had occurred on a Saturday.

While readying her car for the journey ahead, Krea took a few deep breaths and an intense focus on the site destination and the angle of degree from the site to find the babies. There was no time to waste.

She drove to the gas station to fill up her car with gas up and began her drive. It was high noon and Krea would have to make good time to arrive at the site, traverse a two-mile hike one way and get the babies back to the car before the night sets in. This was a solo journey relying on her instincts. With this thought, she instantly received an inner message sent by Myama. Her invisible friends would assist Krea in her quest to find and retrieve the babies. Krea was fully open and grateful for this. Once again the presence of Kobin and Rotussi was present. This gave her comfort for the assistance and protection.

An hour passed and she finally spotted the site. It was a mile off road so her car could not be spotted from the main road. But her faith and inner strength gave Krea an adrenaline rush. She arrived, parked the car, and immediately set out on the hike. The energy level she maintained was above average when the sense of divine purpose coupled with combined spiritual assistance created an exceptional level of passion and desire to be victorious in any endeavor and challenge. Righteous cause would always result in the assistance of spiritual hierarchy. One could not fail.

As Krea stopped for a short rest and water break, she looked behind to see how far she had traveled. From her calculations, compared to the vision, the destination should not be much farther.

She sat for a moment to take a few deep breaths. All was unusually quiet when Krea could faintly hear the cry of a baby and then two. Her inner tank was re-energized and she immediately got up and proceeded to dash toward the noise. Within ten minutes, she approached a small clearing that exposed a huge boulder resting between two stalwart, soldierlike trees. There in front of the boulder were two babies wrapped in blankets and in separate baskets. Krea had dropped to her knees in humble gratitude and thanks for assistance in the search.

She looked around for any clues that might indicate evidence of other people in the area but to no avail. No campfires, no trash of any kind, and no footprints were found near the area. So she grabbed the two baskets of babies and started to hike back to the car. She looked at her watch and it was 2:30 p.m. She had to make it to the car no later than 4:30. Yet her dedication and discipline driven by her devotions to duty kicked in, and her pace remained steady and swift.

When the car was in sight, Krea looked at her watch. The time was 4:00 p.m. *Wow!* she thought to herself as she put the baskets down to open the car. Then she knelt in a prayer of thanks.

On her way back to town, Krea headed for the police station to alert them of the find while out on her hike. Proper protocol had to be followed in case of any reports of missing persons, be it babies or adults. Law enforcement would have to be told where the babies were found so a legal search for the parents could ensue.

Krea's mind was filled with mixed emotions from hoping that the parents would be found safe and unharmed to her dream of always wanting children of her own. How could these babies be abandoned without any trace of adults around? But her logical mind reassured her that the right thing was done and destiny would take over from here. Whatever the case, she committed herself to keep abreast of the situation and offer what other services she could render for these young souls.

After delivering the babies and filing a report with the city officials, Krea headed home and was looking forward to a nice long soak in her tub. She played some soft classical music on the ride home with a pleasant smile adorning her face the whole way home.

Once again, in her heart, a beam of love and gratitude was directed to Myama, Kobin, and Rotussi of which she felt a returning impulse.

As Krea began her bath soak with candlelight and soft music playing in a relaxing mode, an inner message was sent to her from on high.

"Dear one, your search and journey was a success, but the mission is still active. These dear souls are a part of your destiny that will continue on. You are right in your commitment to follow the case!" The dialogue ended as quickly as it had begun. There was a delight in Krea's heart. And then she felt a message from Myama's heart saying, "You have done well and your children are grateful for your actions." And that was it. The rest of the night Krea pondered on the incidents of this busy and adventurous day.

The following morning, Krea, just before awakening, had a dream about the two babies she had found. The babies were in a patch of blue-green grass smiling and laughing while a swarm of dragonflies and hummingbirds were circling them like nature's halo of love and protection. This radiated a warm inner smile within Krea and also with an influence, she felt to ponder on possible names for the infants.

This last thought in the dream ended, but it was her first thought as she awoke from her sleep. Was this a sign that the parents would not be found? Or possibly be found but either dead or in jail? So many thoughts ran through her mind, and then she got her composure to prepare for her morning meditations.

Krea lit a candle, sat on a pillow, and began to take her seven deep breaths to relax and focus her mind/heart rhythm. She projected beams of love and gratitude to all of life and its sentient beings. When this was happening, she instantly received two loving responses: Myama and Miraki.

These beautiful souls informed Krea that the babies would be need a mother soon and that adoption would be an option for her if she chose. Then a message from Kobin and Rotussi followed, informing Krea that whatever her choice was, there would be a person in the future that would come forth and have information about the children and their parents. But no time was given as to when this would occur.

As she received these loving messages, Krea lifted her arms in a receptive manner and poured her heart out as a commitment to love and protect these babies as her own blood children. The four Chosen Ones responded to her light by their blessing back to Krea.

When this communication took place, two names jumped out in bright raised letters: Sara Ann and Jeremy. These names resonated with Krea and pleased her so. In love and spirit, the bond was made with the babies along with the responsibility and accountability for their lives. As Krea's arms were lowered into a prayer mudra, a wave of love and acceptance was being received from the hearts of all twenty-five Chosen Ones. This also pleased the hierarchy.

"Beloved Krea, we salute you as you have just completed a spiritual adoption process through your love and service to these abandoned newborns. Young Sara Ann and Jeremy continue their bond with you from previous lives. You three have a great destiny to fulfill, and the karmic challenges will be a role in some of your initiations in this life. As you grow in their spirituality, glimpses of your past with these children will be revealed to you. Remember this well: the combined power of love and forgiveness can and will dissolve negative karma with any and all beings experienced in life: past, present, and future. And if your initiations with Sarah Ann and Jeremy are victorious, they can be exalted to the status of Chosen Ones as well. Portions of your golden disc will be appropriated to them as flakes of gold within their hearts until enough momentum is gathered to complete their own golden discs. Through the efforts of your sincere loving hearts, you will earn our added protection in this life." The dialogue concluded.

Later that day Krea was contacted by the authorities to inform her of their investigation results so far. There was no sign of any adults in the vicinity of the babies, no trace of any unknown vehicles in the area, and anyone questioned about tourists or visitors in the area was a complete negative. So they informed Krea that their next step was to issue an investigative report on the local networks of any out-of-town friends or relatives having anything to do with a pair of newborn babies. All possibilities were being checked out in a search for parents of the newborn children.

Krea was thankful for the message and returned the call with gratitude for keeping her up-to-date on the latest reports. Now Krea had some deep pondering about that the babies and how, as a preschool teacher, she would be able to commit to the proper amount of time to raise two newborns while teaching. The realization of a major adjustment had caught her whole undivided attention.

She sat down with a pad, pencil, and a candle to contemplate and meditate on what would need to be done for this future, minimal, eighteen-year commitment that was to unfold. She would definitely need the assistance of a nanny and how much money she would be looking at for the new expenses of this position to fill. Immediately a name popped up in her head of a young mother of one of her preschool students. Young four-year-old Tara's mother, Penny.

Penny is a twenty-year-old single mother with one child, Tara, whose father had left the two of them for another woman. Penny and Rob had never married, and he left without any notice except for a simple note saying he found another love and was sorry that they had a child together.

Penny works at the local drugstore as an assistant manager with a bright and bubbly personality to match. She had quickly put Rob behind her to focus on her career and most of all what is best for her four-year-old daughter Tara. Krea and Penny hit it off as good friends, and Penny was really struggling with the one job and taking good care of Tara.

Krea thought things out and saw this as a possible opportunity for the perfect match. When this thought intensified in her mind and heart, the sweet, loving message came into her inner radar from a dear soul, Omer of Norway. He responded with a confirmation. "This young woman you have in mind is a dear soul with a sincere heart and is truly a welcome into the fold. Her love and passion for young children has resonated in my heart and she can be the perfect assistant in our great work for humanity and the Earth." Krea expressed her heartfelt thanks and gratitude to Omer in the figure 8 flow of love and unity through free will for all mankind.

Her next step was to set up a correspondence session with Penny to see if she might be interested in such a proposition as a possible family unit. And she wanted to proceed with caution and respect, not asserting herself too aggressively to where Penny would feel obligated to agree and commit to something way over her head.

The next day Krea called Penny and invited her for a cup of coffee and visit the following day, Saturday, and when the visit would be convenient for her. Penny was delighted to hear from Krea and gave a positive response to the invitation. 10:00 a.m. would be the perfect time as this would be two hours before work. This would allow for a pleasant, non-rushed visit, relaxed and joyful.

Krea and Penny met at the local coffee shop and chose an outside table for two with a beautiful view of Mt. Shasta. Their conversation began with ten minutes of social chit-chat and then Krea supported a semiserious but pleasant look addressing Penny's attention.

"Did you see the announcement about the two babies found off the beaten path of the hiking trail at the base of Mt Shasta?" she asked.

"Oh yes!" responded Penny with an excitement mixed with a concern. "How two newborns like those could be left alone in the wilds of nature with no sign of any parents! I sure hope they will be found safe and okay!"

Then Krea told Penny that she was the one that found the babies while on a hike, but did not explain that the find was from a vision as this was not allowed from a Chosen One.

Penny's face lit up like a Christmas tree. "Oh my goodness!" she exclaimed. "What is going to happen if the parents are not found? Would the babies be turned over to CPS?" Krea responded that that was a possibility. And then she began her possible proposition with Penny.

"If there is an outside chance that the babies could be adopted, I am very serious about applying for the opportunity. However, as a single person with a full-time teaching position, I would definitely need the help of a nanny for a long-term commitment. It would not pay a lot, but maybe I could find someone where we can barter our times with one another to offset the fees I would be able to pay. And then I thought of you and Tara."

She went on to explain her possible ideas and plans that might be feasible for the both of them and emphasized strongly that she did not want Penny to feel pressured into making a quick decision. Krea paused and awaited a response for any interest in the proposition offered.

Penny paused for a moment and then gave her response. "I am definitely interested and would like to think about it. It is important that I get a feeling of how Tara would feel about this. Being a four-year-old, I would not want to chance her being jealous or uncomfortable with Mommy giving too much attention to others and not fulfilling her needs. Can I get back to you in about two weeks with an answer on my decision?"

Krea was pleasantly and positively surprised at the mature thinking and concern that she expressed for Tara that would determine her decision. Being a young mother has a tendency to accelerate the growth of responsibility and accountability if one chooses to be a good parent built from a strong bond between child and parent.

"Of course, Penny. You take whatever time you need and you have my utmost respect and trust on whatever decision you make. You are a great mother to Tara, and nothing should ever sacrifice the healthy bond between you and your child."

Both enjoyed a coffee refill and visited for another half hour. At the conclusion, they embraced one another and parted ways.

Krea acquired a whole new level of respect for young Penny and her maturity as a responsible parent. As she sat in solitude of love and gratitude, Myama, Miraki, and Omer sent vibrations of love and respect to her heart and swore in an internal commitment to support and protect Krea in her role as parent/teacher in this life. She felt truly blessed in this moment of a sacred, profound silence.

But even though her decision was made, it was not 100 percent sure that Krea would even have an opportunity to adopt the babies, contingent on the outcome of the local law investigations in the case. In this moment, a warm and loving signal came to her indicating that what is best for the babies should always be the primary goal and concern in their well-being. Maintaining that thought in mind and heart would contribute to the proper destiny of these souls.

As the days turned into weeks, Penny spent extra time playing with Tara and her dolls. She used this opportunity to observe Tara's actions and attitudes as a parent to a couple of baby dolls. Her favorites were Andy and Su-Su, male and female baby dolls. Tara seemed to be a natural on their care: feeding, changing their diapers, naps, and playing house. Tara would always sing the babies to sleep, rocking each one softly in her arms before laying them in their beds. Little by little Penny would give Tara hints and ideas on the treatment and care of the babies. Tara would listen intently as she approved of Mommy's help with Andy and Su-Su. Penny felt that the time was right to inform Tara about helping out a friend.

During the last two weeks, Krea would check in with the authorities on the continuing investigations of the alleged abandoned babies. So far nothing new is gained, and the babies were being cared for by Child Protective Services. Krea asked if she can see how the babies were doing. She was given permission and made an appointment to see them.

When she saw the babies, they looked happy and healthy and that pleased her. She asked permission to take a picture of them and her request was granted. Krea asked if she could visit the babies to two to three times a week. This was also granted. Lastly, she offered her assistance in any way for the care and case of the missing babies. The authorities were grateful for her concern and offers of contribution.

In the middle of the third week, Krea decided to give Penny a call and see if she would like to get together for another social visit. Krea wanted to tread ground very carefully but yet forward with the momentum directed by the best interest of two young beings and their lives. So she made the call and left a message for Penny.

The following day Penny returned the call and was happy to hear from Krea. But this time Penny suggested a different place to meet. The local pizza parlor with a little playground for children to play in. Krea happily agreed. The time was set for 12:00 noon, the following Sunday.

The day of the meeting with Penny arrived. Krea made sure to take her phone as she wanted to show Penny the latest picture of the babies in the CPS facility. And Krea was somewhat anxious to hear how little Tara was doing. Adrenaline was pumping in overdrive, but Krea needed to downshift her motions to relax in a calm but pleasant state. She arrived at the pizza parlor and was greeted, to her surprise, by Tara.

"Well, hi, Princess Tara!" she said with joy. They both hugged and then Tara took her hand and led them to the table that Penny had reserved for them. Tara ran to the playground while her mom and Krea began their visit.

Immediately, Penny asked Krea if there was any positive news in the case of the babies and the whereabouts of their parents. She saw this as the perfect opportunity to share the recent photos taken of the babies at CPS. But the first response to the question was negative on the investigation. No parents found and no missing reports filed on the babies. By this time the case was reported statewide and just recently nationwide. For many reasons Krea stressed the fact that part of her wished deeply that something would be found in the case of the babies and their family history, but if not, that she would volunteer to step up and offer her services to help them provide a future for the newborns.

"Let me show you a few recent photos of the babies," Krea said. "Oh! They are so darling!" replied Penny, her heart warm and loving like a caring mother should feel. "Would you mind if we let Tara see the photos?" Penny asked.

Krea was stunned and in a state of happy shock. This was a total unexpected response and for a moment Krea froze, bug-eyed. Then she broke with the response "Yes, that would be fine."

It was a thirty-minute wait on the pizza that Penny had ordered for them. In this time frame, Penny described her actions with Tara since their last social visit. She told Krea about Tara playing mother to her two favorite baby dolls, Andy and Su-Su. It seems that Tara has a natural affection for babies to the point where she sings them to sleep at their bedtime. Tara has seen other mothers of her fellow preschoolers bring their babies when picking up their children from school, and her face always lights up with a big smile like a big sister would do.

"I would like for Tara to see the babies so she can sense her own bond with them and then we can observe her reactions before we make her aware of our plans when the time is right."

As Krea gave consent, Penny removed herself to fetch Tara from the play area and to let Tara know that Krea wanted to show her some pictures. They returned to the table and Tara asked to see the pictures, which Krea immediately pulled up on her phone.

"Oh! They are so beautiful and precious!" Tara remarked excitedly. "Are those the babies on the TV?" she asked Krea.

"Yes, they are," replied Krea with a warm smile. "No family has been found yet and I want to make sure that the babies are doing okay. I go to see them twice a week to check up on them." Tara smiled in delight.

"I think that you would be a good mama," said Tara as she looked at the photos again. The approval of Tara meant a great deal to Krea. Penny delighted in the dialogue happening between the two. Things seemed to be coming together in the building of a possible future for the babies.

A few minutes later, the pizza arrived and the three dove in to enjoy their lunch and conversations. Part of the dialogue was Tara telling Krea about how she cares for her two favorite baby dolls, Andy and Su-Su, and that one day in the future she will have her own kids to love and raise. Krea felt the love and sincerity radiating in Tara's being and confidence, trust, and faith in Mama Penny.

The rest of the lunch was a joyful and pleasant visit as the three, unbeknownst to them, were creating a stronger family bond and foundation.

The following morning Krea, relaxed in deep meditation, with a heart filled with love and warmth from the previous day's visit concerning the possible future of two babies in addition to her work as a Chosen One. As her mind expanded more with the unity of the cosmos, more insights began pouring in her new levels of awareness, the most important being the factors involved in the accountabilities and responsibilities of being cocreators in this wonderful universe. Cosmic doors were opening to Krea and the Chosen Ones as each initiation and its victories and, or defeats, were a stage of growth in spirit. Along with the steady growth came more tools of love, wisdom, and power available upon their calls to hierarchy for assistance in their future challenges and assignments.

Krea began to realize more and more the importance of every thought, emotion, and choices we make are the seeds of the future while maintaining the full love and respect of the free will of all involved. She realized the connectedness of all life in the canvas of creation, and that karma, be it good or bad, is a debt to be paid for all as this is universal cosmic law: "As ye sow, so shall ye reap." Many avatars throughout the history of planet Earth spread these teachings worldwide. But they could only share the teachings, and the rest was the use or abuse of free will for mankind. While we are monitored by hierarchy on our growth according to the choices we make on our paths, a true leader or teacher lives the love and light they share and mentors all the destinies of life who are open to these teachings.

She realized that all problems and shortcomings arise when seeds of separation, greed, envy, jealousy, and fear arise and a person veers from the path of love, light, joy, peace, and happiness. So if the creation of one becomes tainted with any of these negative vibrations, we are bound by cosmic law to Mattias of the creation, albeit the original intent was of love and sincerity, to try and encourage the creation back to harmony through free will. This is why spiritual hierarchy continuously emphasizes and reiterates the importance of love, compassion, gratitude,

mercy, and forgiveness as the ultimate blueprint of all beings to strive for in the progression of spiritual growth.

All the Chosen Ones received these important insights in this day's morning meditations. Krea's current situation is what sparked the lessons and the jewels thereof released. All expressed a deep sense of love topped with gratitude toward each and every one. This intense surge of love energy shot out throughout the earth and attracted an equal or greater portion of energy from the Rheyzoun Buddhas and their Guru Ramata. A blessing such as this had not occurred on earth for thousands of years as praise from on high order to the earth.

At the end of the meditation, Krea sat in a serene contemplation of her part in this microcosm of the great macrocosm of the universe. She could not help but exude much love and gratitude for her mere existence on this planet in this time frame. She truly understood the meaning of which the Great Ones of history have repeated to mankind: That we are but a grain of sand on the beach of eternity! But each grain, each blade of grass, has its purpose of being and to fulfill. The beauty of life is the loving power of transformation, like the caterpillar becoming the butterfly, and a baby becoming a child, becoming a young man or woman. One has to pass in order to transform into the next. Love is like energy in its highest form of expression. Krea realized that all of these insights were not separate but a part of her being if chosen to accept, by free will, every breath, every moment as precious as the next, pure ecstasy!

All the more reason now, Krea realized, that she needed to put herself in Penny's shoes. With Penny and Tara possibly in the picture with Krea contemplating adoption of the babies, a whole new level of familial responsibility and accountability would be entered, and the future and well-being of mother/daughter was being added. Was this fair to them? Is this what Krea really wanted?

At that moment in thought, she received a warm message in her heart from Myama and Omer. "When you put their best interest first, the sincere heart will determine the common denominator of the interest of all and choose the outcome in the future endeavor. In this case, all three involved maintain a high level of love, maternal instinct, and the utmost desire to serve one another with unconditional love, love in its highest form."

This loving response solidified Krea's heart and desire to pursue a possible adoption of the babies if Penny and Tara chose to willingly expand their family.

Later that day, Krea called CPS to inquire about a possible adoption option if the time limit of the investigation came up empty. She made an appointment for the next day and would interview with a Miss Dina Emerald. In this way she could begin to learn the steps and qualifications she needed to meet in order to adopt the newborns.

At that moment another realization entered Krea's mind and heart. What about the true parents of these beautiful babies? How and where are they? The thought that she did not offer any direct prayers and affection for the parents made Krea feel ashamed.

Krea immediately sat down and lit a candle to direct a moment of thoughts of love and compassion for the health and safety of the parents of the babies. There is no room for judgment or condemnation in the work of the Chosen Ones, and radiating unconditional love to all is the ultimate anecdote for forgiveness, mercy, and healing that has helped to promote transformations many a time in the history of the Earth and its people.

In this moment she felt the kindred spirits of Kobin, Miraki, and Yoi-Yu flow unto her being. Thus began a dialogue from Yoi-Yu, the Hopi medicine woman. "We are so happy that your heart remembered to reach out to the parents of these dear siblings. Our main mission to save and heal a planet cannot be accomplished without a great portion of mercy and compassion that creates the power of forgiveness to all who experience shortcomings on their individual paths. Though not intentional, many times we are caught up in our own activities and motives, forgetting those who need us the most. And our ignorance of this is unacceptable on the path of unity and purpose. When we direct these energies specifically to certain souls, we set in motion a great quality and quantity of healing their way and the journey to their heart begins. Then our blessings to them releases the energies, leaving the rest up to them and their own free will to accept or reject. You have done well in remembering this by your actions of the heart!" The dialogue ended with Krea bowing her head in a silent reverence to her fellow inner partners.

In the early evening, Penny gave Krea a call to chat about the last visit at the pizza parlor. She began to inform her about a serious conversation with Tara and the babies from the news.

"I asked Tara about you and the babies and what she thought about the visit. Her response was most interesting. She said 'I see that teacher looked like a mama when she had showed us the babies. I think she wants babies but would need help with them. I would like to show her how to take care of Andy and Su-Su if she wanted to.' I was totally stunned at her comments," said Penny. "It is like she saw directly into your heart and wanted to help Teacher on how to be a good mama! And I didn't even tell her anything about what might be happening with our possible plans in the making!"

Krea was in a happy shock as well! What do you know? The student becomes the teacher and vice-versa!

Penny continued, "So I asked Tara if I could invite Teacher to the house to meet Andy and Su-Su? And her immediate response was of course! I think Andy and Su-Su would like Teacher!

"So I am asking if you would like to come over next Saturday for lunch at the house?"

"I would love too!" replied Krea. "What time and can I bring anything over for lunch?'

"No, this is mine and Tara's treat. Is 11:30 good for you?"

"That is perfect. I am so looking forward to the visit." Krea was ecstatic and thankful for everything leading up to this point.

For the rest of the week, Krea was up early for her morning meditations and gave an extra earnest energy/prayer for all parents and guardians in their roles of life's everyday challenges. Her feeling was if we can't help others to forgive themselves for their shortcomings in the raising of their children, then any measure of growth is stunted for the families as a whole. Further developing mercy, compassion, and forgiveness is the spiritual anecdote and Band-Aid that allows for the bumps in the roads of life to be repaved and to move on to further heights.

She closed her meditations with arms held high in a receptive mode as love and gratitude shot out from her heart to all of humanity. It was time to get ready to meet with the representative of CPS, a Miss Dina Emerald.

Krea arrived fifteen minutes early at the facility and the representative, Dina, was already at the front desk. When their eyes met, they knew that within their hearts a special kinship was in the making. They both shook hands as a formal introduction was made.

"You can call me Dina instead of Miss Emerald" was the first dialogue of the CPS representative. Both ladies sported a pleasant smile in exchange.

"It is a pleasure to meet you, Dina," said Krea in response.

"Please tell me about yourself," asked Dina as it was standard questioning for any potential adoptions to incorporate a background check. She listened intently to Krea's life history in addition to her hobbies and goals in life.

Then the big question came: "As a single person, why do you wish to adopt two babies without a father figure in their lives?" A fair question, considering the lives of two newborns with a proper raising and the best care possible.

Krea thought very deeply on how to answer this question. She decided to rely on her heart's intent as she began to give her response. She felt a shift in consciousness as she began to speak.

"While I am a single female, my career as a preschool teacher has served me well in the school. In my many years I have observed firsthand the bond of love between parents and their children. Nowadays, there is a higher percentage of single parents currently in school themselves while their child is being attended to in preschool. These children are well dressed, healthy and most of the time happy. And when the day is over, the children are most happy to see whomever picks them up to take them home. These range from family members, friends, or a significant other that makes a commitment to assist the single parent and the raising of their child or children. I can truly sense the love and bonds of these child/parent relationships for I feel that it is my responsibility and accountability as a teacher to observe and assist in any way possible to ensure that both child and parent are given the best quality and care for the services rendered.

"So, in reality my role as a preschool teacher, I already feel that all the children in my classroom are my family and that they deserve the best care and quality that I and the school can provide. I would never attempt to take on more than I could handle and my strongest quality as a mother figure is that a strong and loving heart will never abandon life's challenges thrown our way. Love will always survive and provide is my model and commitment in life to myself and all that I serve." At that Krea ended her answer to Dina.

It was Dina's turn to respond. *Wow!* she thought to herself. In her mind the whole interview was summed up in Krea's longwinded answer. But the sincerity and the passion of her heart gave a resounding impact to Dina. Nevertheless, protocol had to be followed as she asked Krea the next question.

"Now, what if the parents or relative appeared while the process of adoption was in force. What would your feelings and reactions be in this case?"

Krea thought for a moment and then replied, "My number one concern would always be what is in the best interest of the babies; however, I always pray for the parents or any family member that their well-being is cared for. That being said, abandonment of any kind is irresponsible and always carries a danger with it. Could or would this happen again? Can one imagine the emotional scars tainting these precious little ones? The seeds of fear and loneliness planted in their beings? While I have already accepted the babies in my heart, I have a bond and commitment of proving what is best for these newborns. While my part of the caretaker is bound within my heart and soul, I would raise them to always love, cherish, and honor all and eventually make them aware of their true family and to make their own decisions when they come of age."

"Well, thank you for your time and consideration in this case of the possibilities of adoption," remarked Dina. "We will do a standard background check on you and carefully consider your interest through your answers given to the questions." The interview ended as both ladies shook hands again and Dina gave her card to Krea in case she had any questions or concerns regarding the case.

That evening Krea drove home feeling confident that that the interview with Dina went well. She was allowed to see the babies on her way out in addition to blessing the CPS facility for all that they do in serving the youth through their early years. Then her mind shifted to her next visit with Penny and daughter Tara at their home.

At home in her easy chair, Krea lay back in reflection of all that had transpired since the beginning of the vision to the current moment in time. She felt calm, protected, and fully charged with a higher love shared with all her inner partners. Such a selfless but powerful feeling expressed from kindred hearts! She felt an effortless smile adorn her face as she fell asleep.

That night, Krea enjoyed a dream of love and splendor radiating from her heart to the babies and her entire class of children and their families. To her amazement, she envisioned myriads of smiling faces with wings flying abundantly in the skies and blessing mankind in all walks of life. Beautiful music and aromas filled the land with glory and light. All sense of darkness and shadows melted away from the glowing hearts of all people in the lands. A pure heaven here on earth, she thought. Then a higher message came to her from a Buddha.

"Precious Krea, the vision you are experiencing is the result of the proper and rightfully use of free will expressed by all! When mankind chooses to return to their own unique divine blueprint and realize their unity with divinity, transformation happens. Your vision is the result of this occurring on a worldwide scale. A vision of victory proclaimed on Earth! The blueprint is set in motion! Peace, peace, peace!"

Two days later, Saturday arrived. Krea was excited for the next visit with Penny and Tara. She practiced her meditations early, ate breakfast, and went for a brisk two-mile walk. What a crisp and beautiful morning it was! A cool breeze serenading the singing of birds, dragonflies, and honeybees buzzing in the air and kids playing outside with their friends and pets. Life was vibrantly flowing, fulfilling nature's desires of beauty.

Every breath of fresh air a moment of purity breathing in nature's wonders and exhaling gratitude and love of life thus fulfilling the figure 8 flow of the unity of existence!

Time was moving quickly toward the 11:30 meeting with Penny and Tara. As Krea sat for a moment, a sudden sense of urgency signaled her inner alert system and the name "Jogil" was attached to the message. All were alerted to the call, and a moment of silence was needed.

Deep in the far northern wilderness of Siberia, Jogil sensed a darkness pervading the atmosphere. As he approached the local towns, the people exuded a fear and paranoia, which was not the norm to these friendly groups. People were gathered together talking about weird noises around their homes and their pets started disappearing without a trace. There were no signs of animal attacks; the pets simply vanished without a trace. Fear and confusion was growing like a dark cloud, and the people were like children lost in a maze. What to do? Jogil, being a friend of all towns, looked at his wolf partner, Zac, to observe his mannerisms. The bristles on his neck were standing, accompanied by a low monotone growl. He could sense the darkness and fear that permeated the air.

Sensing this emergency situation, Krea called Penny and asked her if 12:30 would be okay to meet, and Penny consented. This gave Krea the necessary time to focus her energies on the assistance of Jogil's message.

As her meditation began, she picked up an energy signal from Coralea assisting in this urgent action. Then the name Nyla appeared as well, sending an intense focus to the northern hemisphere of Siberia. All were preparing for a major confrontation with the evil forces of Teohta.

Nyla began to speak, "For thousands of years, this area on earth has been the focal point of the dark forces and visitations of alien ships summoned by Teohta. A base has been established, both in the physical and the astral plane. It is an underground base with many secret entrances hidden throughout the lands. I can provide all with a visual of the underground base, but am not privy as to where the secret entrances are located. We must focus our energies on the underground grid to dissipate as much negative energy as possible to protect the physical towns aboveground!" The dialogue ended with all chanting

"Ramtam Om, Shivaya Om!" to protect the small towns and inject light to the underground grid of the evil base.

As this occurred, Nyla made a decree to the hierarchy for assistance in this battle of light and darkness. This created a response of a vision of a breastplate containing bright jewels of rubies, blue and green topazes, and diamonds. "Warriors, prepare for battle!" was an instruction issued from a bright spirit adorned in gold and white with a blue star as a crown. "Charge the atmosphere with victory!" was the command issued. Then the spirit vanished with a golden ball of energy, an orb blazing through the atmosphere.

Immediately, the Chosen Ones envisioned the breastplate of jewels known as the "warrior's uniform," which they immediately adorned themselves on the inner planes continuing the mantra "Ramtam Om! Shivaya Om!" and visualizing legions of light beings filling the underground bases of darkness and a huge blue oval ring surrounding the aboveground towns as a protective shield. They sensed inwardly that their directed energies needed to be an unbroken chain of light to be sustained by no less than the efforts of ten Chosen Ones at a time and for an indefinite period of time, as this was the beginning battle of a stronghold held by the darkness from many centuries; thus, the reason of the extreme cold and barren lands of Siberia.

The assistance of hierarchy was contingent upon the combined efforts and consistency of the Chosen Ones' directed energies to free a people and their lands from the evil grip of Teohta and her legions of doom. Each one adorned a golden crown labeled "victory" along with their warrior breastplate, and became a great conductor of light on which hierarchy could build a foundation when their directed energies maintained a certain level of light vibrations for an allotted time frame. Faith, passion, and persistency were the required efforts of the Chosen Ones as their initiations became greater and more intense to act as one in this spirit of victory through unity.

Meanwhile, Krea gave her energy and blessing as she concluded her meditation session and left for her meeting with Penny and Tara. Eagerness filled her heart as the momentum of her own current situation with the abandoned babies felt positive and encouraging with the progress of today's lunch with Penny and Tara.

As Krea pulled up to the house, Tara was on the porch with Andy and Su-Su to greet her. She approached the house with a bag containing some refreshments and a few containers of baby food for Tara's babies. Tara smiled in gratitude as she saw the baby food and gave Krea a big hug. Krea and Penny exchanged greetings, and then they all sat comfortably in the living room.

"Teacher, meet Andy and Su-Su, my babies," remarked Tara. Krea acknowledged the babies, dressed in blue and pink, respectively. "It is time for their nap, and I will wake them for their next meal," she instructed. Tara dismissed herself momentarily, while Penny offered Krea a cup of tea.

"Tara is quite mature and disciplined as well!" Krea emphasized in a complimentary comment. Penny told her that Tara was anxious and excited for this visit and planned her schedule all week to show teacher what a good mother she is to Andy and Su-Su. "She even has a little playpen and a small TV for them to enjoy," Penny shared.

Tara returned to the living room and told Krea that the babies were happy to meet her. "I think you would make a good mama," replied Tara. Krea smiled and thanked her.

"How old are Andy and Su-Su?" asked Krea.

"One and a half years old," answered Tara. "They are good little babies, but Andy cries a bit more than Su-Su. I give him a hug and a toy to play with, and he calms down."

"It seems that you give them the love and attention that they need like a good mama," Krea complimented with a smile.

"That is what mommas do," Tara replied with a smile of thanks.

"Do you want to be a mama?" asked Tara directly with a keen smile. She could sense the Krea's interest in babies.

"I am thinking seriously about it," answered Krea. "But I can see from your experience that it requires a lot of love and time to raise babies the right way," Krea commented with a compliment directed to Tara.

"Oh yes!" replied Tara. "Mama taught me that good babies can only be as good as we raise and love them!" Tara added passionately. "Mama also teaches me to always be loving even when times are hard, like kids with no daddies; they need more love and help while growing up." Krea was very impressed by Tara's strong convictions and commitment as a parent. And that is a big compliment to Penny on raising Tara as a single mama.

"Would anyone care for dessert?" asked Penny as their conversation continued. She bought Tara's favorite, ice cream sandwiches.

"I think we are ready!" answered Tara with excitement in her voice. This gave Krea and Penny a short break to chat, while Tara enjoyed her dessert.

"I think that this is the right time to tell Tara about the babies and your wanting to be a mama. She is pretty smart and could sense it for a while now. I will let her make the offer to help you if you need assistance in raising them." She smiled, basically implying that Penny was agreeable to the possible new that arrangement. Tara's intuition would seal the deal in assisting Krea in raising the babies. Her excitement was growing more and more because in order to properly raise the babies and do her work as a Chosen One, Krea would definitely require assistance from someone she could trust and have full faith and confidence in. In her heart, Penny and Tara would most definitely fulfill that need.

The next step was to wait on a call from Dina, the CPS representative for a follow-up interview from the previous session. But now, Krea needed the offer from Tara to seal the deal for her own needs. Tara ate her final bite of dessert with a delightful smile, and a drip of ice cream dangled from the corner of her mouth.

"Thank you, Mama! That was delicious!" she expressed. "It is almost time for me to check on the babies," she remarked, looking at Krea intently. "Teacher, would you like to come with me to check on Andy and Su-Su?" Tara asked.

"I would love to," answered Krea. It felt from within that this was the moment that the deal would be set in motion. The love of an innocent dear child would determine the destiny of a Chosen One, with the child becoming the teacher through faith and love. What a joyful moment to be in!

Tara took the teacher's hand and led her into the babies' room, and they peered in the cribs. "The babies are sleeping very good," Tara whispered. "I will let them sleep longer and then wake them for a bottle of warm milk." Tara proceeded to speak as they quietly stepped out of the room, "Babies are so precious, and they expect a lot from us as parents. I love my mama very much, and she has taught me to be a good mama like her. She has taught me how to be good and loving all by herself. She is the best mama, and I think that we could both learn a lot from her." Tara smiled, complimenting Penny with all the love expressed from her little big heart. "If you ever want to have babies, Mama and me would like to help you if you ever need any," Tara offered. Both smiled, their hearts bonding in a covenant of love and motherhood. Tara gave Krea a hug and asked her, "Do you want to be a mama?"

At that, Krea answered a resounding "yes" and followed up with a comment to Tara.

"I would love to be a mama, but my lack of experience would require some help as these babies too would not have a daddy. I would need the love and support from someone like you and your mama to help me," Krea responded, awaiting the final step, an offer from little Mama Tara.

"I would be happy to help you and your babies if it is okay with my mama, and I think she would like that too," offered Tara.

"I agree with Tara and I think that Teacher would make a great mama. Don't you, Tara?" replied Penny, giving her seal of approval and solidifying it with Tara's approval.

"Oh yes, Mama! Teacher has a good heart and is a good listener, and she has learned from me and Andy and Su-Su."

"And," added Penny, "you would be Auntie Tara to the babies if we helped teacher." Tara's eyes were like fried eggs, popping with joy.

"Oh yes, I would be happy about that!" Tara responded with joy. All three celebrated with joy as Penny sealed the moment with another ice cream sandwich to feast on.

Then, Krea told Tara of her intent to possibly adopt the lost babies from the news, but did not reveal to Tara that she was the one who found the babies while on a hike.

"I thought so!" said Tara with a smile, "because you had the look of a mama in your eyes and I could feel it in yours and my heart!" They all smiled happily, bathing in the sweetness of motherly love.

"I have to check on my babies now" said Tara as she politely dismissed herself and left the room. Krea read this as lunch being concluded, and expressed her gratitude and thanks to Penny for having her over. "This would not have been possible for me to consider if I did not have a plan for assistance that would consist of you and Tara," said Krea in a very thankful and grateful manner. "I am eternally blessed to have you two in my life and now pray that the opportunity for the adoption of the babies will be granted."

Penny looked deeply into Krea's eyes and responded, "It will happen, I can feel it." They both embraced once again, then Krea bid farewell until the next time.

When Krea arrived home, she checked her phone for messages, but the box was empty. She sat in her recliner and felt a wave of delight and victory in her ongoing pursuit of the babies while still showing a reverence and compassion for the whereabouts of the parents or any other family members. She put her hands on her heart as she generated a feeling of thankfulness and put out into the universe a statement of "God bless all people and all of life for the goodness that we share."

CHAPTER 16

KREA DRIFTED INTO a calm sleep, but then was awakened by a jolt as Nyla sent out an inner alert to all.

"I have seen a vision of a great, large black crystal sphere underneath the grounds of Siberia that appears to be a great power source of Teohta and her legions. This massive crystal emits and receives signals throughout the galaxies like a queen bee to her drones. Sightings of UFOs are increasing almost daily and the people of the territories are living in fear and panic, which is being magnified by the power of what I will call the great black orb.

"We must focus our energies on the protection of the people's minds and hearts as well as their physical beings, and to also call upon hierarchy for assistance in this intense battle and struggle for the land. If the fear and panic persists, the people will stay in their homes for safety and the local businesses and commerce will begin to fold and thus be victims of the darkness."

Omer responded to the call and offered his services to assist Jogil in this rigorous challenge of the dark forces. "I have a month's vacation available, and I can travel to help Jogil, my brother, in any physical as well as spiritual way that I can be of service."

"This is good indeed," replied Nyla on this inner dialogue. "Your momentum of the Hindu mantras, along with Jogil's spiritual energies, will allow the rest of us to send tremendous amounts of light energy to the two of you as a great focus. You must calm the people and somehow convince them that fear and panic are the enemies, and these need to be converted into courage and passion of pure spirit to erase and dissolve the wickedness surrounding the lands and its people. Encouragement and empowerment of divine justice shall overcome all darkness. This could be difficult since many have different religious beliefs and ways to express them. A common ground must be found for all to focus their own inherent light energies within, for only a tremendous group effort will defeat the dark momentum of centuries past on the physical and the astral level."

Both Jogil and Omer agreed and commenced with a battle plan as Omer was to travel the next day to meet up with Jogil. But the inner dialogue was not over. A Rheyzoun Buddha of immense power interjected with the following offering to the Chosen Ones, and their current battle was just beginning.

"Hail! Beloved ones, I have heard your call and my legions are ever ready to combat the evils of earth! Your clarion light call through your sincere hearts of service and passion has ignited the gates of hierarchy! Jogil and Omer will lead the battle and charge the hearts of a people to a victory crucial for the sustaining of a planet. You must instill in the people that all are 'one family,' and through their faith and passion in unity and power of unconditional love, they will overcome any and all the adversities thrown at them. They must remain and maintain strength in their love and passion of unity in order for my legions to sustain an attack that will assist in a great cleansing of this earth. As the cosmic law 'as above so below' always applies, the physical must initiate the calls to spirit through immense sincerity, love, and gratitude, thus creating a figure 8 flow from hierarchy to the physical in order to defeat and transform any conditions desired. For as you would say, love and truth are two sides of the same coin, and the coin is infinite spirit, for this is the alchemical recipe of a spirit warrior!"

The dialogue concluded and all blessed a moment of great silence with a deep love and gratitude, which created the figure 8 flow to hierarchy and opened the gates of the light armies.

The following day, Omer left on a flight to meet Jogil at a designated city. His arrival time would be noon of that day. Jogil, with Zac, was already within an hour of the airport. As the plane landed, Omer could see a man and his companion, Zac, the wolf, through the window. He exited the plane, then both exchanged greetings with a firm handshake and proceeded to Jogil's truck. Zac hopped in the back as the two entered the cab.

"What a beautiful wolf!" remarked Omer in admiration of Zac. This was his first experience up close and personal with a beautiful creature of the wilderness.

"Yes, he's been a true companion and has saved my hide on numerous occasions," replied Jogil. "You up for a nice hot burger?" he asked for it was lunchtime. Omer agreed, and they went to the local diner to eat. The local people sported a smile as Jogil introduced Omer to a few locals. His keen awareness could sense an agitation from the people, but he remained silent.

However, Jogil began a conversation regarding the people and the culture. "I have observed that the average people of this country are that of a laid-back quality, in that goals of riches and modern industry are not a desire in or of their hearts. This is proof in the numerous towns scattered about with little, if no, technology at all. Comfort with the necessities of life is their contentment through hard work and trade with one another. This attitude and value of lifestyle does not allow for change much at all. They are not very open or accepting of strangers, which I feel prohibits growth and change of any kind. As within their hearts, they would love an easier life, but failure to allow any change for the better is rejected. So, in fact, they become their own worst enemies in their ways of life and attitudes. But yet, they are a kind and loving people with one another within their self-created boundaries of life. I feel that to acquire the light energies of the people, we have to get them to accept us within their inner circles in order to gain their full trust and faith. Then, we can turn the tides of darkness by turning their hearts as a hub of unity, love, and faith in action."

His explanation was most fascinating and also followed up with a strategy, a plan of attack. A natural-born leader was what Omer saw in Jogil. Support for his calling would be a tremendous honor for Omer as he replied, "My brother, I am at your mercy, for we will lead these people to a victory through their own free will and rid this planet of darkness and suffering!" They both agreed as they finished their meal and gave thanks.

As they exited the diner, a brisk wind stirred the air and a charcoal haze enveloped the skies over the town. Jogil had not had this experience before as the breeze created an eerie howling about the area. This ruffled Zac's bristles as he gave a low monotone growl of danger lurking.

Within minutes, a dark, cloaked figure appeared about a hundred yards away and was staring at Jogil, Omer, and Zac. The figure began to speak.

"I am Mattias and I come to claim this town for my master. You would do well to take your leave at once and never to return." Mattias spoke in a low and cold voice that transformed the charcoal air into numerous serpentlike figures as his outreaching tentacles. This was definitely a challenge thrown to the Chosen Ones.

Jogil and Omer, facing one another, generated a fiery passion in their eyes as they chanted five times, "RamTam Om! Shivaya Om!" At that, their inner warrior breastplates were activated as they turned to Mattias and extended their arms, aiming directly at him. Omer continued to chant as Jogil commanded, "You shall not pass!" repeatedly. They could feel the pulse of the inner energy increase as the twenty-five Chosen Ones fought as one in this confrontation with evil.

A bolt of blue and white lightning shot out from their palms and made a direct hit on the figure of Mattias. The contact had fragmented the figure, and the swirling serpents of the wind immediately vanished into thin air as well as the figure of Mattias. "The battle is not over!" howled the voice of the evil figure. "If that's all you have, you will lose!" shouted the voice of Mattias.

When the air cleared, Jogil and Omer peered over to the diner and observed all of the inhabitants aligning the windows as they witnessed what they could physically see of the battle with the mysterious stranger. They all exited the diner and fell to their knees, thanking Jogil and Omer for their courageous standoff with the dark stranger.

"My dear friends, this is not over and the evil ones still exist. We must all pull together the passion of love and light in our hearts to battle the evil ones! This is your home, your destiny, and your families at stake! We can assist you, but you must stand as a force of unity within your hearts, and all together we can and will be victorious!" commanded Jogil. Omer stood stalwartly at his side as they both faced the crowd and, with hands in prayer mode, bowed to the townspeople. They then took their leave and headed to Jogil's home.

When they reached Jogil's home, both agreed that it was necessary for a follow-up meditation session for protective purposes of all the surrounding towns aboveground. But first, Jogil showed Omer his room for the duration of his stay. Both men were extremely compatible in their lifestyles. Omer was both impressed and grateful.

Then, Jogil proceeded to lead Omer to a specific room set up for meditation sessions only. He prepared an extra chair and cushion for Omer. The room was adorned with numerous clear quartz crystals and four large amethyst geodes, two each on both sides of the two chairs. In the center of the room rested a four-foot, column-styled pedestal with a huge amber geode adorning it. Sitting within the open surface of the amber were numerous stones of garnet surrounding a centerpiece of amethyst.

Both men lit their respective candles and assumed their postures of meditation in their chairs. Within minutes, a gentle voice began to address them on their current situations. Both recognized the voice of Nyla as she began her inner dialogue.

"I have been asked courteously of the Rheyzoun Buddhas to address you. A great victory was won today, but the battle will surely heat up as a hornet's nest of evil will surely stir up a reprise to come. But both of you rose to the occasion. Your combined inner strength and light with the assistance of the others prevailed. The Buddhas are pleased.

"As a former sister of darkness, I am very familiar with Mattias and his dedication to Teohta and her agenda. However, the two of you have fought together in previous times as blood brothers about two hundred years ago. This spiritual battle was fought in the Netherlands, and you were victorious. This caused the dark forces to retreat to their mainstay here in Siberia. Back then, you both swore an oath to Ramata to continue the fight against the darkness until a final victory was won. This determination and commitment became a divine blueprint and crown of light that would eventually bring you two together for a final battle and victory. Thus as, Chosen Ones, you are both brothers in arms preparing for that final conflict on this planet. Working together, your combined energies have built up a great momentum of herculean light and power sufficient enough that, if used wisely, will lead to a great victory through your previous sacrifices and service.

"We are close in entering the fourth cycle of this year, 2020. As the Buddhas promised, contingent on the progress and efforts of the twenty-five Chosen Ones, a grant of the cosmic light energies might be released as the fourth quarter of the cycle has always been the most intense and challenging times of initiations and adversities. Working as a unity of hearts and souls in the light will create a great momentum in the battle for a victory on this planet. Keep on keeping on!"

As Nyla's dialogue ended, a resounding "Ommm" filled the air and consciousness of all twenty-five and was complemented by the classical etheric music of hierarchy with big, bold raised letters in blue and gold commencing the phrase, "Well done."

Jogil and Omer reverently sat in silence, hearts filled with love, gratitude, and a fiery passion to match. This created a great figure 8 flow into the cosmos with an unbreakable bond of trust and faith. By the universal cosmic laws of cause and effect, each erg of energy sent out would be multiplied by ten on the return back to its sender, be it good or bad energies. And the qualities of sincerity and mercy would intensify even more on the receiving end. The Chosen Ones would need every ounce of light energy in their upcoming battles as well as dealing with their individual and group karmic debts.

At the conclusion of the meditation, the men agreed to call it a night and turned in for a period of rest and a deep sleep recharging of energies.

CHAPTER 17

YET ANOTHER ENERGY was being activated within the children involved with the Chosen Ones. Byron, Ishi, Taylor, Lizzie, and the twins, Bessie and Trina, all began having dreams of little children in a far-off land, with violet eyes and a higher-than-normal perception and level of awareness. They are scattered about the country, yet can't communicate with one another at inner levels of being.

These children seemed to be new souls of light, untainted by the dark effluvia of modern humanity, being pure of heart and one with nature. Their love for life is boundless and their auras are a light of love, peace, and unity.

They are highly alert and sensitive to any form of danger in the immediate vicinities. One will trigger another, and all will be instantly protected by a cosmic inner force field. Being of pure spirit, anything of less vibrations will be instantly repelled. They are untouchable even to the dark forces of Teohta.

But yet a vulnerability always existed as a potential danger. Any slight dark influence that could creep into one's inner being can act like a virus in a computer system, attacking from within and blossoming in the outer. This was a form of vampirism as the dark forces feed on their stolen light and replace them with a lower negative vibration, eventually bringing the victims under their control and influence.

In this case, the Indigo children up to age sixteen, are continuously protected by hierarchy, while at the same time taught, through the heart on the inner planes of the high spiritual laws and values. how to harness the light within.

The raw and very vibrant light energy of these indigo-eyed children would also automatically charge the nature spirits around them, which would in turn act as a protective shield, a barrier such as a cyclone fence, to ward off the attacks of any dark energies directed their way.

The following day during the Chosen Ones' meditations, a Rheyzoun Buddha addressed to all that the victory of cleansing the earth was crucial as a new race of advanced light beings were already being born on the planet. He described them as the Indigo race and made it clear that they were being born throughout all nations of the world to lay a foundation of highly evolved beings, so that advanced lessons and technology and spiritual awareness could flourish into a new golden age of enlightenment.

But the current low-vibration consciousness of mankind has proved that the technology existing today has been misused in order to profit the corrupt powerful elite at the expense of multitude, thus creating poverty, the middle class, and the elite. There is no excuse for the suffering of mankind that exists today, and much of this is caused by the severe misuse of the competitive nature and man. The unity of right mind, sincerity of heart in humble service to one another alone, is enough to erase all darkness and cleanse the earth of the incredible imbalance that suffers presently.

And the point was made as follows by the Rheyzoun Buddha: "The proper use of competition is that of the individual to use competitiveness within the individual as an impetus for self-growth. To challenge the self by stepping out of the box of mediocrity within and explore new ways and ideas in one's own life experiences. The trial/error, success/failure process is a natural driving force as, to some degree, all strive for a better life on the bumpy road of life's adventures. Both successes and failures are progress on the ladder of life, both inwardly and in the physical aspect."

"Mankind has fallen into the beaten path by dwelling on the failures of self and others. Instead of an attitude of a step in growth, failures have become a stigmata of judgment and have caused severe separation and imbalance of humanity. When others are persecuted, the results become a low self-esteem attitude and the focus therefore is an attitude of 'I can't.' And as that phrase is worshiped as a false God, the negative vibrations becomes the life force, driving the individuals within and equally creating a negative force of dark unlimited consciousness throughout the world."

"The elite evil powers and forces are aware of this universal truth and constantly manipulate mankind into thinking that these are natural in having the various status of mankind, a natural order of things. And mankind knowingly or unknowingly accepts this as truth and reality, thus the web of deceit and darkness grows into a false empire fed by the powerful elite, who lusts for power at the expense of the multitude. And the deception of mankind through the centuries has been too long accepted through free will."

"There have been many through history that have become aware of these truths, thus creating rebellions and battles for truth, justice, and equality. But the monster of darkness and corruption has dominated the earth and her people for thousands of years. The tentacles of evil have controlled the nation's economies, educational systems, and the government's political parties, but even this great level of evil rule will come one day, and they know this."

"But the tide is turning and the hearts of mankind have been crying out from within. This inner SOS has been received by hierarchy, thus becoming the seed of this mission created by the mighty and holy one, Ramata. A cosmic cycle is ending, and the mission will determine the ultimate existence or destruction of a planet." The dialogue of the Buddha ceased.

A new thrust of passion was ignited as the Chosen Ones took to heart the importance of every thought, word, and deed generated by all humans that were the seeds of creation for all that has been up to the present moment. Exposing of the real truth that all are cocreators stemmed from the seeds of thought, emotions, and passion in action, be it of good deeds or bad deeds. This awareness of truth exposes the fact that all by cosmic law are held accountable and responsible for their actions and inactions, and until the good of all becomes a major focus of unity and service, chaos and human discord will remain rampant throughout the planet. All diseases on earth are the result of imbalance, disharmony, and returning karma.

The Chosen Ones also realized that the patience of the cosmic hierarchy for thousands of years to allow all mankind lifetime after lifetime to have the opportunity to grow and evolve through free will was nearing the end of a cosmic super cycle. The evolution of man must reach a certain degree of spiritual attainment, restoring balance within on a planetary scale or perish with his own self-created discord through the improper use of free will and spiritual energies.

As the contemplation of Jogil and Omer concluded, both had sensed an urgency from another nearby town twenty miles southwest of their location. Without hesitation, they loaded their gear and made their way to the town.

During this same time at the ending of September, Myama and Miraki of South America were alerted inwardly by the Indigo children of their country. A gathering of the spirits was commencing to address and assist those of the troubled territory of Siberia. More light was needed for Jogil and Omer as the intensity of darkness was spreading at a rapid rate. While this was occurring, the vision of violent arrows with flaming ruby tips was projected by the Indigo children ready to be aimed and fired in the direction of Siberia. All that was needed was the action of Myama and Miraki in launching the attack by the powers of hierarchy. This they immediately did by the reciting of the mantram seven times: "RamTam Om! Shivaya Om!"

The physical eyes cannot see the launch activated; however, the skies over the waters did produce a slight violet hue. All Chosen Ones focused their energies simultaneously while repeating the mantra, which amplified the attack. In minutes, the arrows reached their destinations, dissolving ashen clouds of evil and darkness. The fallout also created temporary domes of protection over a designated area of the towns. As long as the hues of violet and blue remained in the atmosphere, the towns would be protected. The focus and attention of the Chosen Ones would maintain the force field temporarily until the attacks of the dark forces became more intensified.

Jogil and Omer knew that their plans of attack also relied on the changing and conversion of the hearts of the village people, for they knew from the messages of hierarchy that the combination of strong minds and hearts alike would serve as a stabilizer to maintain the dome barriers for protection.

But to change the minds and hearts of the people rooted in contentment and seclusion from the outside world was no easy task. The only strength of the village people was their unity of separation as their own civilization and way of life. To be able to convert and wake up a few in each territory would be the great challenge. To convince these few would be the turning point and victory over the forces of evil.

As Jogil and Omer approached the town of Bear Paw, a multitude of cloaked figures were surrounding the town chanting and making gestures that created minifunnels called devil twisters. These where human-sized, about five to six feet in height, and would create an eerie howling in the atmosphere. They would travel in circles ranging from a hundred to a thousand feet.

This action triggered an inner alert from Jogil and Omer, which sparked a contact with Vander and Rotussi, and both picked up on a mantram of "Om! Ta-Ju Hri!" being recited by the tai chi senseis. Accompanying the mantrams were thousands of tai chi orbs of blue and gold colors being projected and aimed directly at the "devil twisters" and would explode on contact, leaving a sparkling mist and would then dissolve into thin air.

They maintained the mantram "Om! Ta-Ju Hri! Om!" as they approached a huge double twister of about to twenty feet high surrounding an area of approximately five thousand feet in diameter and only one mile south of the town church.

With the help of all twenty-five Chosen Ones, the mantram was intensified for an attack on the great devil twisters. This also sparked the assistance of the Indigo children worldwide, and thousands of the ruby-tipped violet arrows began raining in on the target.

As a response, Teohta converged numerous devil twisters to form as one mighty hundred foot monster that was now only a quarter mile from the town church. Though the magnified attack was definitely felt by Jogil and Omer, it only intensified their focus and chanting while the visions of the mighty devil twister were being engulfed by the violet arrows and the tai chi orbs. This created an intense howling that filled the air for miles.

Then it happened. A gigantic explosion and implosion happened, which created a huge vacuum dissolving all of the debris leaving a silhouette of what seemed to be the exposure of a portal opening. This remained visible for fifteen seconds and then vanished. The devil twister was finally defeated and also exposed a portal of entry for the dark forces into the physical plane.

The victory of the battle also resulted in a golden hue surrounded by a pink/violet border. This visual also seemed to create an electric charge in the air acting as a freshener full of warmth and love.

The townspeople surrounded the car containing Jogil and Omer, with hands folded in prayer and thanks for saving their little community of Bear Paw and its church.

While they emerged from the car, Jogil emphasized to the people that the war was not over, and after what they had witnessed, they would need to do their part to protect their town. He stressed that through their minds and hearts, coupled with a keen sense of awareness, that their role in winning the war over evil could no longer involve fear and neglect to grow physically, mentally, and emotionally. They must learn to open up and use the tools of creativity, love, and passion for life, not limiting their natural potentials by being independent, aloof, and contentment of isolation.

He explained that their old way of life is what attracted the dark forces who were always seeking those of weakness through isolation, contentment, and no desire for change and growth. This seemed to open their eyes to realize that an evil dominant force preys upon those with no goals in life.

Jogil and Omer agreed to meet with the townspeople at the local high school to educate them on the dangers lurking about. They encouraged the people to gather in groups of no less than three each. Also, to live and love through their hearts in everything they do. By all focusing on the same thoughts and feelings, this in itself would heighten the awareness of any imminent danger arising in the area. More would be discussed the following day in their first meeting.

After returning to their room accommodations, Jogil and Omer discussed for a while about teaching the people on spiritual self-defense and protection, while more advanced teachings were not allowed by hierarchy. Both agreed and concluded the evening with a meditation on their inner strength and the safety of the townspeople. Each lit their respective candles and then entered "the great silence."

Within minutes, a connection was received from Vander and Rotussi, the tai chi Chosen Ones. They began communicating assistance ideas for the townspeople. The elder Rotussi spoke first.

"The first. most important step is to establish strength of the inner core of being. Substitution, not denial, is the proper process to follow. One has to replace fear and doubt with confidence and trust in the true self within, the light of being. Affirmations such as "I am the light of the heart in action within me every day." This is like turning on the light in a dark room. The darkness simply disappears, being replaced by the light. The same goes with the heart. When one affirms to the self: "I am a being of love, peace, harmony, and compassion in action always," there is no room for hatred, dislike, and discord within. These are simply replaced by the "true self," expressing with a sincerity and passion for life and light! These are vibrations of the highest form, and when the groups and multitudes maintain these frequencies, the dark forces become rendered helpless and are defeated."

Then Vander continued the inner dialogue. "The biggest challenge has always been that of fear and discord that have run rampant for centuries as mankind lost touch with his inner nature. The negative vibrations have become the blueprint of man's being today. The rulers and powers that exist today feed off man's dependency on others due to their lack of self-respect and allowing others to do their thinking and decision-making in life. Mind you, all of this happened through continuous misuse of free will and lack of effort to be accountable and responsible in life. Like tai chi, one must simply restore the balance and harmony through practice daily. Gradually, the self-induced limitations begin to fade away, being replaced with confidence, self-worth, love, and compassion. This positive flow with nature will in turn increase the positive momentums of light to the point where there is no room for darkness and evil to exist anymore. It all starts from the heart within and through focus, constant practice, and a strong bond of unity of love, victory will be proclaimed within the heart of life, and the love, light, joy, peace, and harmony of life on earth will reign!" The dialogue ended.

And then a Rheyzoun Buddha interceded. "Mankind in and of itself is a unity of being that was perfect harmony and love initially, abiding by cosmic laws and cocreating with one another. The beauty in concept of diversity allowed each to experience self-expression for growth and the good of all. The idea of competition was nonexistent as each life stream sought to expand their creative awareness as a tool of divinity for self and all. Separation with the Great Spirit was never an issue. Thus, the beauty of ongoing creation with free will stimulated one another, adding countless wonders of beauty and advancement throughout the ages. So, there have been civilizations of past here on earth that were "Golden Ages" and ascended to this spirit realms who continue to create and transcend to higher realms in the cosmos of being. When called upon, they assist planet Earth since they initially began their journey here."

"But then a few on earth began to admire their own creations and very subtly idolized their talents, losing sight of their "oneness" with the "Great Spirit." Then followed the concept of one's creations being better than another's created division by comparison, and the bonds of unity thus began to erode. The seeds of pride, envy, and jealousy were created on a lower vibrational level, dividing the people into groups of like minds. Through free will, each began to think that their way was the best way to follow for spiritual growth and advancement in life."

"Divine inspiration began to dissipate from the minds and hearts of those who chose to fall from grace by selfish needs and desires. By losing touch with the divine energies, a vacuum was created in their beings, leaving them unfulfilled in their desires to create. The first experiences of limitations were born."

"In panic, they strove to promote their creations in a commanding nature, creating more divisions in the world. This lower mentality spread like a virus, and the people began moving further away from one another. They created their own little communities and built up their own sets of rules and laws that further restricted one to live through an expression of free will, love, unity, and harmony. The need to control and manipulate gave a false sense of power and leadership. Instead of a sense of mentorship, the concept of constant monitoring was established. Thus, fear and mistrust went viral, and the leaders began to establish strict laws and rules, limiting life even more in their communities."

"There were a number of people that were still pure of mind and heart, and these souls migrated to the lands where they could still live in unity and harmony with the "Great Spirit." They knew within that, the time was now to separate from their fallen brethren or suffer the consequences of imbalance and chaos. Each had to live their own destiny with the laws of cause and effect. Thus, the earth was split up by different levels of vibrations throughout the planet. Soon, the split in the consciousness of man began to have an effect on the weather patterns of nature."

"Dark clouds began to form and band together, causing destructive forces of wind, lightning, and thunder raging throughout the lands and lasting for days on end. This created floods, landslides, and twisters, destroying all life in its path. Earthquakes became the norm as Mother Earth fought to maintain balance within another surface of the planet. All these—calamities, wars, and pestilence—are due to a long momentum of mankind and his fall from grace through separation with the divine will of love, unity, and harmony. The results of misuse of free will!" The dialogue ended with the words in bold letters: "Love! Peace! And victory! Be with you."

Jogil and Omer concluded her meditation in a reverent silence and retreated to their beds. The time was midnight.

CHAPTER 18

THE FOLLOWING MORNING was the last day of the month. Both Jogil and Omer could sense within that a great stream of light was soon to be released the following day to all the Chosen Ones, the beginning of the fourth cycle in the year 2020.

They had a busy schedule for this last day of the month. A meeting was to be held in the town church to give more guidance to the townspeople. This would be their last day in this town. They felt an urgent call for a neighboring town about thirty-five miles away called Bristle Weed. Reports of a dark, cloaked stranger appearing troubled the inhabitants, causing extreme fear and chaos.

They arrived at the church for the last meeting to remind the people on how to protect themselves and the town. A marker was made on the spot of the location of the portal, the entrance between the two worlds.

Jogil proceeded to speak, "Remember to always assemble in no less than groups of three and be in a state of positivity with one another. Focus on love, peace, and light within your hearts! Be creative and active in your community, dissolving contentment and taking charge of your lives to better one another in unity! Be accountable and responsible! These actions and attitudes will not allow you to be controlled or vulnerable to the dark forces! And above all, make prayers and calls to the Great Spirit for divine intervention and victory for this planet and its people! This is not an option in a great battle such as this. Love and light must conquer all!" The crowd applauded Jogil and Omer, and blessed God and the protection of these two warriors of spirit.

Both men were invited to stay for a luncheon prepared in their honor. They agreed and enjoyed a great meal and the hospitality of the townspeople. They could sense a great, vibrant, new energy in the people and encouraged them to maintain a great sense of victory in every moment of their lives. A great positive momentum was born in the town of Bear Paw.

However, the presence of Mattias was haunting the town of Bristle Weed, and time was of the essence. The men dismissed themselves and returned to their hotel room. They knew that an intense preparation had to be activated immediately. Both readied themselves for a special meditation to call for reinforcements in the next battle with Mattias. Urgency for right action was their driving force, and the need to fulfill their part was crucial. A great warrior must always maintain an alertness and responsive mode to follow.

Jogil and Omer began an intense focus on the town of Bristle Weed and sensed an extreme paranoia infecting the townspeople. Time was crucial as a call was needed to be made to hierarchy for assistance against Mattias and Teohta.

During the focus on the town, Omer could detect a light energy within the town untouched by the pending evil controlling the area. He sensed a feminine aspect in the light. As he felt this, a response was sent as an inner thought of confirmation.

"I am Viola, bearer of light from an ancient town buried beneath this town. I am a protector, but I will need your assistance, Omer." Her voice sounded familiar to his soul, but Omer's conscious mind could not remember. He felt a strong connection with this soul, but the oncoming battle was priority for the moment.

As the focus of Jogil and Omer remained on Bristle Weed, all the twenty-five Chosen Ones commenced with a chant of "Ramtam Om! Shivaya Om!" forty-nine times while projecting the fire within their hearts through the light of Viola's aura and the hearts of the townspeople. This wave of light energy was then magnified by the response of the Rheyzoun Buddhas. The light would be sustained for the following day and until the arrival of Jogil and Omer in the town. This town was three times the size of their Bear Paw. Mattias and Teohta were prepared for a great battle to maintain their control of the territory. The night fast approaching signaled the warriors to get a good night's sleep to prepare for the next day's raging battle.

The following morning of October 1, Jogil and Omer awoke at 4:00 a.m. and commenced into a quick meditation session prior to departing for the town of Bristle Weed. They activated their protective shields from within, then loaded the truck with their supplies and gear. Zac the wolf jumped in the back and found himself a comfortable spot to bed down. A quick stop to gas up the truck, and they were off to Bristle Weed.

Omer closed his eyes and focused on the town and its vibrational patterns, which quickly gave him a vision of what they were to expect. He can only feel the presence of Mattias, but saw a group of what appeared to be ten vagabonds standing in a line close to the entrance of the town. Their eyes wide open in a glare while chanting gave way to what appeared to be swirling barbed-wire barriers from the ground to about ten feet in height. It appeared that this would be their welcoming committee to prevent them from entering the town. He shared his vision with Jogil so they could come up with a plan to break the barrier.

About that time, a tremendous surge of light energy was disbursed to all the Chosen Ones and jolted their physical bodies like that of a Taser. All were charged up by the actions of the Rheyzoun Buddhas along with the following inner message: "A portion of light has been released as part of the fourth quarter cycle of 2020. This dispensation has been granted by the Great Ramata for your first year's momentum of light used victoriously in your battles with the dark forces. Keep your focus as a great unity of action to maintain continuous increments of light to be released when needed."

Following the release of light and the message received, Omer focused on the being of Viola to make contact and gather more information of the dark forces at play in the town. Within minutes, he began to receive the following message from Viola.

"Mattias has released a spell of terror on the townspeople, accelerating their fears and releasing thoughts of suicide and anger, creating mass confusion and total chaos. Four people have committed suicide already, and others are committing violent acts of assault and crime in the streets. Mayhem has run rampant, and people are starting to lock themselves in their homes."

Within seconds, a strong, urgent message was released from Myama and Miraki to all: "We must without delay send out to these people waves of love and light in hopes that they will receive in their hearts the importance of love of life before it is too late. We cannot choose for them, but we can bathe them in love and light and surround it with the blue protective shield." All agreed and immediately released their hearts' love in numerous waves of light to the people of Bristle Weed.

All agreed that the most powerful force in the universe is infinite, unconditional love and the faith to achieve victory within the hearts of mankind. The energy can be corrected and released to mankind, but only received through the act of free will. Man must choose life and the sacrifices that are necessary to earn the right to freedom, for all have debts of karma that have to be dealt with.

Within minutes, the town of Bristle Weed suffered a great quake lasting for minutes that seemed like an eternity. This was a result of the energies of good and evil being released simultaneously in this one physical area that shook it to its roots of being. Some town structures received minimal damage, but the force field of the Chosen Ones protected most of the physical area, thus minimizing any damages.

To his surprise, Omer visualized many groups of townspeople form circles by joining hands while chanting "Love conquers all, for we are love united!" Through their hearts' sincere intent, a protective shield had formed and was surrounded by numerous Indigo children of whose hands were a fiery ruby-red color performing tai chi moves and repelling attacks of the dark forces. And those were many.

At the command of Mattias, hellhounds with black shining eyes and razor fangs with claws to match attacked in packs at the circles of people. But the light of their hearts combined with the Indigo children repelled most of the attacks as the hellhounds dissolved into thin air as they made contact with the energy force fields. Unfortunately, two circles were breached and some casualties ensued. This was caused by the fear that some within the circles had allowed in their hearts doubt of the light, thus weakening the protective domes. But the remaining people closed up the circles and maintained their strength in their hearts. It was a gruesome battle with casualties, but the people and the light prevailed in round one.

As this battle ended, the spell was broken on the vagabonds at the entrance of the town. They gazed at one another and did not understand why they were together or what had just happened. They all turned and waved at the incoming truck of Jogil, Omer, and, of course, Zac the wolf.

As they approached, Jogil asked where the local town hall was and requested that they meet them there in an hour. They agreed and pointed the way of their destination.

CHAPTER 19

MEANWHILE, IN MT. Shasta on this first day of October 2020, Krea received a phone call from Dina Emerald (CPS) regarding the babies. There were still no responses on the whereabouts of any family members regarding the newfound babies, and continuous searches within the area came up negative. However, there were a few more offers of couples interested in adopting the babies, and background checks were being done on them. Krea thanked Dina for the update and expressed again her desire to adopt. She also added that she wanted what was best for the babies regardless of the outcome. Dina agreed and said that she would keep her posted on the case. She admired Krea for her passion and concern for the well-being of the babies.

After the call with Dina, Krea decided to call Penny and update her on the situation. When she called, Penny was delighted to hear from her. Tara was just asking about teacher and the babies too, so Penny thought that she would invite Krea for lunch the following weekend at the house. Krea happily agreed and thanked them for the invite. It would be nice to see Tara and her babies, whom she loves so much.

After the phone call, Krea felt an urgency to take a hike to the area where she found the babies. She felt that with her heighted senses and awareness with a clear mind, she might be able to see or detect something that was not noticed before. So she loaded her backpack with a day's ration and proceeded to her car. It was a beautiful, clear, seventy-five-degree day with a slight breeze.

While driving to her designated spot, Krea recited an inner prayer asking for assistance on the search for clues of how the babies came to be at the spot that they were found. Then, she gave thanks and put her trust in her faith of the light and its divine nature of being. In minutes, she would reach her destination.

As Krea parked the car, a beautiful eagle flew overhead about a hundred yards away. What a beautiful experience! This moment filled her heart with gratitude and a new burst of energy that lifted her being. "This as a sign of a positive day for my hike," she thought out loud. The hike began with Krea humming and singing most of the way.

At about fifteen minutes prior to the spot where the babies were found, Krea stopped her humming and began to focus on anything out of the norm through her senses of sight, sound, and smell. She decelerated her pace so that nothing would be missed by chance. This soon proved to be helpful.

About five minutes before the location of the find, Krea felt a change in vibrations and detected a humming sound accompanying it. She stopped, slowed her breathing, and slowly turned in a clockwise direction. She did this slowly, making a full three-hundred-sixty-degree turn and then stopped. The humming vibrations began to increase in volume, but nothing visible was detected. She felt that she was onto something, so she repeated her actions three more times until suddenly in the two thirty direction of her turns, something visible was occurring. Krea stopped to acknowledge what was happening. Thirty feet in front of her, just over a small mound between two bushes, appeared to be some kind of energy field.

This energy field was about six feet wide and twelve feet tall. It was a pulsating energy with various blurred colors, but very alive. In an instant, she was contacted by a Buddha advising her to keep her distance from it.

"Well done, Krea. Through your focus and new sensitivities to higher vibrations, you have discovered the location of one of many dimensional portals throughout the earth. People and beings of other worlds have been traveling through these for millennia, but not all have the ability or knowledge of these portals and their whereabouts. There have been some that have stumbled upon these, entered them, and never returned to their original dimension from whence they were born. When you hear of missing person's reports with people never to be found, this is one of the reasons why.

"And you have found the source of where the two babies came from. The parents originated from another part of this world and were guided by a light being to a portal not far from where they lived. They were in danger from the evil forces and sought escape for their newborns for safety.

"The parents were truly hearts of light, which attracted the evil ones because of their service to the light. This is where the plan with you came into being. The light being led them through the portal and brought them to the place where you were destined to find the babies. Then, they returned to their homeland and battled with Mattias and his bands of evil. They made their transition, knowing in full faith, trust, and love that their children would be well taken care of.

"Be persistent but patient, and the adoption should sway your way, for the names of Sara Ann and Jeremy are much approved and appreciated by their true parents. Serving the light in the etheric realms of life, you are to remain silent about this information I have given you. Along with Penny and Tara, the lives of Sara Ann and Jeremy are your destiny and responsibility.

"Remember the location of the portal, for in the right time it will be crucial to use its access, but not until then. You will know when the time is right. May love and peace be with you, for you have done well!" As the dialogue ended, the portal entrance dissolved from sight. Krea fell to her knees in a prayerful mode and graciously thanked the Rheyzoun Buddha.

Her heart filled with love and joy about the truth of the babies, that it made her hike back so effortless and euphoric. Her new adventure as a mother pleased her so, including the family bond with Penny and Tara. Her newfound family of five is a blessing she never imagined and yet eternally grateful to be a Chosen One with a soon-to-be extended family.

CHAPTER 20

IT CAME TIME for the town hall meeting in Bristle Weed, Siberian Territory. Jogil introduced himself and Omer, then proceeded to address the townspeople of the nature of what was experienced earlier in the day.

"There is an evil force that exists all over the Siberian Territory, and we must be prepared to battle together. It has been building for centuries and feeding off the fears of all the townspeople across the lands."

One could hear a pin drop as all were totally affixed on Jogil, his four-legged companion, and Omer. He continued, "For too long, the people of this country have fallen behind in any form of growth or advancement of life in general, being content and going backward in any form of evolving forward. Like a pond of water with no fresh flow, the pond stagnates and becomes a source of germs and contaminated water unfit for human consumption."

The people understood the analogy he was making as their heads shook up and down in agreement. Then, Jogil turned to Omer to let him speak.

"When we choose to live in contentment and discontinue to be active in learning more about life and its gifts, possibilities to discover, and improve ourselves and others, this creates a void that attracts those who like to improve themselves at the expense of others. They run for positions of leadership in order to control others for their desires that usually benefit themselves instead of the communities at hand. With very little opposition in elections, they win, band together, abuse their powers, and profit themselves at the expense of others. The more promises they make, the more they take, and situations continue to get worse for the community involved. This negative momentum also happens on a different level in the spirit of man.

"When the people are not able to voice their opinions and ideas, they become morally bankrupt through feelings of no self-worth, disrespect, low self-esteem, and the list goes on. The evil ones feed off of this energy and grow more in their powers of control. They therefore elevate themselves at the expense of others. This is all because a lack of desire and passion to grow gives way to contentment, unaccountability, and irresponsibility, which leads to excuses, etc. It all starts within the heart of humanity and the natural desire to grow and evolve through action and commitment all led by right intentions.

"One person is easily defeated or broken, but many with their right intentions, passionate hearts, and actions to match cannot be defeated by the evils of the world. We must fight for the right things and work together as a community, as a unit, all in one. The heart of a true warrior and all warriors battling together as a single unit. Life with purpose, passion in action built on right, divine intent, the intent to serve one another with prosperity, and love for all! This must be done and accomplished!"

The townspeople all rose and applauded Jogil and Omer for waking them up and rekindling a fiery passion in their hearts. Life with divine purpose will always prevail as long as a bond of unity with love and right intent was maintained and followed through with a momentum of divine action in mankind.

Jogil continued with a closing statement for the townspeople. "My brother is right! Put your minds together and create a positive strategy with a great focus, the right intentions of your hearts, and put into action in a timely manner. Taking charge of your lives without procrastination is a strong bond of unity that is almost unbeaten with passion and desire driven by right intent. Repeating the mantra "Victory is ours!" will drive and strengthen the bonds of unity and bring victory every time. Stay with the fight and make things right!"

The townspeople were applauding the warrior brothers while chanting "Stay with the fight and make things right!" as all joined hands and bowed to Jogil and Omer. They returned the gesture with respect and gratitude.

At that, Jogil and Omer, along with Zac the wolf, retreated to their truck to find lodging for a few days to recharge their energies with rest, always being alert for the next challenge with the dark forces.

CHAPTER 21

MEANWHILE, TYOTAN AND his fiancée, Saraya, had been looking at homes and properties to pursue their dreams of owning and running a bed-and-breakfast. Since they met and started dating, they soon opened a joint savings account, committing 10 percent of their incomes for their dream business down the road. While he being an auto mechanic, Saraya was managing a florist shop.

One day at work, Saraya was talking with a customer and one of their topics was that of searching to purchase a home and/or properties. The young lady named Sylvia is a realtor by trade. Saraya explained that she and her fiancé wanted a six-bedroom and two-and-a-half baths minimum to convert into a bed-and-breakfast business in a nice location, large garden, and ample parking.

The ladies really hit it off as new acquaintances and would soon become good friends. As Sylvia listened to Saraya's wishes and the capital that she and Tyotan had saved up so far, she thought for a moment. Sylvia was currently working in an area that fit ideally with their wishes. Then she made a comment: "I may have a few properties that fit your descriptions, and if you wish, we can exchange phone numbers and I can get back to you. We could set an appointment to view photos of the properties and take it from there. What do you say?"

Saraya's heart began to pound and her eyes lit up like Christmas tree ornaments. "Oh, that would be wonderful!" So, they exchanged phone numbers, and Sylvia left for an appointment with a customer.

Thrilled at meeting Sylvia and the prospect of looking at some properties prompted Saraya to call Tyotan at work with the good news. But first, she bowed her head in thanks and gratitude for this new opportunity. She felt that this was the result of a project that she and Tyotan created about four months prior.

At that time, Tyotan was repairing a vehicle for a young man, and they had a conversation about the same topic. The gentleman offered

Tyotan an idea on how to help their dream and goal to materialize physically. Tyotan's curiosity perked up and he eagerly listened to the man's explanation.

The man, Virgil, began to explain, "An effective tool for anyone desiring a goal requires a little effort and homework to create what is called a 'dream board.' This system has been proven effective for many who have used this system and gave it serious thought on a daily basis. This dream board is a visual creation likened to a treasure map. When one puts an idea on paper to make it physical with your desires and efforts, that the cosmos begins to set in motion invisible energies to assist one in a true, sincere, and positive goal. But once the dream board is created, it is very important to exercise patience, faith, and trust to the universe and its assistance in reaching one's goal. Most importantly, it should never be gained at the expense of another. Your heart's sincere passion and desire maintained with patience and perseverance will be assisted by the cosmos, and the end result, if meant to be, will materialize into one's goal.

"In your case, search for an area that you desire, find a photo of the type of home you desire, landscaping, etc., and create either an actual board or a binder, whichever suits your needs. Will it need minor or major renovations? What is your desired price for the property? How far from a big city? A waterfront or forest setting? Or both? Anything that it may require, think as though you already own this in your mind, making it real as possible: the roof, electric, plumbing, and all the necessities required for your bed-and-breakfast business. Visualize the interior and exterior colors, style of the house, big porch, fountains inside and outside, statues, and a big sign at the entrance. Make your visuals as real as possible, and when completed, review it on a daily basis with a positive mental attitude. Maybe even put a deadline date that you wish to obtain this goal.

"The old saying, you get what you put into something, is a cosmic law that will fulfill one's desires, good or bad. Those that focus on negative energies will receive what they ask for. We can properly use or abuse our free will. The choice is always ours to make on a daily basis." Virgil ended his explanation.

When Tyotan shared the concept of that dream board with Saraya, they both became excited and were grateful for Virgil's idea and insight on the concept. However, Tyotan, being a Chosen One, understood fully that the spiritual hierarchy had a hand in his and Saraya's efforts. Virgil was simply a messenger of the cosmos directed to Tyotan at the right time. His personal meditations on prayers had been answered, and his fiancée Saraya was a like mind and heart, making for the perfect divine complement of his heart and soul. It seemed like prosperity was intended for this happy young couple. Virgil seemed to be the icing on the cake toward their dream goal of a bed-and-breakfast business in the future to come.

Now, it appears that their efforts and energies have proven results with the new connection made with Sylvia, a real estate representative. Things have been set in motion as they will be provided with some actual visuals of properties for sale.

The following day of October 2, 2020, Sylvia gave a call to Saraya at 9:00 a.m. She sent a text with a picture of a property for sale. Saraya answered the phone and greeted Sylvia. She accessed the text to see the home for sale. It was a nice appetizer to look at and she forwarded it to Tyotan at work.

Sylvia had two more properties matching their desired interests. Then she invited Saraya for an appointment to schedule a field trip to the locations instead of texting pictures. It would take about four hours including lunch to see the properties. It would be fine if both Saraya and Tyotan wanted to come.

Saraya said she would call Tyotan and see what day they could schedule off together for a field trip. But first, she asked Sylvia what days she had open, possibly the weekend or during the next week.

Sylvia's response was Saturday afternoon or Tuesday or Wednesday of the following week at noon, whatever best fit their schedule. She is very pleasant and not a pushy person, and Saraya appreciated that immensely. She felt that Tyotan would like Sylvia as well. So they ended the call, and Saraya called Tyotan to make arrangements for an appointment.

Tyotan checked his schedule and it appeared that Tuesday, October 6 would be perfect for him as he only had one appointment for that day at 8:00 a.m. and that would only take three hours for the repair.

Saraya said that Tuesday was perfect for her as well. So they agreed for Tuesday the sixth and she would call Sylvia to make the appointment. Excitement and anticipation filled the air as both were eager to get home, and work and focus on their dream board.

CHAPTER 22

DURING THE SAME time, Hoopti was attending a cultural arts show in her hometown of Saint Petersburg, Russia, of which her parents, Rusev and Nona (Apache female), are currently United States ambassadors. Her love of diverse cultures constantly fed her passion and dream of uniting both the Eastern and Western continents through love and peace.

Thirty minutes into the show, she began to sense some negative vibrations in the air and looked around the crowd. She noticed that throughout the crowd were a certain number of men wearing dark trench coats and sporting stone-cold grimaces on their faces. As the sense of danger grew, Hoopti slowly began to head for the nearest exit, until she realized that they were all being covered by the trench-coated strangers.

So, Hoopti went back to her seat, closed her eyes, and sent out an inner SOS call to her Chosen team. As soon as this occurred, shots were fired in the air and all were commanded to stay in their seats or else. Then, three trench coats grabbed three people from the front row and ordered them to drop to their knees.

Without any warning or hesitation, the trench-coated men shot and killed the three people. The remaining trench-coated men numbering thirty shouted "Death to the infidels!" with their guns held high in the air.

Somehow, a group of terrorists slipped through the building security guards to carry out their surprise attack. Evil was at its worse in the action taken today, but Hoopti remained calm and focused, and she received an inner response from Nyla.

"There are good forces in place and ready for a counterattack on the trench-coated men. Keep your focus on the light, and they will make their move shortly through you. Visualize the locations of the trench-coated men and hold the thought as a blueprint. Then, within yourself, chant "Ramtam Om! Shivaya Om!" nine times!"

Hoopti did as Nyla directed, and within minutes, shots were fired simultaneously for five seconds. People screamed out, but remained in their seats. Then, a dead silence followed.

Everyone slowly began to look around and did not see any trench-coated men standing around, that is because they were all shot and killed without warning. The terrorist attack was over.

People stood up in confusion, and within minutes, law enforcement began entering the building and escorting them to the exits. When they were outside the building, the authorities began questioning some of the people about the attack and about how the trench-coated men were taken out. This inquiry bewildered the crowd. They thought that the law officers had shot and killed the trench-coated men, but it turned out that the law enforcement had just arrived after the men were taken down. So much confusion in such a short time created mass confusion in the people.

No one at all had a clue as to how the terrorists were defeated. And Hoopti was also curious, but had an inner sense that divine intervention had played a part in the rescue.

Hoopti began to ponder how the men were eliminated without any other innocents being harmed or injured. As she fed on this thought, the Buddha began a dialogue on the answer.

"Within hierarchy residing in the etheric planes of this earth are a spiritual order likened to your Secret Service. They constantly patrol the world of all the evil happenings taking place. And they are also bound by cosmic law not to interfere unless called upon by physical beings—humans. We appointed Nyla as the main physical coordinator in the policing of all world events. So, when an activity involved that of a Chosen One, the one who sent out an inner SOS signals an immediate assistance to Nyla and the Secret Service. Then, in an instant, a plan is set in motion, enacted with extreme precision, and always undetected. They cannot be physically seen as they reside in the vibrational state slightly above the human senses.

"So, cosmic justice can be called upon for this special group as long as the cause is contacted by one of pure sincere spirit serving the light with a higher purpose and the good of all mankind." The Buddha blessed Hoopti as the dialogue ended.

And this dialogue was received by all the Chosen Ones within their hearts and beings. This greatly intensified their momentum of light energy as the beginning of the fourth cycle of 2020 was entered.

CHAPTER 23

MEANWHILE, TUESDAY MORNING of October 6 arrived, and Tyotan prepared for work after his meditations. He was excited, for today was the day for his and Saraya's appointment to look at some properties after his early work day.

For five minutes, he and Saraya focused on their dream board once more. Then, both commenced with their half day until the appointment time. Both supported a good feeling for what was to come.

The time arrived for them to prepare for the appointment with Sylvia. Tyotan was minutes away from home, and Saraya was prepared for the day. At that moment, Saraya's phone rang and the call was from Sylvia.

She offered to pick them up at their residence, and both agreed. Adrenaline was flowing as Sylvia would arrive in about fifteen minutes. The rest of their day was free, so no worries or stress was involved for the journey ahead.

Tyotan and Saraya had their financial figures prepared and were ready for any possibilities of negotiations should the right property fulfill their dream and requirements. They embraced one another and stood for a moment staring at one another as they heard a vehicle pull up in the driveway.

Before Sylvia was halfway up the sidewalk to their porch, they opened the door to greet her. Saraya gave an introduction, and in moments, they were all aboard Sylvia's Lincoln Navigator and on their way to the first property. Sylvia offered to spring for coffee at a local coffee shop along the way. They delightfully agreed while listening to soft music in the background.

Sylvia commenced to the drive-through for the coffees, then proceeded on the trip to the first property. It would take approximately twenty-five to thirty minutes to the property, which allowed the three to get acquainted with one another. The company was pleasant indeed as Sylvia asked what prompted the idea of doing a bed-and-breakfast business for the two, and Tyotan happily explained their desires and dreams.

"Since we met and started dating, the most common thread of virtue shared is that of pleasing and serving one another as best as we can. This served as growth for a strong, unflinching bond and respect for each other and, most importantly, an unshakable love for one another and for life itself."

Saraya could not be more proud and touched by the way Tyotan was describing their dreams and goals in life. Tears flowed from her eyes—tears of love and reverence for the life they shared—as he continued with his answer to Sylvia.

"As we looked in one another's eyes, without a word, we realized that we could not keep this unconditional love in a bottle for ourselves, that we had a purpose and responsibility to share this with others. And as we had already decided to start saving for a property, an idea came up at that same time in our heads: a bed-and-breakfast getaway. What better way to share and serve others and to provide a vacation spot, where couples can escape the stress of everyday life and relax in beauty and a loving peaceful environment. We both agreed that to share our happiness is the ability to help create an atmosphere of peace and happiness in others. This has become our purpose and goal in life, and we will fulfill our dream." There was a deep silence as he finished his explanation.

Then, they both asked Sylvia about her career as a realtor, and she responded, "I have been doing my dream for about ten years now and I most enjoy helping others to find what makes them most happy in their lives. I, too, have a home I love, and that is what compelled me to expand that feeling of love and happiness by sharing the joy through service to others. Apparently, this as an extreme passion with a goal and focus that drives us to accelerate our lives in service to others. Tyotan, your beautiful explanation of your and Saraya's dreams is the same treasure in my heart that I value greatly. Oh, here we are at the first property!"

As Sylvia approached a small dirt road on the right, about 2500 feet sat a beautiful two-story semi-mansion on the right side and a four-car garage straight ahead constructed from brick. The house was fifty-fifty: the first level composed of rock and brick, and the second story is of brick and wood.

Tyotan and Saraya's first glance was in complete awe. Such a beautiful setting nestled well enough off the main road, which pleased them both. And the front yard was beautifully landscaped with lawn and various boulder rocks scattered about evenly and complemented with pansy and marigold flowers around each boulder.

As Sylvia parked the car, Saraya prepared herself with a pad of paper to list the pros and cons of each property. Sylvia was impressed and admired their attention to detail and making notes, so they could discuss their opinions about what they want in a property and a things-to-do list for any additional enhancements that would be necessary to make. Saraya already made a note that more ample parking would be needed to properly accommodate a bed-and-breakfast business, and Tyotan agreed.

Then, Sylvia asked them what they would like to see first: the grounds or the house. They chose the house first, and so the tour began.

Sylvia encouraged them to ask any questions they had at any time of the tour. She began, "The former owners had resided in the home for at least thirty years. The children have grown up and moved away to pursue their lives, leaving only the parents. They decided it was time to move on. The husband is now a retired engineer and the wife is a traveling businesswoman. They raised four children, were very active in the community, and liked by all around the community. Now, they wish to travel the world for their retirement years. They are willing to negotiate on the price of the property with the right prospects. They are a very humble and well-respected family for all their years of residence.

"As you can see, the entrance is very spacious, with the huge, wooden double doors, stained glass windows, and huge vases on both sides to complement the very spacious porch. As we enter, one can appreciate the marble flooring of the entrance way, complemented with high roman columns topped with dome lights on each side. Also, on each side are coat closets to provide ample space to support convenience of guests.

"Then, to the left is the staircase leading to the six bedrooms, each with full bathrooms and a concourse area for entertainment or various activities. You can see that most of the home is consisted of hardwood flooring with the exception of the entranceway, the bathrooms, and the kitchen along with the laundry room.

"The living room area is well equipped with two beautiful, large chandeliers, complemented with a fireplace and a very roomy built-in entertainment center that can support an eighty-inch television with a nice Bozeman surround sound system to match.

"Further down the hall on the other side of the wall supporting the fireplace/entertainment center is a huge library area ideal for a capacity of up to twenty people comfortably. On the other side of the hall parallel to it are three spacious rooms that the children used for study rooms for schoolwork, etc. Are there any questions that you may have?"

Both Tyotan and Saraya shook their heads "no," but appreciated Sylvia's respect and manners. They were strictly in observation mode. She continued on.

"Very well, then. Let us continue on to the other side of the staircase. To conclude, the first floor is a master bedroom at the end of the hallway and two additional rooms off the hallway of which was the personal area for both the parents. I personally sense a very pleasant aura in the living environment of this home. Would you agree?"

Both Tyotan and Saraya had the same feeling. This seemed to be a very loving atmosphere supporting positive vibrations. Peace, serenity, and harmony definitely resonated in this beautiful home.

And during the tour, both were taking pictures on their cell phones, which Sylvia noticed. It was a very pleasant tour so far. Then Sylvia asked, "Are there any questions thus far or are you ready to see the grounds? We shall move to the kitchen area on the way out if you are ready." Both nodded their heads in agreement and gave motion for Sylvia to lead the way.

"Very well, then. Let us move on to the kitchen. All the kitchen fixtures have been updated, supporting a nice island centerpiece equipped with cutting board, drawers for silverware, etc., and power outlets to run toasters, blenders, crockpots, etc. A well-equipped kitchen with two overhead microwaves, an eight-burner gas stove, dual sinks with garbage disposals, plenty of counter space, and all the wooden cabinet space you will ever need. This is definitely a good-sized kitchen that can provide for a good-sized banquet!

"And here to the right is a large dining area that can comfortably accommodate a group of up to twenty occupants and is complemented with another beautiful chandelier and sconces on the end of the walls for a nice ambience! An ideal space for two tables or a nice, long assembly-type table. Are we ready to venture outside? Oh! Almost forgot to show the pantry and the laundry room! Oops!"

Tyotan and Saraya giggled and were shown to the last part of the inner tour. "This beautiful pantry is equipped with shelves galore and a nice overhead light to match. Then, to the left of the pantry is the laundry room spacious enough and set up to equip two washers and three dryers. Then, you have one large sink, a good-sized folding table, and some upper and lower storage cabinets. The owners really were almost fanatic about the upkeep of all the house and its maintenance schedules.

"A new roof was done three years ago, and the septic system was updated two years ago and definitely up to code. The home is equipped with satellite hookups for entertainment. All the electrical and plumbing issues have been updated currently. I really enjoy showing this property that has been well maintained by a beautiful and well-respected family of the community."

So far, Tyotan and Sarah were speechless and motioned for Sylvia to continue. "Very well, then. Let us backtrack to the kitchen and I will fetch us each a bottle of water. Then, we will continue on outside to explore the beautiful property. Are we ready?"

With a grin like a child with candy, both nodded their heads "yes," and off they went through a sliding glass door through the living room area adjacent to the dining room. And what a beautiful picturesque garden they stepped into! It began with a beautiful redwood deck, approximately ten by twenty, that led to a plush green lawn with a stone path throughout the yard. After the first six stones, they veered off left and right and then diamond-backed to form a diamond shape. In the middle of the diamond stood a fountain with a statue of Atlas holding up the world on his shoulders, an awesome message of strength and beauty for oneself to contemplate on. Then, in each corner of the yard, there were angels with trumpets sounding off. Then, the surrounding area from angel to angel were variations of pompous grass, heavenly nandinas, and various ground covering consisting of blue, yellow, and purple flowers. Beyond the back oasis of the yard lay the open wilderness, with scattered benches surrounding the yard. The boundaries of the property went two acres into the wilderness, with a nice natural path for strolling.

The grand tour was concluded for this first property. To her amazement, they only had one question: "Were there any potential buyers at the present time?"

Sylvia answered that only two other couples have taken a tour, but so far no one has qualified financially for the market price. And then their next question was, "Can we now prepare to see the next property?"

Sylvia nodded yes, and they started back to the car for the ride to the next stop. On the way, they passed through the kitchen to take another bottle of water for the ride. As they headed back down the road, Sylvia informed them that the ride would be thirty minutes to the next property. And then she asked Tyotan first, "What did you like best about the first property?"

He replied, "The fact that the house sits well off the main road is a major plus. The second is the first floor layout plan. The area where the parents resided was the perfect feature for a married couples quarters. And thirdly, the backyard landscape, a perfect setting for contemplation and meditation."

Then, it was Saraya's turn to answer. "I, too, love the backyard with Atlas, the angels, flowers, and the benches surrounding the yard, which acts as dividers separating the garden and an actual wilderness. But my favorite is the house interior as a whole. I can visualize happy couples relaxing for a nice getaway being served like the royalty they are, free to roam about on the property and relaxing in a beautiful stress-free environment at a reasonable price. And above all, precious memories to cherish and always a sincere 'welcome back' whenever they desire for a retreat for whatever purpose."

Tyotan nodded his head in agreement as Sylvia can truly sense that their goals and dreams are truly an expression of their hearts' desire to please and serve their fellow man, and to assist others in fulfilling their hearts' desires is definitely what Sylvia loves about her calling.

Both added that the price was in the upper range of their budget, but hinted that their plans were for something a bit bigger. Sylvia just smiled and replied that they would be at the next property in fifteen minutes.

During this time, Tyotan and Saraya were comparing pictures from their respective phones and taking notes in the pad that they brought with them. For their first-ever showing, they rated it an 8.5 out of 10. Now, they were prepared for the cream of the crop and, by the way Sylvia was reacting, saving the best for last.

For the next ten minutes, the trees on both sides of the road became larger and denser. A majestic feeling filled every pore in their bodies as the anticipation grew from within.

"Two more minutes on our left is the entrance," remarked Sylvia. Such a beautiful drive. How much better can this get? And then the inner voices answered, "Be prepared for a moment of awe!" Just up the head was a sign with the address 8578 etched in the wood.

"Here it goes," said Sylvia as she made a left turn. Mattias crackled on the gravel payment, with tall trees still abound on both sides of the driveway for the first thousand feet and then transformed to moss-covered boulders lining both sides for the next two thousand feet. Then, the last two thousand feet were lined with various shrubberies on both sides. This all led to a huge arch made of stone and covered in vines. Such a beautiful entrance way left Tyotan and Saraya speechless.

Then, she stopped the car for a minute to let them take in the beauty for a moment as they experienced a beautiful trance of wonder. And then it was time for the main course. Through the arch she drove, and in another thousand feet appeared a breathless moment that sucked the air out of the couple's lungs.

"Oh my goodness!" they gasped in harmony. The most beautiful mansion lay before them with an otherworldly wonder about it. They've never seen a home with a blend of two tones of brick, blended with marble columns and stained glass in every other window, culminating to the most beautiful stained glass designs on the double doors of the main entrance of the house. Like bookends of the whole front of the house, there were two large fifteen-feet-tall eagles with wings fully extended. "Wow!" was uttered.

As they exited the car, Tyotan and Saraya walked to the middle of the huge front yard to take in a full frontal site of the glorious mansion that excitingly radiated their hearts like nothing they have ever seen or witnessed.

Just inside the eagle statues were the outermost windows, each with stained glass windows that were pictures of morning glory flowers. Moving inward, the next windows were plain glass windows outlined with gold leaf frames. Then, the next windows moving inward were stained glass designs of a dove and two roses, one pink and one red. Then, next were the plain windows. The next were stained glass designs of angels with trumpets, then plain glass leading to the final stained glass being the upper portion of the double-door entrance. The grand entrance was a big beautiful rainbow with glowing open hands, palms up, indicating "welcome."

They turned toward each other realizing that, without looking any further, this is the one that felt just right for their dream bed-and-breakfast.

And then, without hesitation, Saraya said the words "Hidden Mist" while looking through Tyotan's eyes and to his heart. His response to her was a loving smile and nod, indicating that it was a beautiful fitting name for their business.

"Shall we enter the house to continue the tour?" suggested Sylvia. "Yes, please!" They both responded like synchronized twins. So, Sylvia unlocked and opened the double doors, and they took their first step into this glorious residence. That's when Sylvia told them that the address is 8578 Whispering Winds Drive.

Immediately, they noticed that the entranceway was about fifty feet in diameter in the shape of a scroll. The flooring is a beautiful stone-tiled design, appearing like a parchment scroll with a wonderful "welcome" calligraphy etched on it.

The main floor throughout the mansion were of marble varying in different shades in different parts of the home.

Hanging overhead just past the entrance was the largest, most beautiful chandelier they had ever set their eyes on. To complement that was the most amazing staircase ever!

There were two staircases, left and right, that spiraled up and connected to the top, which was a long combination hall and bridge as the second level of the place.

The second floor, they would learn, consists of six master bedrooms with windows providing beautiful views overlooking the scenic wonders of the property.

"Let's begin to our left, and we will work our way to the right," suggested Sylvia. Both agreed, and the grand tour officially began.

On the extreme end was an office space on the left, and the right is a master room with bathroom attached. Just outside in the hallway on both sides are cabinets for storage. Then, moving down the hall toward the main entrance on the right is a laundry room with hookups for four washers and four dryers. Opposite on the left of the hall is a supply room stocked with shelves, with tables underneath both sides and a sink basin at the end.

The next room on the right is like a medium-sized reading room with four comfortable chairs surrounding a table in the middle and a beautiful little water fountain with rocks and a few bamboo shoots.

Across the hall on the left is a library area, with bookshelves on all walls of the room. There is room for two chairs, of which one was occupied by a gentleman perusing a book.

"Good afternoon, friends," addressed the man to Tyotan and Saraya with an inviting smile. "And how are you doing so far on the tour with my dear friend, Sylvia?" he asked. Tyotan smiled as he somewhat remembered the face and offered his hand in greeting.

"I am Virgil, a good friend of Sylvia and the former owner of this wonderful house and property." As he looked back at Tyotan, he remarked, "And my car is working very well, thanks to your excellent repair job!"

Then, the full recognition lit up Tyotan's face. "Honey," he said to Saraya, "this is the kind gentleman who shared the idea of a dream board as a tool for our dreams and goals." They exchanged greetings, and then Virgil excused himself so the tour with Sylvia could continue.

Continuing down the hall prior to the staircase at the entrance were two more rooms opposite one another. These were smaller master bedrooms that would easily accommodate one person comfortably. Both thought that this would be perfect if a single individual wanted a getaway and relaxation.

Then, they were back to the center of the house. Sylvia suggested that they continue down the hall on the right side of the home. The first two rooms on the hallway are master bedrooms that have similar styles of a colonial decor. All the bedrooms were equipped with two chairs with a small table and a large set of chester drawers. And the walk-in closets were a nice feature as well.

Just past the first two rooms were more cabinets for storage space, and recessed between them were small bench areas as well. They noticed that one of them consisted of a stack of small-sized carpet pieces all square in shape.

Sylvia explained that these were used as mats that the former owners provided for guests since the floors were all marble and would be too cold for some while getting out of or into their beds. Continuing down the hall, the next set of bedrooms sported themes of Native American and frontier motifs. This had a nice appeal, and both smiled in approval.

Then, a long stretch remained down the hall that opened to a well-sized amphitheater room for entertainment. Sylvia explained that this large entertainment area was used for holiday celebrations, even some weddings for friends, ballroom dancing, yoga, tai chi, and the list went on. There were plenty of power outlets throughout the large room. There were sconces on all walls with the capability of dimming or brightening up the lights for different occasions.

Topping off the wonder of this huge, glorious amphitheater were four of the most beautiful chandeliers in European style. In all the corners of the ceiling are hooks if some would choose to hang some chimes. The total size of the room reminded them of the size of a school gym. It was definitely a splendor to behold.

"Any questions up to this point?" asked Sylvia. Tyotan responded, "Can you tell us a little about the house and any upgrades, reports, etc.?'

"Definitely. Glad you asked," responded Sylvia. "Inspections have been done, and all passed as exceptional. The plumbing and sewage were inspected and passed last year. All the electrical wiring and fixtures are functional and safe. The roof is three years old. The appliances were all updated two years ago. The owners preferred gas stoves and dual sinks with a garbage disposal, but no dishwasher. Both front and back sprinkler systems are fully functional. There is a brand-new portable barbecue grill in a storage unit in the back. There are five portable fifteen-inch TVs available upon request, but are not used much. Most prefer less of a modern-day technology and more peace and quiet. If I forgot anything, please do not hesitate to ask me, and anytime I cannot answer immediately, I will find answers and inform you by phone, text, or e-mail, which ever you prefer."

Tyotan and Saraya both were impressed by Sylvia and her attention to detail, and so far, their questions were satisfied.

"Are you ready for the second floor tour?" she asked, smiling. Both nodded yes as they proceeded to the left staircase. While ascending to the second floor, they were admiring the steps that matched exactly with the flooring. The railing was that of a rustic wrought iron that complemented both the flooring and ceiling respectively. And Tyotan counted a total of twenty-eight steps leading to the second level. Then, he took a photo of the first floor from above. Such a breathtaking shot to behold!

Moving on to the first room on the far left, they approached like little children on a field trip. Sylvia opened the door, and a cool breeze caressed their faces as they entered the room. The window was slightly cracked open for some fresh air. This room is a mellow peach color with a nice queen-sized bed and dresser to match with an ornate dark brown mirror. The bathroom provided the options of bath and shower with a marble top sink and wooden storage space beneath. A small divider wall separated the commode with a well-sized walk-in closet. To complete the room are two comfortable chairs and a medium-sized octagonal table. Upon exiting the room is a little decorative sign on the door that reads "No random act of any kind, however small, is never wasted. -Aesop."

At that point, Tyotan and Saraya shared a loving glance with each other. They were communicating without words that this is a special sacred atmosphere that started to really resonate within their hearts.

Then came the second room. Sylvia gestured for Saraya to open the door. As it opened, a gentle breeze activated a small hanging chime just above the window opposite the door. It made for such a pleasant welcome that they were speechless. This interior sported a pleasant light turquoise color, and a beautiful dream catcher hung from the upper left corner of the room. Above the king-sized bed hung a beautiful picture of a young Indian maiden with a crystal ball in one hand and looking at a dove in the other hand. This room had a soothing and mystical feel to it.

Placed between the bed and the window are two chairs dressed in beautiful animal furs accompanying an attractive driftwood table. These are facing a nice little fireplace on the right half wall. Between the fireplace and the main entrance wall are the bathroom and a walk-in closet with ample storage space made of cedar wood and chester drawers to match. Hanging from the ceiling in the closet is a Native American medicine wheel laced with various colored feathers bound by beads.

Turning toward the door to exit is a four-foot column with a perched, majestic-carved wooden eagle. A small sign on the door read "May the Great Spirit bless your life with love, peace, and harmony."

Moving on to the third room, Tyotan led the way to take a turn and open the door. As it opened, he felt a strong but loving presence within his heart and a voice that spoke, saying, "Welcome." As this occurred, he looked directly across the row, and centered in front of the window on a small platform sat a statue of a Buddha sitting in silent meditation in a lotus posture. His immediate reaction was to bow his head with hands clasped in a respectful manner. After a brief moment, Tyotan directed his intention to Sylvia with a question, "Are any or all pieces of artwork included with the house or are the owners still moving things out?"

Her answer was immediate. "The artwork on display in the home is included at the discretion of the new owners if they choose. The original owners did not want to interfere with the ambience and spirit of the home as it had been since their moving in thirty-five years prior."

Tyotan and Saraya smiled with joy as everything they had experienced thus far was extremely acceptable and attractive. Then, the Saraya spoke with a question, "Have you had many viewings of this property thus far, and if so, any offers?"

"As a matter of fact, you are the first to tour this home since it went on the market that day before I met you in the flower shop," Sylvia replied. It almost sounded too good to be true! At this point, the happy couple knew within themselves that this was the chosen product that their dream board had materialized for them. Not one thing so far had any reservation in the negative column of Saraya's list. As a matter of fact, her notebook had not even been opened since the moment Sylvia pulled up into the driveway.

On with the third room were two amethyst geodes measuring up to three feet tall opposite one another in both corners on the same wall of the Buddha in front of the window. This room was accentuated with wallpaper, and the design was a bamboo garden-like nature. Adorning the wallpaper were dragonflies and various colors of frogs scattered about.

One sensed that feeling of peace and tranquility in the air of which Tyotan immediately felt. This was enhanced by the two rattan chairs covered in cushions and completed with a glass-and-tile table with a yin-yang design on the surface and a beautiful candle in the center. Saraya could see and feel in Tyotan's eyes and heart that this was his favorite room thus far.

The beautiful wallpaper also adorned the bathroom and walk-in closet. Making full circle to exit the door, a most beautiful saying was surrounded by a simple bamboo frame that read "May the lotus in your heart forever be filled with joy, peace, and serenity to share."

Moving down the hall to the fourth room was like walking on air as the happy couple embraced each and every moment of this most wondrous tour of what they felt was like a piece of heaven on earth. How could this get any better than what they have already experienced?

At that thought, Sylvia opened the door of the fourth room. To their surprise, the room offered no particular theme of any kind. The walls were an off-white color and the standard furnishings were of earth tone colors. For the most part, this room was plain, and Saraya smiled at that. This offered the opportunity for them to have at least one room to exercise their own creativity for a theme if they chose to do so. They breezed through this room and proceeded to the fifth room. As they entered, it was the same as the fourth. This kind of brought them back to earth a bit as now each could have a room to create a theme for.

Finally, the time came for the sixth and final room to complete the second floor. Tyotan led the way and proceeded to open the door. Once more, their eyes and heart were transported to the realm of wonder and awe. In the left corner of the window wall stood a five-foot-tall statue of Pythagoras, and in the right corner was a five-foot statue of Voltaire. The ceiling design was that of night blue sky with the stars shining, and wallpaper of old school maps of the old world adorned the room. A small table underneath the window was decorated with an old cutter ship inside a bottle.

The two chairs complemented the wallpaper, and the table in between was black with a square frame, and ingrained in the middle was a picture of the Dead Sea Scrolls. What a wonderful way to complete the tour of this most precious mansion! Exiting the room, a frame with a very inspirational message read "The creativity and potential of man is one step closer to all that ever was, is and shall be. May he remain humble and devoted to the service of life. -Unknown."

As the three began to descend down a staircase, Saraya and Tyotan informed Sylvia that they were very pleased with the tour and would like to make an offer on the property today.

Sylvia nodded okay as she led them through to the backyard to experience the landscaping. What an experience it turned out to be!

The most beautiful, huge redwood deck led to the path of the yard. The deck supported six tables with four chairs each, and a large barbecue grill sat to the right. Just beyond the deck was a very large circular yard separated by a curved path in the middle. This brick path consisted of recessed circular lights built in and activated by timers. On both sides of the paths were the most beautiful pink, yellow, and red roses.

At opposite ends of the yard were two willow trees about fifty feet in height. The right side of the path consisted of bluegrass lawn. The left side of the path was all ground covered with tiny flowers of various colors.

It was then that Tyotan and Saraya realized that the whole yard was in the shape of the yin-yang symbol. What a beautiful and marvelous idea! They both began to wonder about the owners, what they were like to have such a place designed, and what motivated the concepts.

About the time they finished that thought, Virgil appeared seemingly out of nowhere with a gracious smile as Sylvia addressed them, saying, "I will kindly let Virgil explain about the history of the residence and its previous owners as he was closely involved with the gentleman, Ellis Windsor." At that, Sylvia excused herself and told Tyotan and Saraya that she would start up some paperwork on the property for them.

"And how do the both of you feel about your tour through this home and property?" asked Virgil. His demeanor was the most pleasant that they have experienced with anyone, and they felt most comfortable being in his presence.

Saraya replied first. "Words cannot express our appreciation and gratitude for your most generous assistance in sharing the idea of the dream board as a positive tool to work and strive for one's goals in life. I have learned an important lesson of focus and consistent attention on the desired goal. Every cell of my being is filled with excitement and joy, and it is most necessary that we express our most sincere appreciation in the matter."

Virgil smiled as he bowed his head in respect with hands in a prayer mudra to Saraya and Tyotan. He responded, "I sense a deep reverence for life and service to others within your hearts, and it is quite an honor to assist the both of you on your journey and destiny of choice. Now, I would like to share with you the history of the residence and its former owners, Ellis and Charlotte Windsor."

He continued, "I met Ellis forty-five years ago in a small spiritual order where our similar desires and goals brought the two of us together. At this time, we resided in a small town in New Zealand. You might say that as of the older eras of time, there appeared various secret orders that never broadcasted their whereabouts or practices due to their nature. The reason being that their philosophy of all mankind as a great brotherhood consisted of no boundaries or limitations, thus no specific labels. This is most unacceptable in the current world orthodox churches.

"Our emphasis was on the transformation of the inner efforts and works through the sincere heart-driven passions of all who dedicated their lives and various kinds of service to one in other. When Ellis and I performed a focus of love and service in our meditations, we both felt a sense of urgency in Austria and sensed that a void of love and unity of life had germinated in certain areas. The mission of our order was to seek out these dark holes and serve the communities with love, sincere passion, and sacrifice, if necessary.

"Ellis was fortunate to have gained wealth through his family inheritance in addition to his top-notch education, degree in philosophy, and major in history. However, through all of his success, humility and the passion to serve his fellow man are and have always been his dedicated destiny of which his wife and soul mate, Charlotte, is a dedicated servant to life also. It is very rare that in an order of this nature, there are very few married couples bound to the same oath of a society dedicated to the rebirth of the heart and soul of mankind through countless opportunities of service.

"Forty years ago, we traveled here and found this property through a vision shared by both of us." Tyotan and Saraya were both mesmerized by the historical account that Virgil was sharing with them. He continued.

"The structure of the home needed a lot of updating and work, so the property was offered at a low price. As cost was not really an issue with Ellis, the purchase was made for a higher purpose, and together with other members of the fraternity, reconstruction was soon underway. This became a hidden headquarters for our group, but eventually available to all as an assisted living residence. It took five years for us to complete a total renovation. And one of the key members was an architect by trade. His name is Seth Goodwin.

"Seth experienced a wondrous vision of what you have seen and experienced on your tour this afternoon. He felt that the positive vibrations of this created environment would attract the right couple when the time was right to vacate, to relocate, and sell the property."

Virgil sported a slight smile as both Tyotan and Saraya gasp for air as their eyes opened wide. Virgil continued, "My assignment here will be completed when the property is sold and our mission will continue on in our new location. But we will always send prayers of love and light to this location as this is but one continuous point of our network on the planet. I feel strongly that we share similar values and interests that will allow for continued communications to remain between us."

Tyotan reverently bowed to Virgil in gratitude along with the following comment: "If this is to be ours, we promise to always maintain an integrity of love, service, and gratitude to our fellow man to abide and peace and harmony."

Virgil returned the gesture with a final comment before his departure. "Most precious ones, we highly approve of the name that Saraya thought of for the home." At that, Tyotan and Saraya turned to one another in total amazement, with Sylvia approaching on their left.

"At your convenience, we will run your credit check while you decide your offer" Sylvia stated. Then they turned to their right to thank Virgil once more, but he was gone. They turned back to one another, bewildered, as Sylvia cut in with a remark. "That's just Virgil, such a sweet and kind gentleman. He's there one moment and gone the next. I am used to it," she said with a slight grin.

Tyotan and Saraya both knew instantly that the Hidden Mist was to be theirs. After the well-told history of the place was shared by Virgil, they decided that a fair price should be offered even if it's over their budget a bit, for the history and aura of this magnificent place is a sacred honor and priceless in its created purpose for loving service, and to continue and maintain the aura of love, peace, and harmony.

Sylvia and Saraya agreed to start the process of their bid and filled out some paperwork on the dining room table, while Tyotan went for a stroll on the back side of the property. He needed some alone time, and Saraya fully understood that.

He began to wonder beyond the borders of the yard until he was out of sight. He took deep breaths while admiring the lush forest, its majestic aura, and vibrations. Ten minutes out, he discovered a little creek winding its way across the property. Then he bent down with hands cupped to take a drink from this pure source of liquid.

"Hmmm!" He sighed as the coolness caressed his throat and silently quenched his thirst. Right beside him was the perfect flat rock convenient as a resting spot. At once, he sat and began to focus on his heart while giving thanks from within and expressing his gratitude for this wonderful opportunity of a lifetime to serve his fellow man with the woman of his heart. This created a silent and stillness of extraordinary peace within, and in response, a voice from within began to address him.

"My son, we have been waiting for this moment of celebration! The ones you know of as Virgil and Ellis have been devotees of the Rheyzoun Buddhas from many centuries, preparing the way for the Chosen Ones and the final battle between the light and dark forces here on earth. They serve on a different level of the brotherhood just below the level of the Chosen Ones, but no less dedicated and committed to the service of life. They are of a level known as the Preparers and strategically set out to create and maintain blueprints throughout the earth.

"These Preparers have spent countless lives of sacrifice and service since the times of ancient Egypt and before. They have been very crucial in their work and service to the light. If not for them, the earth's balance would have tilted the axis, thus creating more destruction on a cataclysmic scale. Now is the time for stepping up of light vibrations to overcome the heaviness of the dark forces to maintain a proper balance of the planet, thus averting a major catastrophe.

"Today, we celebrate the passing of the torch that amplifies the positive energy grid here. You and the others will share a huge responsibility to maintain the vibratory level here, and we will always be able to assist when help is needed. Just make the calls for assistance as always. One more thing to show you." As the last comment was made, a subtle humming noise pervaded the air.

As Tyotan opened his eyes, he witnessed an opaque oval approximately twelve feet tall and twelve feet wide appear. Then, the Buddha spoke once more.

"This is a portal that allows dimensional travel. Its purpose is for a higher work and not meant to be for recreational purposes. Make no mention of this to Saraya or anyone else. We are making you and the other Chosen Ones aware of these as your growth and heightened sense of awareness allows. There will be times when they will be necessary for your work to combine forces with one another. You must also carefully guard these areas of entrance from the dark ones. We will advise you in your meditations on how this is done. It is crucial that the energies here maintain a high frequency of love, peace, and harmony. This is why you were destined to have your bed-and-breakfast business here. When you return to the house, Sylvia and Saraya will inform you that Ellis, Charlotte, and Virgil signed a letter of agreement to accept whatever offer you make on the property.

"Gratitude is definitely in order for Virgil as he was our messenger to assist you two in your goals, and you definitely qualified through your passion and desires in pursuing your dream to serve. We congratulate you in your determination and success! May the fire in your hearts eternally burn and serve in the light!"

In ending the meditation and dialogue, Tyotan took one more soothing drink from the creek and then headed back to the house. When he returned, Sylvia and Saraya were sitting at a table on the redwood deck of the backyard.

Saraya stood and approached Tyotan midway of the yard with a paper in hand. She wanted to verify with him about their offer amount for the property prior to their signature. He remembered the dialogue of the Buddha and was bound to offer a fair amount since he knew that the place would be theirs. He looked in Saraya's eyes with a serene smile as they both agreed to pay the asking price, but he agreed with one condition only.

"And what would that be, my love?" she asked in a happy and somewhat bewildered tone. His smile grew wide as he put his hands on her soft and supple shoulders and asked, "That we get married here two months from today: December 6, 2020!"

"Oh! Yes! Yes! Yes!" she responded with such an excitement and joy. "You totally caught me off guard with that proposal! I am so happy and thrilled for our dream to be sealed in the bonds of love and matrimony, my love!" They both shared an embrace that touched Sylvia's heart dearly as she sat and witnessed this momentous event.

Then they both approached the deck where Sylvia was sitting and shared the good news. Sylvia stood and congratulated them both with a big smile and hugs. She expressed that the previous owners also had their own wedding there, and if Saraya needed any help or assistance for the event, she would be honored and privileged to be of service.

They both thanked her and said that they would definitely keep her in mind. Then Sylvia asked one more question. "May I offer and treat you two to dinner tonight in honor of your double celebration? I would be most happy to!" They immediately accepted the offer, and Saraya was anxious to share the name of their new business venture. Sylvia gathered the paperwork and suggested that they depart the property so Tyotan and Saraya could enjoy some time together before the dinner treat.

"How does 4:30 p.m. sound, and do you both like seafood?" asked Sylvia. "I have been wanting to try the new seafood restaurant in town, Clambouyant. I've heard nothing but positive comments and recommendations from the townsfolk, and it has received rave reviews from the radio."

They smiled and looked to Sylvia with a big yes painted on their faces. "Would you like me to pick you up or do you want to meet me there?" she asked. Tyotan and Saraya said that they would meet her there promptly at 4:30.

"Perfect then!" she replied as they exited their soon-to-be new home and business venture. From the midyard, they looked back once more to take a picture of the lovely home on 8578 Whispering Twins Drive.

The drive back to their home was a joyful ride as they chatted about the new home, wedding, etc. Then Sylvia asked Saraya if they thought about where they might want to go for a honeymoon. Immediately, Saraya spoke up and, to Tyotan's surprise, blurted out, "I always wanted to visit the Canary Islands!" He was pleasantly surprised for that was something they haven't even discussed. But he knew from within that it would be a great opportunity for him to meet Nyla in the flesh. He nodded his head in agreement. "What a wonderful choice!" remarked Sylvia with the radiant smile on her face.

Then Saraya quickly interjected that they might have to postpone their honeymoon for a while due to funds mainly going toward the preparation of the new business and all. "Don't I know it!" responded Sylvia. "New business startups can eat up one's time and funds real quick." At that, they pulled up to their home from the end of the most joyous and successful home tour.

"See you both at the restaurant soon," said Sylvia as she rolled up the car window and drove off. The time was 2:00 p.m., which gave Tyotan and Saraya a little unwinding time to relax. Saraya told Tyotan that she needed a little nap before dinner and quickly retired to the bedroom. He responded that he would join her in a bit. This gave him some time for a little meditation session to show his love and gratitude for the great assistance in the purchase of their new home and business venture.

Tyotan changed into some relaxed clothing and then lit a small candle for his meditation. Within minutes, he was centered in his heart with a focus on the love and gratitude of the Buddhas and his devout Chosen brethren. Then, a loving response came from within, which he knew was Nyla, and she shared, "Congratulations on your new home and proposal to Saraya! I am looking forward to your visit here in the near future!" The message ended. He had mixed emotions of joy and puzzlement. "I guess somehow we will be going on a honeymoon." He pondered as he bowed his head in respect and gratitude. A plume of love burst forth from his heart to hierarchy and his Chosen comrades. Just before his meditation ended, he had a vision of Virgil and another of which he felt was his partner, Ellis. As they returned a warm smile, the meditation ended. The time was 2:20 p.m. Then he went to join Saraya for a quick nap.

Time flew by as they readied themselves for the dinner with Sylvia. Tyotan decided to wear a nice lavender shirt with blue pants, while Saraya's choice of clothing is a pastel-flowered blouse with peach-colored pants.

They arrived at the restaurant five minutes early. Sylvia was being assisted by the host as they entered the restaurant. "Good evening, friends!" greeted Sylvia. The host took the lead and escorted them to their table. There was a beautiful flower arrangement as a centerpiece accompanied by two tall candles. The table was for four, but they were only three. They were a little puzzled but happy as they sat down, admiring the wonderful table arrangement.

The waiter introduced himself and said that he would return shortly with some water and menus. As the waiter walked away, a gentleman approached the empty chair and politely asked if it was taken. Both Tyotan and Saraya's face lit up like a Christmas tree. "Virgil! What a pleasure to see you here!" they remarked excitedly. He sat himself down, holding a most beautifully designed envelope in his hand.

"I am so delighted to be here to congratulate the happy couple on your new home purchase and your announcement of your wedding!" he happily remarked. "On behalf of Sylvia, myself, and my partner, Ellis, I would like to present you both with a small token from our hearts on this special occasion."

Virgil handed the envelope to Saraya with the warmest smile as she asked, "May I open it with your attendance here?" He nodded yes, and she carefully opened the beautiful envelope with reverence and respect.

When she removed the contents, her eyes filled with tears of joy as she shared it with Tyotan. "Oh! My goodness! Things could not get much better than this!" A pair of tickets to the Canary Islands for a week delighted the happy couple. "And," Virgil added "with your permission, I would like to offer my services and tend to the Hidden Mist while you're temporarily away." They happily agreed and were left speechless in this momentous occasion.

For a moment, Saraya looked a little puzzled as she did not recall sharing the name of the business with anyone other than Tyotan. However, that quickly subsided since Virgil felt like a longtime friend in just the short time they were acquainted.

October 6, 2020 proved to be a victorious and glorious day for Tyotan and Saraya. They really felt honored to have made new friends in Sylvia and Virgil. Realizing that two months would fly by, they had much planning and work to do in a short time.

Tyotan had quite a bit of vacation time saved up, so that would not be a problem to put in for the week off. Then, he had to figure out a plan on how to slowly phase out of his job as a mechanic and transition to the bed-and-breakfast business. He was happy that he maintained a healthy and positive relationship with his employer, Arnie, and Boyd, his assistant-in-training who is a quick-learning young man.

Boyd is a part-time employee but has been working toward becoming full-time. His quality and work ethics proved to be a blessing to both Arnie and Tyotan. There is no doubt that he would receive a positive endorsement and recommendation from Tyotan to become the number one head mechanic.

So, Tyotan decided on cutting down to three and a half days of mechanical work after the honeymoon. He felt obligated to try and help to find a part-time helper for Arnie and the shop. Arnie felt like family to Tyotan for the many years of his employment with him. The loyalty and trust between them was solid.

Saraya began to plan as well with her job at the hotel she was managing. She would have to begin training someone to take her place while still working part-time for a while. She two decided to cut back to three and a half days. Both wanted to be able to spend at least two days a week together on the Hidden Mist. Not to mention that they still needed a steady flow of income for a bit until the bed-and-breakfast was running.

Since things happened faster than expected, they had to quickly apply for a business license and whatever permits were needed for their new venture. Here again, Sylvia stepped up to the plate and gave Saraya a list of everything they would need to start up their business. This was very helpful and saved them a tremendous amount of time and energy.

Tyotan and Saraya were so grateful that they agreed on a special gift that they would impart to Sylvia for all her help and friendship. She would receive a full two weeks of free time at the Hidden Mist whenever and however she wished to use it.

CHAPTER 24

MEANWHILE IN THE Canary Islands, Nyla and her companion, Brandon, were enjoying a beautiful day on the beach. This brought happy memories of her pets, Motley and Dart, who recently passed on from a battle with Teohta. But she felt their spirits within her heart that was very soothing and warm. Brandon could sense this as he held her hand with affection. Then something unexpected happened.

Brandon fell back and became unconscious. He blacked out with no warning signals at all. Nyla, with lightning speed, drew from within and activated an inner protective shield for Brandon and herself. She then projected an aura of pink and green light to absorb within his being. This was surrounded by a thick blue ring of light for protection for both of them.

On a deeper level, Brandon became aware of being on a bridge enveloped in total darkness accompanied by a choir of obnoxious negative vibratory tones. But a loving voice within said, "Be strong, my love! Resist the darkness, for you are protected!"

As he heard this message, he could see and feel the strength of the blue protective ring within and around his being. Then immediately, an apparition began to appear about thirty feet in front of him on the bridge of darkness.

It began as a small ovoid of smoky gray that grew into a six foot six male figure dressed fully in black and a cape to match, with a fiery red collar and a long staff that he held by his side.

While this was happening within Brandon's inner being, Nyla immediately received inner messages from Vander, Kobin, and Rotussi. All responded to Nyla's activation of the golden disc within her being, signaling an SOS alert. This quick response clearly showed the growth of the Chosen Ones as an emergency situation could occur at any time without warning. The difference between victory or defeat could be determined by mere seconds if one is caught off guard and fails to act immediately. "We are with you, Nyla!" was the message she was most happy to receive.

The energies of Vander, Kobin, and Rotussi immediately intensified the protective shield for Brandon in his inner battle on the bridge of darkness. As the apparition took form, it addressed Brandon by his name. "My dear Brandon, before you lies the opportunity for you to decide on what to do with your ordinary, mundane life in the earth. We here have much to offer if you choose to live an extraordinary life."

The voice of Mattias ceased to allow Brandon to absorb what was just offered to him. Nyla was deeply concerned that Brandon was alone in his confrontation with her nemesis, Mattias. She knew their strategy of getting to her through Brandon and was upset at herself for being caught off guard for this kind of attack.

That being said, she knew that a great lesson was learned from this and she quickly had to dismiss this attitude of self-persecution of shortcoming as this would dissipate her light energies in assisting Brandon. She knew from within that this is a direct perversion of the light forces that could destroy their cause for the victory of a planet and its people. She would have to remain an observer without interference in Brandon's confrontation with Mattias and the dark forces. His use of free will was at stake. The light protection was all that could be offered.

Mattias continued on with his offer to Brandon. "Your life as a tour guide is a nice form of service, but is it something that is totally satisfying for your wants and needs? We offer a power and opportunity to expand your life skills into something greater and more satisfying than the ordinary. You owe nothing to others, but don't you owe it to yourself to be rich and successful and a prosperous life to live?"

Again, he paused briefly to allow the words to be absorbed. Then came the eye opener. "At one time, Nyla was a part of our great team and she prospered greatly. Unfortunately, her greed became overwhelming and she took what we gave her and then left the team. Her vows and commitments were dissolved of her own choosing and has chosen to fight against us. Yet, we still would welcome her back if she wills it. The invitation is always open once you have become a part of the team."

"What deception!" Nyla thought as she realized why the rank of Prince Mattias holds under the Kingdom of Darkness held by Teohta. Mattias continued with his dialogue. "We will leave you now to ponder and decide what you choose to do with your life. We shall meet again in a while and hopefully await your decision to join us and leave behind you the mundane life of ordinary and at the mercy of others." At that, Mattias dissolved into thin air, leaving Brandon alone on the bridge.

Then slowly, the darkness began to fade away, being replaced by a beautiful violet and pink hue radiating his being. The next thing he knew, he was lying on the beach with his head in Nyla's lap.

"My dear Brandon, you blacked out and have been unconscious for ten minutes. How are you feeling?" asked Nyla. "I guess I'm okay. No pain or headache, but a little dizziness," he uttered. "I think we should go to the urgent care and have you checked out." Brandon agreed, and they left the beach.

During the drive, Brandon began to relay to Nyla about what appeared to be a dark dream, but yet felt very vivid and real to him. She listened very attentively as he gave a very detailed description of what occurred. He emphasized that even though it was like a nightmare, he felt safe and protected the whole time. In this dream, he himself never uttered a word. He was just an observer.

When they arrived at the urgent care center, Nyla was happy that the presence of the others was still engaging in their energies directed to her and Brandon. The bond of the Chosen Ones was growing ever stronger in the light.

As the doctor was seeing Brandon, Nyla sat in the waiting room in silent contemplation of love and gratitude of her compadres. They all sent figure 8 flows of light to each other and then concluded with thanks and gratitude to the hierarchy for their sponsorship.

Then, a Buddha sent an inner response to Nyla: "Your friend Brandon was an easy target for Mattias and his legions. Any and all connections with the Chosen Ones will always be an easy or susceptible way to thwart the agenda of hierarchy. Your immediate action and that of your brethren was crucial and precise timing in his protection.

However, this is his personal battle with evil and will be determined by his own free will. You will need to maintain his protective force field constantly, and, at your discretion, explain more of your not-so-pure history to test your love and to give him a better understanding of what is happening to him without divulging your world mission of the Chosen Ones to save a planet. You both have a previous history, and he greatly needs your assistance for a much needed victory. The choice will be his."

Nyla understood the nature of the circumstances and graciously thanked the Buddha with heart and soul. The same response resonated from her brethren, giving love and thanks to the Buddha. A wave of light was reciprocated back to them from the Buddhas, stepping up the vibration levels of their individual golden discs.

The urgent care doctor completed her prognosis of Brandon, and only detected dehydration and recommended more water and rest in addition to a follow-up visit with his own personal doctor. So, Nyla took Brandon to her home and suggested to him that he stay with her for a while, which he agreed.

They reached home at about 4:00 p.m., and Nyla prepared a light dinner consisting of soup, hot tea, and water. Brandon was a bit tired, so he chose to retire early for a good night's rest. Fortunately, the next day was an off day from work as well.

This gave Nyla some quiet time as she prepared for a special meditation time. She lit a candle and relaxed into a state of contemplation and quiet. Her heartbeat became her focus and was soon followed up by the chanting of "Om" nine times softly, but intensely. She then followed up by some deep regulated breathing. This created a connection with a Buddha for some additional higher lessons in her initiations as a light warrior and a leader of the Chosen Ones.

A Buddha then began a discourse: "Nyla, your mission at this point is to assist Brandon on the inner planes for his next confrontation with Mattias. You must make him aware of the parallel bridge of light that exists, being the path of righteousness and love for all sentient beings. His career as a tour guide is an honorable service to others and can have a positive growth potential toward his destiny. Your relationship with one another complements both your destinies, provided that the right choices and actions are blended in heart, soul, and being.

"Your fondness for one another has grown to higher levels of love and will be tested as such. As both are always vulnerable, one must lead by example with an unconditional love and respect for the other's space and free will without sacrificing right virtues and understanding of the higher laws of cosmic life and light.

"This also requires patience, since other's decisions may cause them to stumble at times. Yet, stumbling blocks are always an opportunity of wisdom through experience as one studies the path of growth and understanding in life. Compassion and empathy, when acted appropriately, can heal wounds, thus creating a stronger bond in a relationship. This act also draws up the lesser to the greater levels of vibrations, creating a clearer mind and heart.

"This is a bridging of heart and soul between two, united together. As the positive growth continues, this bridge then spirals up to an even higher bridge, until the bonding of two hearts beating as one is attained. Once this height of oneness is reached, the final journey to the ultimate bridge of light and victory begins.

"This is not an easy path, for many initiations will test both souls in order to fully strengthen the bond of unity, which requires sacrifice, service, selflessness, and surrender when necessary.

"Remember to always seek the light within to draw upon its strength, while also calling upon hierarchy for assistance. 'Ramtam Om! Shivaya Om!' repeated will create an inner figure 8 flow and an exchange of cosmic energies with a sincere, humble, and passionate heart to always do right. The call will always compel the answer! Make sure that all the efforts of light work are always to the benefit of life and service to mankind.

"A friendly word of caution and warning: the more all of you twenty-five begin to resonate with one another, the bond between you strengthens but also your karmas start to intertwine, both good and not so good.

"Even though some may be raising their vibrations higher than others, if some stumble and fall a little bit, that action will cancel out the positive momentum. So, if one feels a little dissipation in light energy, this would likely be the case. This could range from an incorrect decision on an event or issue, or a lack of focus and meditation time, causing a drainage of light energy in your newly acquired grid of energy, your bond in unity.

"It is crucial that a minimum of three times a day that a focus of twenty-five beings immersed in a flame of passion and victory is visualized and filled with love, gratitude, and mercy toward one another, for this is the unguent of which reignites the fiery purpose of light over darkness." Nyla acknowledged the discourse and gave a heartfelt thanks.

The following morning of Thursday, October 7, 2020, Brandon awoke with a slight headache and quite thirsty. A bottle of water was left at his bedside by Nyla earlier that morning. As he gulped the water down, he perused the room and noticed a nice picture of Nyla and her now deceased pets. His heart sank a little for her loss.

"Good morning, dear," said Nyla and she entered the room upon his waking. "How are you feeling? Did you sleep well?" she asked.

"I feel pretty good," he replied. "Thanks for the bottle of water. I was pretty thirsty and could probably drink some more." Apparently, the urgent care doctor was correct in his dehydration status.

"Do you feel any nausea, dizziness, or pain anywhere?" asked Nyla. "Whenever you are ready, we can call your doctor to make an appointment if you would like," she offered.

Brandon grabbed Nyla's hand and gazed into her eyes with a smile of gratitude. "Thank you so much for being here for me." He kissed her hand ever so gently. She smiled in return and bent down to kiss him on the forehead. Their bond was growing stronger.

"Come, I will fix us a nice to breakfast," she suggested. She led Brandon to the living room couch and sat him down as she went to the kitchen. He began to admire her crystals and noticed a nice little Buddha incense burner in the middle of the coffee table. Then, he noticed a small book on an end table titled *An Introduction to Crystals* that piqued his interest. He recalled that in his recent dream, certain colors gave him a sense of comfort and protection. Maybe this would give him some insight as to their meanings. Nyla peeked into the living room to see how Brandon was faring. She noticed him absorbed in the little book, and that made her smile.

"Breakfast is ready," Nyla called out to Brandon. He ventured into the dining room and sat at his designated chair. In front of him was a plate consisting of two scrambled eggs, two slices of wheat toast, a small bowl of fresh fruit, and water. "Thanks, sweetie," he addressed Nyla with the radiant smile.

They thoroughly enjoyed each other's company down to the last bite, and then Brandon offered to do the dishes. She consented on the condition that he made a doctor's appointment right afterward, which he agreed to.

An appointment was made for later on that day with Dr. Amelia Cruz. This allowed for some more quality time for the both of them. They retired to the living room to sit and chat a bit. Brandon proceeded to inquire about the nature of crystals and their usage. This made Nyla felt comfortable and confident in her ability to properly educate him, which would also offer him tremendous support for his own protection.

Nyla began her little discourse to Brandon. "The first and most common is that of the clear crystal quartz; this represents the purity of light and clearness of mind and spirit. Green is both emerald and aventurine; this represents energies of healing, abundance, and prosperity. The pink is rose quartz and represents the energies of love and creativity that is usually expressed through the arts and music."

She paused a moment to allow the information to be absorbed by Brandon and to answer any questions he may have for her, and he did have a question. "Is there a special meaning of these crystals if used together besides individually?"

"Good question!" she responded. "For example, if white and green are surrounded by blue, it indicates that the healing quality of mind and spirit are being protected by the outer blue ring." She paused to allow the answer to sink in. Then she continued a bit more.

"Yellow in the form of citrine or amber represents the energy of wisdom and understanding. This is also related to mental creativity, discipline of mind, and organizational skills. These are all tools of focus for prayers and meditation or mental exercises."

"Wow!" exclaimed Brandon. "This is very fascinating, and I would love to learn more!" "Please take the little book as a gift, and we can schedule another time to talk some more," Nyla offered.

"What do you say we go for a nice little walk?" Nyla suggested. "Do you feel up to it?" "Yes, that is a good idea. I could use a breath of fresh air," Brandon responded.

Nyla grabbed two bottles of water as they headed out the door. Brandon glanced back at Nyla's home and noticed a slight blue hue surrounding her house. No wonder why he felt safe with her, learning about what the color blue represented. He decided to keep this to himself, but Nyla could sense this and just smiled.

It was a beautiful day of partial clouds and a gentle mild breeze riddled with dragonflies and butterflies. A mini swarm of hummingbirds adorned a beautiful bush of bright red, purple, and orange flowers. Close by is a little neighborhood park buzzing with little children, their pets, and local squirrels running to and fro. All felt like a mini paradise filling the air with joyous energy pleasing to mother nature's canvas of life.

They approached a park bench and sat for a moment to enjoy the surrounding life about them. With her heightened awareness, Nyla noticed a figure of a Buddha floating in the air with a lotus flower in one hand and a beautiful dragonfly perched on the other. She closed her eyes and bowed her head with reverence and respect for the presence of the Great Being. While this occurred, Brandon squeezed her hand in a loving manner. This is an experience Nyla would value and treasure forever.

It was a little over an hour before the doctor's appointment as Nyla and Brandon headed back to the house. So far, he felt fine, but felt it safe to pursue the appointment to rule out any type of illness or possible virus. They arrived at the doctor's office ten minutes early and signed Brandon in, but he was called up in five minutes to see Dr. Cruz. He was told to go to room 3 and the doctor would be with him shortly.

Nyla chose to use this quality time in the waiting room to do some contemplation about the incident thus far. While chanting some mantras within herself, a strong inner alert almost broke her concentration. It was an uneasy vibration that she had not experienced for decades. So strong was the alert that her inner golden disc produced a deep blue protective ring surrounding her whole physical being. Then, she visualized a dark entity that was an old nemesis, the one she finally defeated in her battle to return to the light.

And he was the worst of the worst, a lieutenant to Teohta and son to Mattias. He could take many forms while creating webs of lies and deceit. His shape-shifting fooled many in battles and was responsible for numerous victories in his battles with the light.

The legions of light in themselves are indestructible, but as they come to battle through the calls and actions of the physical human race, the chaos and confusion created by the dark forces have been effective in cutting off the legions of light—the ultimate plan of divide and conquer.

By cosmic law, if decisions of the human race are made in error, even though the intent is to make the right call, the assistance of the light forces must withdraw and allow the battles to be fought by humanity alone. Mankind's worst weakness is their susceptibility to deceit and lies intertwined together by the dark ones.

Contingent on one's attunement with the hearts, combined with a strong faith and passion to match, no room in exists for any slight feeling of fear and doubt. These are the loose threads that can easily dissolve one's force field of light, enabling a great vulnerability and eventually defeat in battle.

As Nyla's defenses lit up, her fellow physical warriors had responded to her SOS and ignited their guards as well. Another major confrontation with Mo-Dru was building, and his thirst for her blood and light was strong.

However, the last time they battled, Nyla did not have the luxury of twenty-four fellow comrades to fight with, albeit each of their vibrational levels of light vary, not being the level of Nyla's. Yet, her confidence is strong, as day by day their levels are constantly growing through their practice and commitment of their meditations, and the passions of the heart radiating brilliantly in their auras.

With the access and availability of Ramata and the Rheyzoun Buddhas, more than enough tools and weapons of light are at their disposal as long as the purity, intensity, and the passions of heart are maintained in the service for all mankind in the saving of a planet.

As she sat waiting for Brandon, Aton reached out in response to her SOS signal. Along with Zeera and Amara, they projected a strong blue protective ring protecting the area occupied by Nyla and Brandon. Their sensitivities detected a threatening vibrational pattern and reacted not a moment too soon, for Nyla sensed and could see on a higher level a smoky haze filling the air except for the spaces surrounded and protected by the blue energy rings.

Almost instantaneously, the blue shield magnified as the forces of all twenty-five Chosen Ones were fully activated.

"I've been looking forward to this reunion, Nyla, and this time, the victory will be mine!" was the voice of Mo-Dru addressing his former foe with intensity and extreme aggression. His anger created a fierce wind outside, sending objects flying through the air for two minutes and then subsided. There were no clouds or any indication of inclement weather that would account for a logical explanation of this nasty wind. It was so nasty that numerous car alarms were set off. This was only a warning.

Dr. Cruz and Brandon had entered the waiting room and inquired about all the ruckus going on outside. Nyla responded that a gust of strong wind came out of nowhere and created chaos outside, but only for a minute or so.

"Are you sure you are okay?" Brandon asked Nyla, noticing a little discomfort in her demeanor. Their advanced feelings for each other had increased their attunement to one another and made for a little more difficulty for Nyla not to expose her part of a battle with the dark forces. But she quickly gave him a response of truth without specifics that would not make Brandon suspicious or ask any further questions.

"I am just concerned about your welfare and what is best for you, my dear. You mean a lot to me, and it has become my responsibility as we grow closer that we share a long and healthy bond as a couple."

Brandon was deeply touched and so grateful for their friendship that was getting stronger day by day. He responded with a warm smile and a hug, followed up by soft kiss on the lips.

In the hidden spheres, Mo-Dru grew more angry and vengeful of Nyla as their bond was growing stronger, for at one time before Nyla's transformation into the light, Mo-Dru and Nyla were very close in the forces of the black brotherhood. They were to be deemed the prince and princess of the shadows. They fought and thought as one in the bonds of evil, until that went away. Even though it was a victory for the light, Mo-Dru grew stronger through the jealousy and extreme hatred that blossomed from the event. This pleased Teohta, that Mo-Dru, son of Mattias, had been advanced to the rank and title of "The Legionnaire of Darkness," which gave him full access to the powers of darkness. This would take the oncoming battle to a whole new level that Nyla and her comrades had to be prepared for.

Nyla knew of his growth in the ranks, which put her on high alert for anything and everything that could happen in a moment's notice. All twenty-five were alerted to this, and that from here on, their senses of heightened awareness would have to be consistently maintained at higher levels without tipping the scales to the point of paranoia. The stakes were growing higher, and so was the level of spiritual warfare.

On the drive back to Nyla's home, they chatted about other things while listening to some beautiful Strauss waltzes on the radio. Enjoying the music gave Brandon an idea as he proposed a question to Nyla.

"What would you think about maybe taking a class in ballroom dancing together?" he asked. Their taste in music is a perfect match and they both loved the classical music of the masters.

Nyla thought for a moment and then responded, "Why, that is a great idea, my sweetness!" she replied. "But we will need to check our schedules to see what days we both have available, and most classes are taught at night. It will be much easier for me to adjust my schedule to complement yours." Brandon agreed as at times his job as a tour guide exceeded normal hours depending on weather, traffic, etc.

"Thursdays are usually my days off, and I might be able to work out Tuesday nights. I will have to inquire further on my weekly schedules before confirming Tuesdays"

Nyla responded that it would work out okay for her. Then, she had another idea that seemed kind of a bold move, but seemed appropriate at the time due to events and the ever-increasing level of their relationship. She then popped the question.

"Since I have plenty of room in my home, how about possibly staying at my place for a couple of months to see how things work out? The convenience of each other's company and being together to help one another would be a big plus, and you would have your own room for your privacy. My office space is easily able to accommodate two people with separate desks and chairs. Please consider this and take your time. I love your company and feel more complete as a person with you around and in my presence." She stopped to allow Brandon to ponder the question as she pulled in the driveway of her home.

Brandon smiled as they walked to the door for he felt flattered and was very touched by Nyla's advance. He experienced a few butterflies in his stomach, but in a positive manner. He loved the fact that Nyla always had some beautiful music playing through her home, and his new interest in crystals and semiprecious stones had been aroused. Their food habits were pretty much the same, however, once in a while, he needed to feed his craving for a nice, big, juicy steak with potatoes. He also was concerned for her since the loss of her pets, Motley and Dart.

While Nyla was in the kitchen preparing some tea for them, Brandon was busy perusing the little crystal book she gave him. At that moment, his mind and heart agreed that her invitation, given so sincerely with love and compassion and no pressure whatsoever, was a positive and an "all systems go" move to advance in their relationship. The approval for the next step was given from within.

Brandon advanced to the kitchen to assist Nyla in fetching the tea as they moved to the living room to enjoy their drinks. He ever so gently and lovingly held her hand and proceeded to ask, "Would this weekend be too early to start bringing my things and organizing my room?"

Her eyes lit up with a smile to match as she reciprocated by grabbing both his hands with excitement and joy. She, too, was experiencing butterflies in her stomach as though they were each other's first date. But her mature side was also happy, as being together in the same home would be much easier to help and protect Brandon from what was to come, knowing that Mo-Dru would unleash a full attack against any and everything that could weaken and wound Nyla.

She bowed her head with much love and gratitude to hierarchy for her role and opportunity to serve such a righteous role for humanity. When she did this, a warm jolt shocked the body of Brandon as he jerked like that of a hiccup. They never had that experience before, but it wasn't a painful feeling, It was like touching someone with a static buildup, but only a little bit stronger. They just laughed together as they celebrated with their tea.

After the tea, Brandon suggested that he take a nap for he was a bit tired. He retired to his room, while Nyla decided to use the time for a meditative recharge. She kicked off her shoes, lit a partial candle, and sat quietly and comfortably on her meditation cushion. As she composed herself, she made sure that her blue protective shield was up and also included Brandon in the protection. The realization that since he is now a part of the household, a consistent protective focus should be maintained in, through, and around the home for the both of them.

She took some deep breaths and focused intently on the flame in front of her and her heart flame within. As she opened her mind, a warm and familiar loving presence appeared in her vision.

"Beloved Ahtimo! My heart is filled with joy to see you, master!" she uttered within. Ahtimo was her personal sponsoring Buddha that assisted her in the final battle and victory from the dark side. They acquired a karmic bond and relationship of master/teacher that will last for a cosmic cycle. Ahtimo began to speak.

"Dearest Nyla, your advancement is well noted, and I am very pleased with your progress as captain of the twenty-five Chosen Ones of earth. Now, we must prepare for a major battle with Mo-Dru and Mattias. You know well that the intensity of the level of battle is beyond compare to any previous confrontations experienced to date. Timing and preparedness is everything in order to create a momentum for victory in the light. The honorable and mighty Ramata will activate a release of light for the fourth cycle of the year. This will be directed to Rheyzoun-45, and the cosmic beings there will magnify the current according to his will, then emit it directly to the earth. You will all feel a tremendous surge of light energy within and a portion will be also distributed to all other beings on the planet according to their merits and deeds. The light will only be absorbed by the intent of good will, but what people choose to do with it is of course by choice and free will. This release must be used wisely and not squandered away.

"Know well that Brandon is a much-added responsibility now in your household. That the little jolt he experienced earlier was a small portion of your personal light and, aware or not, he is responsible for its proper use or abuse. The web of karma grows on, be it good or bad, in the strengthened bond that you both share.

"It is good that he has acquired a thirst for knowledge in the use and knowledge of crystals, and an excellent introduction to the light and its principals. His desire to learn and his love for you will be his greatest asset for growth and preparedness in the near future, for Mo-Dru will definitely target Brandon to try and weaken you and your emotions. Know that your strong bond with Brandon cannot allow for unbalanced emotions in the upcoming battle. You must detach from your personal feelings for yourself as well as the others, so that the bonds in your chain of light remains pure and strong.

"I have been granted permission to extend a greater portion of my light if I choose to do so. My decision was not made lightly, for a portion of light from my master is risked as well, for the master/student relationships continue up the evolutionary ladder of light and its cycles. This is where the test of faith and love in action creates a momentum of fiery passion in action toward the victory of love and light in the cosmos. Thus, the micro continuously moves to the macro, like a drop of water aware of its oneness with the ocean.

"I am confident in your faith and sincerity of being and grant you an extra portion of my light. Guard it well and use it wisely, always remembering the causes and purpose of hierarchy! We happily sponsor you and your advancing momentums in the light. Maintain your caution and alertness at all times, and when necessary, call upon us for assistance for you represent the light of hierarchy upon earth through love, mercy, compassion, and right action at all times.

"Be now at peace and greet your partners, Tyotan, Namko, and Pyrena, for they will play an integral part in the up-and-coming events." As this the discourse ended, Nyla bowed her head in thanks and gratitude to Ahtimo Buddha.

She began a few chants of "Om" before exiting the meditation session and then enjoyed a great vision so wondrous to behold. She experienced a vision of a most beautiful dragonfly, with bright yellow wings outlined with green and spots of three different shades of blue adorning its presence. What a majestic beauty it was! Then, below the dragonfly were three wondrous ruby-colored frogs staring up at the winged being. But what was this experience for? What did it mean?

Then, a loving response was answered by Ahtimo. "When the time warrants, you will understand the nature of the vision. Now, be at peace for your Brandon has awakened." At that, her meditation ceased and she gently extinguished the candle with reverence. Then Brandon entered the room. He sported a smile like that of a child as he began to speak.

"I had the most beautiful dream while napping! I was calmly sitting on a flat rock beside a smooth-flowing creek when a group of red frogs began to serenade me. Then, a swarm of dragonflies surrounded my body in a most friendly and comfortable manner! It gave me a sense of peace and serenity. This attunement with nature and its wonders is something I truly treasure and value. This can only enhance my life as a tour guide and as a person in general."

Nyla was deeply moved and impressed by Brandon and this sharing of his heart of the emotions. She was speechless as she just nodded her head with a warm smile. This positive mood of his created the perfect state of receptivity for her to work with while continuing to educate him about crystals and their many values and uses.

"'I am excited to learn more about crystals and semiprecious stones!" Brandon added, as though he was picking up on her thoughts. "I will have to return back to work tomorrow as I am feeling much better now," he added, and that was perfect for Nyla as she wanted to ready herself by reorganizing her home to accommodate Brandon's move-in. She also wanted to focus more on her meditations for the release of light on October 10, 2020 as Ahtimo referred to.

"Brandon dear, could you run to the store and fetch some groceries for dinner? I made a little list for tonight," asked Nyla. "Sure, I will go now and stop by my place on the way back for a change of clothes for work tomorrow. I will return in about an hour and a half, give or take," he replied.

"That will be fine, thanks," she responded, giving her some time to arrange some things around the house for more protection in the upcoming battles with Mo-Dru and his army.

As soon as Brandon left, Nyla proceeded to retrieve a large box filled with crystals and incense that she knew would someday be needed for this type of occasion. She began to strategically place the crystals and semiprecious stones around the home. Some were in visible site, while others were not visible for anyone to see. The visible ones she would teach Brandon about, so that his energy would be reinforced for both their protection.

Now, Zeera, Amara, and Aton responded to Nyla's recent attack almost instantaneously due to the fact that in their own histories, they had battled Mo-Dru and met defeat. They were fellow monks in a battle with a warlord that attacked their homeland and raided numerous other towns in the lands of Tibet. As they met their demise, they left their bodies and swore an oath to one another that in the future, they will come together to battle the warlord, defeat him in honor of their fallen ones, and become victorious in the fight for truth and freedom.

It was their vicious murder by Mo-Dru that allowed an opening for Nyla and her rebellion and assistance of light warriors to defeat the dark forces. In this embodiment, the three have once again come, and this time, they were the first to come to the aid of Nyla. A debt was paid, and now their combined forces as Chosen Ones form a great battalion of light along with the assistance of hierarchy in the coming battles.

Nyla sat silently and projected a heartfelt figure 8 flow of thanks and great love as the three of them reciprocated with a mighty flow of light energy.

CHAPTER 25

ON THE SAME day in Rugby, North Dakota, Kobin's wife, Vanessa, was in the middle of homeschooling the twins, Bessie and Trina. While working with them on their vocabulary skills, she felt a slight sharp pain in her temple, but it quickly faded away. Then, she experienced a slight chill, followed up by a blurred vision in her left eye. This too passed. Trying not to worry, she took a few deep breaths to clear her head, and none of this was noticed by the girls.

At the same moment while Kobin was outdoors at work, his senses detected a slight disturbance at home and immediately projected a blue ring of protection for the home front. This also signaled the other twenty-four to be on high alert any time the protection shield is enacted. He still had three hours left on his shift, so he made a call to Vanessa just to check in. Vanessa responded, "Things are fine, dear, and you?"

"Just want to finish my shift so I can come home to my lady and girls," he replied. "Will see you in a little while." "L-E-O-P-A-R-D," Bessie spelled out the last word for today's homeschooling. "That is correct, dear. You have both done well today," Vanessa responded as she gave the girls an assignment for tomorrow's schoolwork.

On the same day, while Rotussi was in the middle of a tai chi class, his phone rang and went to voicemail. While he cannot hear it, a message from his brother in New York was left about his sister. Apparently, she was struck by a truck while crossing an intersection, resulting in a broken right leg and some bruises from the fall. She had the right of way, but the vehicle ran a red light.

However, during the class, he felt an inner urge of something that activated his protective mode to assist the others in an instant. This was also an inner reminder that his responsibility for all around him, his students especially, needed a portion of his protection in their lives as well.

When the class had ended, he listened to the voicemail and returned the call to his brother Joel. "Sasha will be fine as the emergency room did not detect anything life-threatening. It was definitely a hit-and-run situation, but a bystander got the license plate of the vehicle and a few others were witnesses to the incident."

"Thank goodness she is okay," replied Rotussi. "I will get a plane ticket and fly out there tomorrow to see you both for a couple of days." "That would be awesome, as Sasha did ask about you," replied Joel. "It has been over a year since we've seen one another."

"Yeah, I know," remarked Rotussi. "I will see you all tomorrow." After the call, he retired to his special room, separate from the class, where he would sometimes perform some of his meditations.

Meanwhile, in Stuttgart, Germany, Vander was teaching his tai chi class minus four students who called in sick. It seemed that a virus was going around causing nausea, fatigue, and dizziness in his young students. After a short class session, he dismissed the remaining students to go home, eat an early dinner, and get plenty of rest to strengthen their immune systems. Vander, too, felt his protective senses engaging, and realizing that from here on, their protective abilities would have to be magnified for all beings involved within their lives as a karmic duty and responsibility. The focus of alertness and high awareness was required for the next release of light energy from hierarchy.

As he sat in a meditation posture focusing on a clear crystal quartz, he entered a state of attunement with the Chosen Ones. In that moment, the names "Aton and Russi" flashed in his mind and heart. Then, a vision of what appeared to be a black centipede was beginning to surround itself on Russi's body.

Vander, without hesitation, shouted out three times "No! No! No!" and shot out a blue dart with a fiery ruby-red tip that struck the centipede. Then, numerous other darts followed up, striking the enemy in several other regions of its being. The shadow creature dissolved away, but left a portion of its essence attached to Russi's being.

In that moment, Russi, in the physical body, had suffered a cold sweat and a heavy fatigue. His energy was drained as he lay down on a couch in the home of Aton. Aton was in his home office working when an inner alert told him to check on his father. He immediately went to the living room where Russi had fallen asleep on the couch. Aton could see that he was breathing and let him rest.

As he turned to walk away, Russi started to talk in his sleep. "No, no, I don't know!" He was saying like a response to someone badgering him about something. Aton stopped to listen for more dialogue, but Russi immediately said, "No! No!" and then stopped and began to snore.

Aton sat in a chair opposite the couch to observe his father, to make sure that he was not in any danger. He could see with his inner eye the blue ring of protection around Russi. Then, he projected a calm green cloud saturating his body in case of any internal damage inflicted. He sat for fifteen minutes more and then returned to his office to continue his work.

It seemed that one after another, incidents were occurring simultaneously that ruled out coincidence in Nyla's mind and heart. This is definitely in the work of Mo-Dru trying to use his divide-and-conquer tactics. She immediately sent communications to Kobin, Rotussi, Vander, and Aton. Her message was to step up their force fields directly to all family members and acquaintances that could divert or compromise their focus for the oncoming battles. It was an all-out alert to be on guard twenty-four-seven, but not to the point of paranoia.

When all were put on high alert for Nyla, an extra surge of light energy was felt and absorbed by all. This was due to Ahtimo's blessing to Nyla. And not a moment too soon, they all felt their inner golden disc step up their energies and stamina. Their inner armor had been strengthened.

Meanwhile, Brandon had retrieved a couple sets of clothing and was now in the grocery store with the shopping list given by Nyla. As he was gathering the foods from the list, he noticed a section of plants over by the produce section.

He perused the garden area and noticed a bamboo plant adorned with two dragonflies. This brought a smile to his face, so he put it in the cart along with the groceries. This would make for a nice little gift for his lady. He grabbed a few more items and then headed to the check stand.

Brandon exited the store and was heading for his car when a vehicle was speeding through the parking lot and almost hit him. Someone yelled out to him, "Are you okay?" "Yes!" replied Brandon. "That was a close call."

He loaded the groceries and the plant in the car while he caught his breath and gathered his wits about him. He slowly and carefully exited the parking lot and onto the street, ever so watchful of his surroundings. The music he had on in the car helped to calm him down and regain his composure.

Only two blocks more of stop signs and then he would be at Nyla's house. As he approached the first four-way stop, a car flew across the intersection, running the stop sign. It never even attempted to slow down at all.

He took his turn and advanced across the intersection safely. One more stop sign and then home. As he was pulling into the driveway, Nyla was outside the door to greet him. He grabbed the two bags of groceries and gave one to Nyla at the door. They advanced to the kitchen, and Nyla began to unload and put away the food. Brandon went back out to the car to fetch the plant he bought for Nyla.

He quietly snuck into the dining room, but as soon as he put it in the middle of the table, she looked over from the kitchen. "Oh, how nice, my dear!" she blurted out, admiring the new addition to the room. "I love bamboo plants, one of my favorites for interior decor!" Her excited smile was like that of a child with ice cream. Brandon was pleased that she was happy.

Yet, Nyla could detect that Brandon was a little uneasy about something, but she let it go, deciding that if he wanted to talk about anything, it was his choice. She did not want to be a pest or seem to appear overprotective to him. So far, things were going okay.

And at the same time, Brandon decided to keep his near misses to himself. He did not want to overburden Nyla with every little thing. Her concern for his well-being was much appreciated by him, and he felt the same about her.

CHAPTER 26

THE SAME DAY at 2:00 p.m., halfway across the globe in Rugby, while resting, Vanessa felt a headache coming on while the girls were playing in their room. The pain started to steadily increase, causing a sensitivity to the lights in the room. She turned off the light and lay back on the couch. The clock read 2:15 p.m., and she knew that Kobin will be home by 3:30. After a little drink of water, she laid her head back and immediately fell asleep.

At the same moment, Kobin felt his inner protective shield flare up and sensed an uneasiness about Vanessa. As he approached his truck to head home, he made a phone call, but no one answered at the house. He made one more attempt at calling, but to no avail.

While heading home to check on Vanessa, further northeast in New York, Rotussi's sister, Sasha, lay semihelpless with a broken leg and some nursed bruises from her hit-and-run incident. Her brother Joel visited her every day and assisted in the paperwork for her medical benefits.

Sasha was anxious to see Rotussi and felt that he could be of help in her situation, especially on an emotional level. He had always been a calming effect in the family and was missed so greatly, almost to the point that they had become too dependent on him. That was one of the main reasons that his tai chi sensei had recommended that he relocate.

Back at the plantation estate of Aton, Russi was still in a sleep state. Aton came to check in on him again, and he appeared to be fine. He sat for a moment to observe and focus on his father. He did notice a little more intense blue ring around his being. He could sense that his dad was experiencing a dream, so he closed his eyes with a few deep breaths. Then, he had a visual experience.

Russi was on a dark bridge being addressed by an entity surrounded in a charcoal cloud. The voice appeared to be friendly, yet very cunning. Russi allowed the entity to speak, but he only responded with a "No!" every time he was made an offer. His blue protective shield blazed brightly.

Then, finally, the entity began to fade out and was replaced by a magnificent, shiny dragonfly hovering over the spot where the entity had occupied. This great wonder made Russi smile within as the dream slowly faded away.

Aton also smiled within himself as his father had just experienced a victory in his personal battle with the dark forces. Now, he knew from direct experience the importance of the focus of protection of all around. It acted like an equalizer for mortals to do battle with the dark ones on all levels. Aton bowed his head in gratitude for the assistance of his compadres and hierarchy.

As Kobin entered the house, he saw Vanessa on the couch and heard the girls playing in their rooms. He walked a little closer and noticed a cold sweat covering her body and he felt her head. As he did this, she made a slight moan, but her eyes remained shut. "Can you hear me, honey?" he quietly asked her. The response was another moan, but she squeezed his hand in acknowledgment.

From his senses, her blue ring shield was not quite the intensity that it should be. He placed his left hand on her head and his right hand on her heart and within himself chanted "Ramtam Om! Shivaya Om!" nine times, visualizing a green cloud surrounded by blue. As he concluded, her body experienced a jolt and then went limp.

As this occurred, he noticed a slight visible cloud of a dusty residue exit her body. Her head was cooling down, and it seemed that the sweat had stopped. Slowly, her natural color began to reappear.

Kobin grabbed a dining room chair and sat beside his wife for about twenty minutes. Then, her eyes began to slowly open, followed by a slight smile seeing her husband beside her.

"How are you feeling, honey?" Kobin asked her sweetly. "Okay, I guess," she responded, "but I am pretty thirsty." He retrieved a bottle of water from the kitchen. "The last thing I remember is dismissing the girls for today's lessons and then I felt a slight sharp pain in my head. Must have been fatigued and fell asleep. Then, I woke to see your charming smile."

"I called home, but got no answer," he commenced, trying not to show an extreme emotion. "You must have been extremely tired," he added, not commenting on her damp clothes due to her sweat. Then, she gave him a semiserious look as she began to address him.

"I did experience somewhat of a strange dream that I want to share." She paused for a moment and then began. "I appeared to be on a dark bridge, and someone or something began speaking to me. It offered me a chance to change my 'mundane' life as it was called. I could be a leader of people instead of just an ordinary mother with family. I could have wealth and fame, having others serve me instead of me always being the servant. The voice seemed pleasant, so I requested that it show itself. My request was not granted, but the voice continued on.

"Your lives have always been just average and even sometimes lesser than that. We want to offer you more, for there will always be the average beings that do not desire any more than what is comfortable to them. They just exist and require those who can lead them to take control of the environment. Ponder our offers as we ask for little in return.

"As the voice stopped, four figures, each in and ovoid outlined in a deep blue, appeared all looking directly at me. It was three men and a woman, and I felt in my heart that they were friendly. A smoky substance tried to get to them, but they would dissolve as it made contact with their blue-ringed ovoids. At the same time, the four would gave me an invitational gesture to join them, but I could not move from the spot that I was at on the bridge. Then, the voice addressed me again.

"These people that you see have rejected our offers for a life of mediocrity and will return empty-handed.

"The voice this time had a tone of resentment and disgust. That told me that something wasn't kosher about the offers made. So, I finally uttered the word "No!" three times while the four figures continued to signal me with an invitational gesture. Then, the voice made one last attempt to recruit me with an offer.

"Don't be a fool and accept our offer of power over the ordinary life! We offer this one last time!

"And then some kind of tentacles began advancing my way, and I shouted a firm and final 'No!' But the tentacles were still advancing until I felt a jolt, and in an instant, the four figures surrounded me as a protective shield. Then, I woke to see your smiling face!"

Kobin immediately sent a heartfelt thanks to the spiritual associates for the assist through Vanessa's dream experience, for he knew that her battle would only allow a certain level of his energies that was not quite sufficient for the task. Kobin, Rotussi, and Aton responded with a figure 8 flow of love and service back to her. And the woman was Nyla.

Kobin also knew that his involvement was crucial as he provided the "jolt" that allowed the four to surround her in protection from the tentacles of Mo-Dru.

"How are you feeling now, my love?" asked Kobin in a very concerned tone. "Just a bit tired and thirsty, but okay," she responded. Then, she added, "Can we keep this between us as to not alert the twins?" Kobin nodded his head in agreement, then added, "You rest some more, and I will take care of dinner and the girls tonight. Agreed?" She nodded as acceptance.

What followed was a violent rumbling that lasted a good thirty seconds that shook the house and set off car alarms outside in the neighborhood. A few items in the house fell to the floor, but nothing was broken or damaged.

The girls had let out a yelp and hugged each other tightly through the incident and then ran into the living room to Vanessa afterward. All seemed okay inside the house, so Kobin advanced outside to check for any damages of the property. As he did this, Vanessa turned on the radio to see if the incident of the rumble had been addressed yet. Reports were just starting to roll in on the news. The earliest report was that an earthquake was registered at 5.8 and was centered directly in the heart of Rugby.

Kobin discovered some fractures in the ground that seemed to be minor with no other major damages. He went back to the house to check in with the girls and Vanessa.

The radio had reported that there was a major sinkhole on a major street heading out of town, but no accidents or injuries reported. So far, a major earthquake without injury was good news. But Kobin's inner senses knew that Mo-Dru was behind the incident, and that was just an appetizer for things to come.

"If you guys are okay, I'm going to check and see if any of our neighbors have suffered any injuries or damages to their homes," said Kobin. The girls gave him the okay, and he went outside to offer his assistance to the neighbors if needed.

As he was walking, an inner message began to relay to him, saying, "Be prepared for a strong aftershock within the next two hours," and then he continued his trek to assist the neighbors and thus now able to prepare them for any aftershocks that could occur within the next couple of hours. He also explained that it is not uncommon to have many minor quakes after a major one in an area. For this, they were all grateful.

Kobin found a semisecluded spot and stopped for a quiet meditative moment. He made a call to hierarchy and his compadres for a protective shield around the town of Rugby. A voice of immediate response greeted him with a warm and sincere warning. "You must remember that due to misuse and abuse of free will for thousands of years, an almost unstoppable momentum of negative karma is in play and unfortunately is a plus for the hordes of darkness as they look for ways to accelerate destruction on this planet. This incident that just occurred is a combination of both aspects. Therefore, your energies and efforts as a whole, combined in unity of hierarchy, have overwhelming odds stacked against us.

"But the right use of power and intent of the light with an intense desire and focus to match can overcome great odds when aligned with cosmic laws and the great heart of harmony with the universe. When the laws of vibrations are released more and more through the meek, sincere hearts of the world, a great positive shift can occur in the mass consciousness of mankind. But it takes a certain amount of advanced spiritual mentors to wake up people to realize that they have to stand up and fight for their hearts' true, sincere, and loving desires to be free with the right use of free will, and the bond of unity in action can turn the tide of a troubled planet and its people. This has to be a consistent, continuous effort, creating a strong and loving energy to reverse the tides of darkness through self-inflicted limitations that have helped mankind in bondage for far too long." The inner dialogue ended, leaving a great sense of strength and urgency for the Chosen Ones to step up their efforts and energies to be more proactive. Up to this point in time, they have only been reactive, but now they must learn to team together and launch themselves against the dark forces. In two days, on October 10, 2020, hierarchy will release a portion of light to the Chosen Ones according to their deeds thus far in their first year as a group of spiritual warriors assigned by hierarchy.

As Kobin headed for home, a realization came to his mind. When a Chosen One's town is in a threat of danger, they are all in a similar threat, so the solution is for all to remain on constant guard of their towns. Then, when a protective shield was activated through them, the intensity is multiplied by twenty-five. With the right timing and a call to hierarchy, the negative energies could be repelled back on itself.

When he gave this thought energy, it was instantly shared with the others, making them also realize the importance of shared focus of energy multiplied as a unity of the man's energy, light vibrations, when used correctly, to ward off and defeat the attacks of the dark forces. This higher level of thought signaled the hierarchy that a new release of light could be stepped up a bit more than was anticipated.

As sunset began, another strong rumble hit the town of Rugby measuring 5.2 and lasted for twenty seconds. Kobin and his family were in the center of the living room huddled together, riding out the quake.

A few minutes after the rumble, they all stood up and went different directions to check the house for damages on the interior. The girls accompanied Vanessa, while Kobin started in the kitchen. One of the girls' rooms suffered a cracked window and a slight fracture line running across the ceiling, but nothing was broken. The hallway was fine, but the bathroom also suffered a cracked window. So far, the floors all appeared fine.

Kobin observed some dishes shifted in the cupboards, but nothing was broken. However, he noticed a crack in the porcelain sink, but nothing major. He turned on the faucet, which worked okay and no leaks in the pipes. He noticed the refrigerator had shifted about four inches from its normal position, but other than that, all the food inside was fine.

He slowly turned on the gas burners one at a time, and all was well. He sniffed to make sure that no gas leaks were happening, but decided to make an appointment to have the lines checked out as a safety precaution. He perused the floors, walls, and ceilings for any damages, and all appeared fine.

He then entered the garage to assess any damages and found that the side door window had cracked. He checked the washer and dryer hookups, and they seemed okay. The ceiling and walls seemed fine, but there was a long crack/fracture on the concrete floor that went halfway to the middle and then forked left and right through the rest of the floor. They seemed minor, but he would have it checked out as well.

Then they all met in the living room to share and assess the damages done on the interior of the house. Vanessa wrote down everything as this would be needed to file a report with their homeowner's insurance coverage. As she did this, Kobin once more went outside to check the exterior of the house and property.

He entered the backyard first and discovered a big tree branch cracked and landed partially on the roof. He would have to get his ladder to get a close-up look if any major damage had occurred, but would do that a little later. One end of the fence was leaning out as a post had cracked near the bottom of the ground. Again, nothing major had happened in their home.

Then, once again, he made a trek through the neighborhood to assist anyone who may have suffered any severe damages or personal injuries. Three doors down from his home was a house whose garage roof had partially collapsed in and the garage door was severely damaged and ruined. He knocked on the door, and a young man answered to greet him.

"I noticed that your garage was damaged and wanted to make sure that no personal injuries were suffered. Is everyone in the household okay?"

The gentleman's name was Ricky. He and his wife, Brea, were the only inhabitants in the house, and both were fine. There were a few cracked windows and a leak in the bathroom plumbing, but the garage had the worst damage. It was fortunate their car was parked outside in the driveway.

A little farther down the street at the intersection, a corner house had suffered a large fracture and cave-in at the front lawn. It also broke a main line in the sprinkler system that would need some serious repair. The owner was a man, six foot two, and his name was Alfonse. He shook Kobin's hand.

They chatted for a few minutes. He offered his services to Kobin and said that if anyone else needed assistance, make sure to call him and he would be of service to the neighborhood. Alfonse was a certified handyman with many skills and twenty-five years' experience to back his credentials. Kobin was very appreciative and said that they would be in touch.

Then, Kobin crossed the street as he was heading in the direction back home. As he made his trek back, people were coming out of their homes in their front yards to see if any major changes had occurred from the aftershock. He made sure to address each family to make sure that all were physically fine. He made sure to encourage them to make a list of any and all damages for their homeowner's insurance representatives, and also offered his and Alfonse's phone numbers for any assistance that they might need. They were all grateful and thanked him for his concern and generosity.

As he crossed the street back home, he turned and looked back at the neighborhood from whence he just came from. A smile adorned his face as he realized that good can always rise out of any adversity or opposition that life events present to us. He just met all these fine people of the neighborhood.

Vanessa and the twins, Bessie and Trina, were very proud of Kobin and love him greatly. His unlimited concern and acts of kindness for others had driven him to be a natural leader in any adverse or emergency conditions, and enabled him to calm others with the confidence that he exhibited in their personal beings. It is no wonder why he was a proven candidate for hierarchy to consider him as a Chosen One, for such a pivotal point location-wise in the geography of the work required an extraordinary soul advanced to the caliber of a great spirit warrior.

CHAPTER 27

IT WAS AN arduous day with all the unexpected happenings. Kobin decided to fire up the barbecue in the front yard, and the girls were ecstatic for some hotdogs and burgers. Vanessa responded with a wink and a slight smile to Kobin. As well as a great dad, he had the ability to calmly transform a not-so-good day into something special for the family. As a matter of fact, he suggested to the girls that this was a "tough house" celebration since the house suffered minor damages of two above-normal quakes.

Some of the neighbors observed Kobin firing up his barbecue and decided it was a great idea. Within twenty minutes, three of Kobin's neighbors had set up their grills and set out some lawn chairs and portable outdoor tables. And to Korbin's surprise, Alfonse drove up in his pickup truck with a couple of ice chests full of bottled water and soft drinks to offer to the neighborhood. People were smiling as he pulled up to each house and offered the family some refreshments. He wisely also offered his services as a handyman for any repairs needed due to today's shake-up. It was a win-win situation for all as neighbors were able to meet one another through a crisis and pull together as a unity of care and service to one another.

Kobin introduced Alfonse to Vanessa and the girls and then offered him a choice of a hotdog or a burger. The girls said that he could have one of each. Alfonse smiled at the girls, bowed like a prince to a princess, and remarked, "I am totally at your service, my ladies." The girls giggled, while Kobin and Vanessa snickered at the performance.

Vanessa, like Kobin, was admiring the camaraderie of the neighbors and was amazed at how a semidestructive day had turned out to become a blessing in disguise. Then, out of the blue, Kobin walked to the middle of the road with a drink held high in the air addressing the neighborhood with the toast. "Here's to all our strong homes, strong hearts, and a strong community!" And all responded in return as though a victory chant was in order. Yet in that moment, a bond of unity was born that connected these souls together in spirit as well as friends and families.

As the neighborhood barbeques wound down and the sun had begun to set, everyone began to retreat into their homes for the night. What a day it was! This would be a day in the history of Rugby to remember, especially for this neighborhood and the new bonds of friendship made.

Vanessa put the girls to bed, kissed Kobin good night, and had retired early herself. Kobin sat in his easy chair for rest and contemplation. His emotions consisted of love, gratitude, and admiration, for these have all humbled his heart in the faith and hope for humanity.

As he entered this calm and relaxed state, but now with the continuous protective shield for the whole community, a friendly and loving voice within began to address Kobin.

"You have discovered a profound understanding through this experience of the potential transformation of humanity when certain activities trigger a chord in the human soul. You see, when a person's attention is brought to the current moment, all else becomes trivial due to the nature of the event currently happening. Things such as likes and dislikes, opinions, discriminations, and such take a backseat to the reality occurring, putting the being in survival mode. Barriers are temporarily set aside as the higher instinct from within begin to respond like a reflex. When two or more souls are connected from an event of this nature, no questions are asked, for quick response will determine the fate or survival of all involved.

"In cases such as devastation from tornadoes, the main focus and energy is directed to the safety and survival of all souls affected by the disaster. Many people's lives have been transformed by their actions and deeds to assist those in need. So intense is their focus and actions that they become totally unaware of their own safety as they put themselves in harm's way, potentially sacrificing their lives for another's to be saved. Only later after the fact do they realize what risk they put themselves at, but then they realize that they would not have done anything different if the situation had happened again.

"The people who live mostly in this natural state of the heart are your law enforcement, firefighters, and all the branches of the military forces. Their purpose of existence, chosen by free will, is to live a life of sacrifice in order to protect, serve, and save the lives of others. These are the true warriors of life that would put themselves in harm's way without any hesitation whatsoever. Their acts of selflessness, sacrifice, and service are unparalleled, and no amount of pain can affect or deter their bonds of trust and unity of heart. In true reality, they live to unite all of life to a state of love, peace, and harmony.

"Hierarchy are pleased by your actions and deeds in this current event, with the true victory being the uniting of all hearts within your neighborhood. Things physical, such as homes and possessions, can always be replaced, but the transformations of souls' hearts are the nectar of life, and its many blessings bring to fruition love, peace, and harmony that through time and persistence can raise the consciousness of mankind. This is the ultimate recipe for spiritual evolution and the saving of a planet. Keep on keeping on!"

Kobin bowed his head in reverence to this teaching and felt the love flow from all the others in gratitude.

CHAPTER 28

THE NEXT MORNING, Saturday, October 9, 2020, all the Chosen Ones extended their meditations, readying themselves for the following day when hierarchy releases and increment of light according to their individual as well as group growth. From here on, this would be a semiannual occurrence through their mission to try and transform a planet through the improvement of mankind's growth and evolutionary progress as a race. So when, one by one, man finds balance from within, the planet begins to restore its balance through nature and the right use of cosmic energy of the universe.

As all were in their meditations, an experience of pain in the feet began and slowly increased to a point of semiagony. But something from within told them to increase their breaths while giving the "Omm" chant. As this occurred, the pain slowly subsided, leaving a slight numbness and then back to normal.

They did this for a full ninety minutes, sometimes experiencing slight headaches and pain in the hands as well. But they did not even question the experiences in their minds, knowing that there were some necessary experiences that would reveal itself when the time was right. This mindset prepared them for an explanation from a Rheyzoun Buddha almost immediately.

As their last breaths were being expelled, a warm and soothing greeting was announced within their hearts and was followed by a vision of a Buddha who began a discourse on their preparations for the next day's release of light.

"Blessed ones, your commitment to serve the light and life does come at a sacrifice of yourselves as all great leaders of true service to humanity have experienced. This planet has suffered a great burden of pain and suffering at the hands of mankind and their abuse of free will. By cosmic law, the pain that has been dealt out makes full circle and returns to its makers tenfold, and this karma must be balanced out on all planes of existence.

"As Chosen Ones, you were dealt an extra portion of this karma in this meditation session. These five points of the human body—hands, feet, and head—are the physical active tools of the mind that are the causes of misery and suffering brought upon the earth. When acts are destructive, pain is created. When acts are constructive, balance and harmony is gained.

"So, this process has allowed the negative karma to pass through you as a purification process, creating a vacuum within your physical vehicles that could immediately be filled with light. You all have become conduits of divinity that help to filter and transform life, creating a positive momentum of the victory of the heart, mind, and soul.

"All good things, at one time or another, have come at a great price of sacrifice and service. Change does not always come easy, and the brave of heart all willingly assume the risks involved. So, rejoice as candles of light in an ongoing battle for truth, justice, and purification of mind and heart for mankind."

The discourse ended with a glow of wondrous purple and gold lights replacing the vision of the Buddha. All had projected an aura of love and gratitude from their hearts to the souls of mankind and veneration to hierarchy.

Soon, another vision appeared in their minds. It appeared to be somewhere in the Pacific Ocean, where the waters were bubbling forth, like a large, circular ring and then subsided. That concluded their ceremony of the morning meditation.

It seemed that this meditation had triggered a spark of creativity within the heart and mind of Tillow. She could hear some beautiful etheric music and instantaneously began to play her violin along with it. So beautiful was the music that she lost herself and became one with the music. She was absorbed in the etheric realms of divine music.

In the same moment, Zeera of rural North Canada had picked up on the waves of this wondrous music taking place. She began to hum in harmony with the heavenly sounds, therefore connecting their respective homelands of Alaska and Canada. This divine symphony had reached out to Fioriya of Beijing, China, touching her heart and causing her to dance with the lovely music playing in the ethers. They were all aware of one another in this most miraculous moment of oneness—a divine unity.

CHAPTER 29

BACK IN THE territories of Siberia, Jogil and Omer were busy helping the townspeople of both Bear Paw and Bristle Weed. They felt responsible to assist these wondrous souls in their slow but steady evolution of growth and expansion with the economy and current technologies.

They introduced them to computers and other up-to-date tools of life, such as blenders, power tools for auto and appliance repairs, and cell phones. But with cell phones, it would be necessary to install cell towers spread out across the lands for proper usage.

The convenience of these technologies would help to enhance their lives with more comfort, production for the economy, and also to create jobs, providing commerce. This would also provide more effective communications with other towns, thus helping to restore confidence in the people and their potential for growth and success in life.

But the most important point to remember is truth and sincerity in their new ventures. A growing and thriving community needed close monitoring and security from any devious or corrupt activities. The dark forces were always on the lookout for weak links in any system or individuals who allow fear, doubt, and uncertainties to absorb within their beings. Maintaining a strong passion of confidence loaded with purity of mind and heart creates the perfect force field to ward off and defend any attempts of the dark forces attacks.

While Jogil and Omer broke for lunch, both experienced a sudden feeling of urgency coming from the northeast direction from Bristle Weed. Jogil knew this town well and its reputation as somewhat of a badland. Briar Valley has been a homeland of thieves, murders, and total chaos, a perfect breeding ground for the dark forces and a stronghold of Mattias.

But the intensity of evil had alerted the defenses of the golden discs within their beings. This was a sign that an army of darkness was on the move and a battle would soon ensue.

They ate a quick lunch and immediately began to pack the truck with supplies and fuel tank. It would be an hour and half drive through some of the most rugged terrains in the country. And there was only one midway point for gas, food, and lodging half an hour before Briar Valley.

As they veered to the northeast, a band of dark clouds had formed and was expanding in size. It appears that a rough trip was awaiting their drive, and Zac was anxious and eager, with his bristles raised on his neck and a low moan under his breath.

After firing up the truck, they sat idly for a moment, with eyes closed and chanting "Om" for a few minutes. Then, they felt the amplified energy of their compadres expanding their inner protective shields. They opened their eyes, and then Jogil put the truck in drive and the journey began.

In that same moment, Amara of Perth, Australia was experiencing a vision of a patch of blue whales out in the Pacific Ocean traveling toward the middle of the ocean where a ring of bubbling water had previously occurred. Then, the vision faded away.

Young Myama of Ecuador, South America was out collecting some herbs when a vision came to her from her invisible friends. It was about four different herbal plants in the area that needed to be harvested and blended together, forming an important herbal tea. She knew these herbs and began to collect them immediately.

Now, Miraki of the southern tip of South America picked up on Myama's vision and felt the urgency of the vision. Still not knowing the purpose of this blend, they acted on faith that the vision was a preparation for something far beyond their comprehension at this point.

Meanwhile, on the dark side, Mattias was readying for a major battle in the stronghold of Briar Valley. A strategy of divide and conquer, Mo-Dru was building a momentum for an attack in the lands of South America. He would direct his tactics toward the youth of the lands. Apparently, it had already slowly begun.

In the northern small towns, children began to fall ill, experiencing fatigue, delirium, loss of appetite, and numbness. Their ages ranged from three to twelve years of age. Doctors and shamans tried to diagnose the symptoms to no avail. There were also rashes that would develop throughout their bodies. Schools were closed to prevent any spread or epidemic of any virus.

The same began to happen in Miraki's area in the deep south of the continent. They both began a deep focus on all children as a direct contact began in their hearts and followed up with a vision of a blue force field of protection. This was magnified by the efforts of all the Chosen Ones. A major challenge of two oncoming battles was being waged on opposite sides of the planet.

Teohta thrived on the combination of chaos and confusion to instill fear and doubt in the hearts of puny humans, as she liked to refer them to. Ever since her fall from the heavens, an eternal bitterness against Ramata had festered in her dark heart, knowing that eventually her demise will occur since she was given ample opportunities to repent and once again serve the light.

But her fall, in addition to legions of followers, attracted beings from other systems that have rebelled against the light and soon looked at her for leadership to control other planets in this galaxy.

Some of these were invisible beings involved in the plethora of chemical warfare. It appeared that this is what was being launched in the country of South America. In order to annihilate a race, an attack on the youth would become the focus and concern of the parents and all communities involved to try to heal and protect the children. It would simply appear that this was just an outbreak of something possibly as serious as the plague that almost wiped out a country in the past. Myama and Miraki understood the visions they shared of the four herbs to be blended and used when necessary. Now is the time.

The recipe of herbs was apparently designed to act as an anecdote to reverse the effects of this specific, unknown viral attack on the children. Hierarchy had foreseen this attack coming and relied solely on the intuition and faith of the Chosen Ones providing an inner strategy to counter.

This powerful blend would be disbursed as three drops per eight ounces of water per child. Time was of the essence. They sensed within that the antidote would have to be taken within four days of infection. There was no telling how far the virus has spread. Urgency of the dispensing of the tea was crucial.

Miraki and Myama put the word out that this potion had to be distributed immediately and given as soon as possible. Runners were contacted and came to gather the batches of potion. They quickly set out while the towns were informed of their travels to deliver the potions and directions of the dosage to be given.

While they began their treks, more batches of the tea blends were mixed for the next set of runners to pick up and deliver. A race against time was the counterattack of the light to hopefully defeat Mo-Dru's germ warfare.

While the battle was being fought, the other Chosen Ones focused an intense energy of love and protection in, through, and around the entire continent of South America. A focus of energy had to be maintained for the oncoming battle of Jogil and Omer. Then, a great insight came to the minds of the Chosen Ones. They all acted without haste.

When they focused, a mighty light as a bridge united South America and Siberia. Hierarchy would intervene in the assistance of both battles, but it was contingent on their focus, faith, intensity, and passion of the heart.

As the mighty focus was maintained with the chants of "Ommm!" a great surge of light shot forth from the middle of the Pacific Ocean to Siberia and South America, forming a triangle from all points.

This invincible triangle of light lit up the sky and emitted a long humming sound for about three minutes before disappearing from sight. A pattern, a force field of light was made that would be accessible for the light warrior when necessary.

When the cosmic triangle faded, it sparked another vision that Amara experienced. Again, she witnessed a group of blue whales traveling toward the center of the Great Pacific. This time, she counted twenty-five of them, and further ahead of their destination was a large ring of bubbling water of which the source of this action she could not detect. Then, the vision vanished. She was curious as to why she, in particular, was having these visions.

Meanwhile, Jogil and Omer were trekking their way to Briar Valley as Zac let out a robust howl that grabbed their attention. He could sense a strong smell of fear and evil in the atmosphere as the bands of dark clouds ahead were expanding and intensifying in their size. At that moment, Jogil applied the brakes to a complete stop. He looked at his watch—it was 3:00 p.m.

Suggesting that he and Omer pitch tent, he pulled off the rugged bumpy road over to a spot fifty yards away. There were three boulders grouped together forming a pocket perfect for making camp. Here, they would meditate, strategize, and rest until they felt the time was right to continue on with the battle.

Thunder and lightning made for a show, indicating the rage and fury of Mattias and his hordes. Omer and Jogil quickly focused and chanted for an intense deep blue ring of protection surrounding the camp. While doing this, they also invoked and visualized their protective armor, expanding their golden discs outlined with a ruby-red intensive tone. They protected this as well for the safety of Zac.

A small meal of various nuts, jerky, and water was in order. This would allow for some very active and intense chanting for assistance from hierarchy for the upcoming battle. The request to visualize the strategy of attack from the enemy was made in a call, and this drew immediate attention from the other twenty-three fellow warriors. Fighting as a complete unity of one was increasing the intensity of energy flowing. As they focused their minds and hearts on the newly established triangle of light, this energy would multiply and provide the defense necessary for the invisible battle being waged against Miraki and Myama in South America.

That battle was swiftly moving as now all children in the central part of South America were falling ill faster than the herbal potion could be distributed. By now, word has gotten out to most cities of the recipe, so fewer runners were needed to trek across the country. It became a major battle of time and implementation of the potion to the children.

They needed to be given the anecdote within four days of contracting the virus plaguing the nation.

Myama made a specific call to all of her invisible friends to assist her in the protection of all children throughout the lands in a swift manner. She also projected a blue ray of protection that they could inject into the young victims for protection of their souls.

This action triggered a message to all of the Indigo youths of the country to project their essence in the assistance of the healing process. Their ages ranged from sixteen and older, providing for more strength and focus in their projections of this powerful light energy.

Myama noticed that all of her personal amethyst crystals had been activated by vibrations and was emitting a bright glowing field that she had never experienced before. But she knew this to be a positive action unleashed.

CHAPTER 30

MEANWHILE, THE CHILDREN of the Chosen Ones were having an experience of the visions accompanied by a warm and loving energy flowing through their beings. A friendly voice in their head addressed them to see all these children being bathed in green and gold clouds of joy and happiness. But they were to tell no one of what they were doing, not even their parents.

This was the beginning of a new, strong, light bond between North and South Americas being established by the authority of the hierarchy that would be crucial for future battles and a steady growth of light on the planet.

In Mt. Shasta City, Krea was making a visit to see the babies before going to lunch. As she peered through the window, she noticed the light violet color surrounding them and sealed in a blue protective ring. She could sense that hierarchy had plans and a purpose for these young ones in their futures. This excited her and confirmed within her being that their adoption by her was just a matter of time.

Again, Amara experienced a vision of the blue whales, but this time, they were singing in harmony during their travels. As they sang, their bodies would resonate in different colors from white to yellow-green and back to blue as they grew ever closer to the area where the ring of bubbling waters were activated. As the vision ended, a loving but firm voice commented to her saying, "Soon, very soon, it is coming," and ended at that.

In this dire emergency situation, Nyla projected a great vision of the continent of South America being immersed in a green-violet ovoid surrounded by an intense blue ring signifying the healing and purification process being protected by a force field of the blue ring. Then, she reached out to hierarchy through her golden disc within and chanted "Ramtam Om! Shivaya Om!" twenty-seven times to draw upon the light from above. In her mind's eye, she could see and feel this light descending and saturating the continent with so much love that the whole land shook for thirty seconds before subsiding.

Then, she realized that this momentum of cosmic energy needed to be transferred to the assistance of Jogil and Omer against the mighty Mattias and his hordes of darkness. As her focus turned toward them, the light connected the two points together, and that activated a line once again to the mid-Pacific Ocean and a line back to South America, forming a great triangle of light.

This connection of cosmic energy flow was barely visible to the human eye, but was very real and powerful through the inner eyes of the Chosen Ones. Within two minutes, the cosmic triangle had ceased and left a great charge in the auras of the spirit warriors, thus creating an immense momentum for their actions. Given the right strategy combined with exact timing and focus, this assistance should be sufficient to win both battles against Mattias and Mo-Dru.

This also had an adverse effect. It had brought out the worst of the dark forces that would test and challenge the merits of the Chosen Ones. The dark ones knew that once the assistance of hierarchy subsided, the twenty-five are left to battle on their own. They would bet against the growth and advancement, assuming that dependency on hierarchy had always been their crutch. This is the ultimate strategy of the dark side always—divide and conquer.

Nyla knew this from her previous life on the dark side. She knew that the strength and potential from within was enough to constantly remain invincible and indestructible against the forces of darkness, but all had to eventually earn that attainment.

Now, Mo-Dru had summoned a wicked infantry of aliens called the Dastards. If there were any weak areas in the light force fields, they were the experts to infiltrate and attack with swiftness. Once human contact is made, any open sores, disabilities, etc., would be accelerated until crippling or death would ensue.

Unfortunately, a few areas inland were weakened, and infiltration of the Dastards had occurred. The youngest and weakest children were attacked. The Dastards went on traveling to find and attack other areas of weakness, but not all was totally lost.

Some Indigo children appeared and were attracted to the weak and ill children. They would they approach the child and put their left hand on their forehead and the right hand on the heart. Then, a beautiful tone would be activated like a humming radiating an aura of pink and violet, encompassing both beings in and ovoid. This would last for seven minutes and then dissipate. Then, the Indigos would move on to assist others in need. This was a last chance effort to try and save the inflicted ones.

Some had survived, but unfortunately some have passed on. There was no time for sorrow as the battle continued on. The virus of the Dastards must be dealt with swiftly. But as quickly as they struck, the Dastards disappeared, leaving a path of death behind. 40 percent of the children attacked did not make it, and the bodies had to be burned right away to eliminate any residual germs in the air.

It was now 5:00 p.m. as Jogil and Omer observed the fury as Mattias was moving closer and stronger. They had a plan that would allow for a closer approach before the launch of an attack. The golden discs were fully charged with an army of blue with fiery ruby-tipped arrows ready to be launched combined with a mighty call to hierarchy, and finally the intense heart focus of the people of Bear Paw and Bristle Weed. They figured that playing possum while the enemy advanced closer and closer would cause a greater impact when they unloaded with a full arsenal of light force. Then, something changed.

The hordes of darkness suddenly stalled about a mile from Jogil and Omer's camp, almost as if it sensed something ready to happen. Then. a dark shadow arose in front of them, about two hundred feet in the air. Its long, dark cape flapped viciously in the air of the howling winds.

The figure of Mattias focused directly at Jogil and Omer. He could detect their protective light force fields with his advanced psychic abilities and sense their preparedness for a full-blown attack. Then, he began to address them in a firm and threatening tone.

"You humans think that you can match the powers of my hordes who have conquered many battles of ages past on this helpless planet? You are merely prolonging the misery and suffering of a pathetic race of humans who have proven their inability to coexist with one another and will always allow fear to be their master. Give up your fight for them and join the ranks of Teohta, Mo-Dru, and I, and we shall rule this earth with unlimited power forever!"

Jogil and Omer just looked at one another with a big smile of confidence, then shifted their focus to the floating father of darkness and proceeded to respond in synchronicity, "Meet your defeat this day, for you shall not pass!"

Their response infuriated Mattias, and as he raised his hands above his head, a dozen alien ships of a green octagonal shape appeared bright and glowing. Then, he lowered his arms, pointing directly at Jogil and Omer. The ships began to slowly advance forward and stopped only a quarter mile away from their location.

As Jogil glanced at his watch, it read 6:00 p.m. straight up. They then turned their heads forward, raised their arms up, pointing straight to Mattias and let out a loud vocal commanding sound of "Ho! Namo Ho!" three times in sync. This launched an unending barrage of the fiery ruby-tipped arrows directly into the menacing dark clouds of fury. As they made contact, some of the clouds dissolved into thin air, only to be replaced by the remaining surrounding clouds and grew darker.

This action only provoked the alien airships to advance closer to Jogil and Omer. The battle had definitely come to them, and they just kept smiling directly at Mattias.

Mattias's focus was definitely directed to what was in front of him and his hordes. Then, all hell broke loose. A massive wall of bright light appeared right behind Mattias and his army of darkness. The massive wall of light began to fold itself over and around the army from top, left, and right, smothering and extinguishing the negative energies within minutes. Mattias managed to escape while his army of green spaceships had crumbled to the ground below. Within a few minutes, the winds died down and the skies cleared up.

It appeared to be a victory this evening, but they knew that they would have to travel onward to Briar Valley. A stronghold of Mattias would not be an easy one to break, and it had to be defeated. Right now, the momentum appeared to be on the side of the light.

A valuable lesson was learned by Jogil and Omer from their previous battles with Mattias in other lifetimes of defeat. Patience with no fear had beaten Mattias at his own game, but it would take a lot more than that to not only defeat but to totally destroy Teohta's commander of darkness.

The brother warriors bowed their heads with reverence, respect, and thanks to hierarchy, and then immediately focused and redirected their energies to the lands of Myama and Miraki.

Another two hours passed as the two separate battles had ended for the day. It was only a short time before a release of light would be implemented by hierarchy.

Another vision was activated within Amara, and she was in a meditative state. Again, a pod of blue whales were nearing the center of the Pacific Ocean where a great ring of bubbly water was maintaining its momentum. As she looked to the skies above, it was pulsating with a lavender hue oscillating back and forth from a mellow peach and lavender again. The sky was mimicking the pulsations of the whales changing colors, while they continuously sang while trekking to the center of the ocean. The vision faded away with the words "All are loved greatly."

With the battle being over in South America, a great healing process had been initiated by Myama and assisted by Miraki. Even though they exercised herculean energy and efforts for a whole continent, the death toll of children was estimated at about twelve hundred. Most of the victims that were given the herbal potion were well on their way to recovery.

All twenty-five Chosen Ones simultaneously projected a wave of gratitude and love to hierarchy for their assistance in the recent battles. The love was projected throughout the earth for all of humanity. A great response was activated back to them and the rest of the earth.

CHAPTER 31

THE TIME HAD come, and the Great Holy One, Ramata, began the fourth quarter transmission of light energy to the beloved light warriors. A great pulsation began to be transferred, first as a golden fluidic substance entering the top of the head, flowing through the body's Chi channels, then to the bottom of the feet, out of the physical body, and into their individual auras.

Next followed a stream of pink with violet hue energy journeying the same track as the previous and then out into the aura.

Then, a green energy followed next. Then, an energy blend of violet and ruby red traveled the Chi channels, then out to the auras. The final injection was of a deep blue fluid that completed the transfer of light energy within each individual.

All were experiencing an expansion of passionate vibrations filled with love, mercy, hope, and faith. This magnification of the light accelerated in their cells, atoms, and electrons to a higher resonance of frequency. In order to maintain this new level of energy, their focus and sincere intent to serve unwaveringly and faithfully had to remain as a greater unified effort consistently. The glow within their beings would continue for three hours until the transmission was fully completed. During this intense transfer, a great Buddha of immense light and love began to speak.

"Precious hearts, you are the final chapter of faith and hope of a planet that has been lagging too far behind in its opportunities for spiritual growth and a healthier, happier way of life. The abuse and misuse of free will has polluted the planet and its natural habitat of balance and harmony. This, according to hierarchy, has stunted the growth and prosperity of its galaxy.

"There have been enough discoveries in technologies provided to restart balance through love, peace, and unity for all of mankind. But the elite and powerful have thwarted these efforts in order to control through fear, doubt, greed, and a low self-esteem of mankind. But through free will of man, this has been accepted as the norm. And as long as mankind accepts the self-made fact that there will always be the rich and poor, this cycle of control will remain as the main stronghold of the dark brotherhood.

"There are many loving and sincere people on the planet, but they lack the faith and passion to fight for their freedom and rights. So as they sow, so they shall reap. You cannot allow any longer the disintegration of cosmic energies to flow in a downward spiral of discord, disease, and death. The passions of faith, hope, and determination in action must guide them to turn the tide of darkness into light!

"Love and truth have been perverted so much that various religions have become enemies of one another instead of living the life of love, truth, and respect of the diversity of life. A rose does not condemn a lilac because of its shape and color, for nature is the perfect example of beauty and balance in all things. Some trees are larger than others, rivers pour into the oceans, creeks feed rivers, and so forth. All of creation has a purpose and a connection of unity. All are composed of the same cosmic energy, the difference being only the different levels and rates of vibrations.

"A ladder is not a ladder unless it has a certain number of rungs to make it complete. Therefore, the bottom rung is no less than the top rung. They are one in nature. The same applies to numerous cars stopped at a red light. The first car in line is no better or worse than the tenth car in line. Both await the green light and will advance when the time is right.

"This also explains the importance of patience and understanding. All good aspects and virtues of life must be understood, maintained by right actions, and respected by all. For 'united we stand' or separate we fall. But you have passed these initiations of life that qualified you to represent hierarchy as the Chosen Ones.

"We are grateful for your actions of love and sacrifices that have allowed for the potential growth and hope for humanity. Maintain your hearts' sincere desires and passions to act when necessary to lead mankind back to his destiny of love and devotion through growth and service to all. This gift of the light will be maintained and expanded within your hearts as long as the focus of love, faith, and unity is the fuel for a full blossoming of your higher selves to ascend the higher understanding of infinite love and victory of life." The discourse concluded with a great symphony of the etheric music filling their hearts and minds with cosmic light.

CHAPTER 31

AS THE TRANSFER of light was complete, all were blessed with the same vision that Amara had been experiencing. A pod of twenty-five blue whales were within minutes of their destination in the middle of the great Pacific Ocean. The ring of bubbling water had reached a height of six feet as the intensity grew due to the approach of the whales. Now, the ring was changing colors to match that of the whales.

Each of the Chosen Ones could feel within the singing of the great mammals stirring their hearts with love and ecstasy. All began chanting a great "Aum" in unison. As this began, the whales began circling the ring in a clockwise direction. This action had caused a rainbow of colors to expand far beyond the exterior of the water ring. Then, a rumbling began to slowly occur that spread throughout the great Pacific.

The eastern coast of Japan began to experience this rumbling as well as the western coast of the United States of America. It was a steady shaking that went on for fifteen minutes, but not cataclysmic in nature. Both countries alerted their emergency broadcasts and prepared their people of any impending danger. The worst threats would be any tsunamis advancing to the coast.

It was in this moment that they realized the vision was, in fact, really physically happening! But they kept their flow of chants and focus of love, feeding the vision as long as it occurred. The skies were emitting hues of pink, yellow, and lavender oscillating to and fro. Then what followed was the highlight of the whole experience.

A great glow of white light filled the ring within the waters of the Pacific. Bubbling waters grew higher and higher to a height of three hundred feet. Following the walls of the ring, an immense silence fell upon the scene.

And then it came.

**THE END
BOOK 1**